To Teresa
Enjoy The
Deb Marlowe

Death from the Druid's Grove

THE KIER AND LEVETT MYSTERY SERIES
BOOK 2

DEB MARLOWE

DRAGONBLADE PUBLISHING, INC.

ARE YOU SIGNED UP FOR DRAGONBLADE'S BLOG?

You'll get the latest news and information on exclusive giveaways, exclusive excerpts, coming releases, sales, free books, cover reveals and more.

Check out our complete list of authors, too!

No spam, no junk. That's a promise!

Sign Up Here

www.dragonbladepublishing.com

Dearest Reader;

Thank you for your support of a small press. At Dragonblade Publishing, we strive to bring you the highest quality Historical Romance from some of the best authors in the business. Without your support, there is no 'us', so we sincerely hope you adore these stories and find some new favorite authors along the way.

Happy Reading!

CEO, Dragonblade Publishing

ADDITIONAL DRAGONBLADE BOOKS BY
AUTHOR DEB MARLOWE

The Kier and Levett Mystery Series
A Killer in the Crystal Palace (Book 1)
Death from the Druid's Grove (Book 2)

Chapter One

Shoreditch, London
October 1851

"LET ME HELP you with your mask."

Miss Kara Levett held the piece steady. The thin metal, cool against her face, warmed quickly as sure fingers tied the mask in place.

Finished, Mrs. Imogen Berringer walked around her, examining her with a critical eye. "My dear, job well done. You look magnificent." Frowning in concentration, she bent down to peer at the skirt of Kara's gown. "Hold a moment, are those ... mathematical equations?"

"They are," Kara confirmed. "Mr. Towland instructed me to prepare a ceremonial gown that I would wear for my own initiation tonight, but also for other formal functions of the Order. He said it should reflect the Order's interests, as well as my own."

"Sensible advice," Mrs. Berringer said. "You can expect several formal functions a year, and there is always plenty of wine, so be sure you are comfortable, as well."

Kara spread her hand over the rich, sky-blue material of her skirts. "I worked with a modiste to incorporate acorns, oak leaves, and Celtic knots into the embroidery. That took care of the Druidic elements of the group. And I asked for a few significant equations and tiny representations of my most used tools, to represent my own work." Her fingers traced a line of the embroidery, done in white and silver that complemented the color of the gown.

"Well, it turned out beautifully. You look magnificent. And that mask! Arthur will adore it. Niall crafted it for you, I presume?"

"He did." Her friend, Mr. Niall Kier, was an artist and a fellow exhibitor at the nation's Great Exhibition, currently winding down its wildly successful run. "He's been so busy, I'm grateful he found the time for it."

She loved the mask he'd made for her. It was crafted of several interlocking Celtic knots and had been painted midnight blue. On the forehead blazed a silver triquetra.

"I predict Arthur will be pestering him for a similar one," Mrs. Berringer said.

"I'm sure Niall will accommodate him. We are both so thankful for Mr. Towland's help earlier this year."

Arthur Towland was a magistrate of the police courts and had been incredibly helpful when Kara was wrongly accused of a gruesome killing. His intervention had given them the time to discover the true murderer, and Kara was so grateful, she'd given him a gift from her heart—and from her mind, fingers, and long hours of detailed work. She'd crafted him one of the elaborate automatons she was becoming known for.

Towland had been enchanted and promptly invited her to join his Order of Druidic Bards. He'd led her on a short study of the group and their ideals—minus the secret bits—and now here she stood, ready for her initiation.

"He'll be thrilled," Mrs. Berringer assured her. "Just as he's thrilled to welcome you into the Order." Her gaze passed over the carved symbol. "And you know, the triquetra is particularly meaningful to him, and to me as well."

"Is it?" Kara asked.

"Indeed. I am particularly intrigued at the idea of several facets or faces, all representing one being." She went quiet for a moment, clearly thinking, before she gave herself a shake. "In any case, it's time we went down. Will you help me with my own mask, my dear?"

Kara did, helping Mrs. Berringer don the exquisitely feathered likeness of a snowy white owl. The rest of Mrs. Berringer's gown was made to match it, trailing net and feathers in a suggestion of wings. An appropriate choice, as Kara had found the widow to be both wise and an astute observer of human behavior.

"Thank you," the lady said. "Now, let's go down and collect your fellow initiate." Her tone was neutral, but Kara noted the slightly grim look in her eye.

Niall had told her of the whispers floating amongst the members of the Order, that this new initiate might be replacing the widowed Mrs. Berringer in Mr. Towland's affections.

"Surely it's no one's business but their own," she'd answered tartly. She'd grown a little sensitive on the topic of gossip, since their own unusual friendship had set tongues to wagging in the last months.

"Oh, ho. You should prepare yourself," Niall had answered with a laugh. "You think Society gossips? The Druids put them to shame. After the Great Secession, the different factions naturally gossip endlessly about each other, but they are also merciless with their own. The thing is, because so many of the members possess such interesting talents, positions, and beliefs, it makes for far more fascinating tittle-tattle than anything Society can dredge up."

He'd been right, too. Kara had heard a great many whispers about the woman who would be initiated with her this evening, but this was the first time she'd laid eyes on her.

"Good evening, Miss Ottridge," Miss Berringer said briskly. She made the introductions, and Kara eyed her counterpart with curiosity as they exchanged greetings. The other woman was tall and thin, with dark hair left hanging down her back. She had a long face and a sharp chin, but that was all Kara could tell, as her mask was already in place. Eschewing an original design, Miss Ottridge had dressed as Lady Justice, complete with a small scale hanging like a chatelaine from her waist and a mask that resembled a blindfold, but cleverly left openings among the folds so that the lady could see.

"An interesting choice," Mrs. Berringer remarked when Kara complimented the inventive arrangement. "Especially as the introduction of the blindfold to the figure of Justice was first made satirically."

"Indeed?" Miss Ottridge asked coolly.

"Oh, yes. It was intended to show the lady as blind to the injustices going on all about her."

"Fascinating," the woman responded. "Fortunately, there is no danger of that here."

The tension in the small anteroom flared. Kara held her tongue and watched as silent battle waged between the two women.

Mrs. Berringer at last turned away to pull open a pair of double doors. They let in air from the garden outside. The cool evening breeze swept in, bringing the scent of juniper and freshly turned soil. Kara could see a path of crushed stone coming right up to the door.

As if the opening of the portal had been a signal, twin torches flared to life across the garden. They flanked the door of a low structure with many windows. A summerhouse?

Mrs. Berringer tossed a look over her shoulder. "Line up together, ladies. Follow me. It's time."

They stepped out onto the path behind her, the gravel crunching beneath their feet. Lights continued to spark into life behind the windows. As they neared, the door opened and they filed in.

The interior was lovely, filled with wooden tables, low couches, classical art, plenty of foliage, and a multitude of candles.

It was also quite deserted.

"Where is everyone?" Miss Ottridge sounded startled.

"You have been honored with an invitation to enter the Druid's Grove," Mrs. Berringer intoned. "Miss Levett, you will go first. They await you."

A gate stood at the far end of the of the building. It featured a graceful outline of a bard's harp and garlands of leaves and acorns as borders. Kara recognized Niall's work when she saw it. It swung open, and she moved to step through—and gasped at the sight before her.

She stood on a stone patio. Before her spread a large, circular wooded grove that looked like it might have been transplanted from Mount Olympus. Soft light shone everywhere among a variety of trees and through a multitude of blossoms. A large flat spot in the middle actually had a stream running through it. Around it rose ascending terraces, broken up into sections, some rising slightly higher or lower than its neighbor, each terrace unique and filled with different plantings and garden architecture.

It was a stunning space. Otherworldly. And filled with masked figures, all facing her.

"You are welcome in the Druid's Grove, Miss Levett."

It was Mr. Towland approaching. He was dressed in a long white tunic tied with a gold cord. His outer robe was forest green and decorated with embroidered Celtic knots in gold thread. His mask resembled a stag, complete with holly-bedecked horns.

Bowing, he offered his arm and led her in a stately walk through the throngs of masked members, over the stream on a path of steppingstones and to a flagstone circle on the other side. He placed her in the center and stood to one side as the crowd gathered around them.

"My friends and fellow Druidic Bards, I hereby offer up Miss Kara Levett as a candidate for our august Order. Should anyone have reason why she should not join our ranks, speak it now or keep forever silent."

Kara glanced over the assembly, stopping with a smile when

she recognized Niall Kier. Not in Druid's robes, thank goodness, but clad in his formal kilt. Her heart thumped. In part because he was so … substantial in his black coat, white linen, and the red, green, and black tartan of Clan Kerr, but perhaps also because she was taken back to the events when last she'd seen him in it—to the night she'd nearly died when a madman tried to run her down.

She dragged her gaze up and away from the sight of his sturdy, bare knees, only to startle a little at his mask—the beady-eyed, sharp-beaked face of a golden eagle.

"Excellent!" Mr. Towland announced. "Now, we have something truly unique in store tonight. As you know, every candidate is asked to carry on our revered musical or storytelling traditions of the bards. Usually, this takes the form of a song, a poem, or an occasional dramatic piece. Miss Levett, however, has gone to a great deal of trouble to gift us with something special."

He raised his hand, and footmen filed in. Two carried a small table and two more held a covered figure. They set them up next to her, and Mr. Towland stepped close to grab the corner of the fabric covering.

"I present to you"—he pulled away the cover—"a facsimile of Taliesin himself!"

Kara straightened a little with pride. She'd taken great care with this representation of the famed bard bent over his harp. His expression was absorbed, his long hair carefully crafted from thin, curled metal. She'd selected two ancient songs, one a ballad and one a drinking song, and once cranked, her bard would nod his head and pluck the strings of the harp while the music box encased inside would play the selection.

Mr. Towland spoke in a hush to the crowd as he wound the figure and bade them listen.

He played both songs, and the crowd appeared impressed. Some even sang along. When the second song finished, Mr. Towland took her hand, kissed it, then raised it high, presenting her to the assembly. Wild applause rang out, along with a few shouts of welcome.

"I think it's clear we all agree on the suitability of Miss Levett as our newest member." He dropped her hand and led her back across the stream, where masked figures gathered around them, congratulating and welcoming her.

"I must admit, I am relieved," she said to Mr. Towland. "I had a song prepared—a children's song popular in the north, in case I needed to sing as well—but honestly, everyone's ears have had a lucky escape."

"Your Taliesin is a rare accomplishment and more than enough to secure your membership, my dear." He sighed. It sounded heavy and full of resignation. "But now we must see to the other, I suppose."

He crossed back to the flagstone circle and called for order. Kara went to stand with Niall as the door opened again and Miss Ottridge appeared. There was no escort this time. She walked alone to the circle, where Towland moved aside so she could take the center.

"Miss Ottridge has been nominated as an initiate to our Order. She has completed the requisite study. Should anyone object to her, please state your reasons now."

"He sounds almost hopeful," Kara whispered to Niall.

No one spoke. Mr. Towland breathed deeply. "The lady will be given the chance to showcase her talent, and the company will decide."

Miss Ottridge straightened her spine and raised her chin. "I will recite an original poem," she announced. "The title is 'Secret Justice.'"

Squaring her shoulders, she spoke out in a strong, ringing tone.

Lies and secrets fill the air
Sinister half-truths found everywhere
Among the great and the low
Every layer has its own to show

Not far to seek
Betrayed by a flinch, a look, a peek
Rarely hid for long
Told in a whisper, shout or song
Those among us with a nose for such
At home in shadow, never ask for much
A long-held tradition, old as sin itself
Misdeeds never long hidden on a shelf
To the seeker dispense a token, sinners must
If ever they seek the sleep of the just

She finished, and for several long moments, silence held. Abruptly, everyone began to speak at once. A few applauded. Others asked loud, angry questions.

"You need to work on those middle stanzas, my dear," someone shouted.

The noise level rose. A few masked members approached the girl. Several looked agitated, rather than welcoming.

"She's put the cat amongst the pigeons now, hasn't she?" Niall leaned down to speak in Kara's ear. "At least she's giving them something else to talk about."

"Has she?" Kara asked. "We are all meant to conclude that she's blackmailed her way in, are we not? She's being rather blatant about it. After all the gossip, won't they all assume it was Mr. Towland who has had to *dispense a token?*"

"Some might assume he's let her in to keep her quiet," he replied. "But he did say she's been nominated, not that he nominated her—not the way he implied it was he who invited you. So perhaps it is someone else that she's put the screws to?"

Kara looked back to the entrance to the Grove. Mrs. Berringer stood near there, surrounded by several members all talking avidly. She held herself silent and still in their midst, clearly watching Miss Ottridge.

"Or perhaps she merely wants access to the group?" Niall

continued to muse. "It's an eclectic collection of personalities, to be sure. Ripe for blackmail, I'd wager. Maybe she's merely putting them all on alert."

There was no heraldic moment of welcome, as Kara received, but it appeared Miss Ottridge had passed the test. She'd been led out of the circle and stood answering questions near the stream.

Niall put a hand to the small of Kara's back and led her beneath the drooping boughs of a willow.

"Welcome to the Druidic Bards, Kara."

"Thank you. It is an honor, and I mean to enjoy it." She breathed deeply, glad of his familiar, stalwart presence. "You did make me promise to widen my circle of acquaintances."

"*Friends*, Kara, not acquaintances," he corrected her.

"That's ever so much harder," she complained. He laughed, and she gave a sigh. "Honestly, if you had asked me months ago about joining a semi-secret society, I would have predicted it to be at Lake Nemi," she confessed, referring to the women's social club to which he'd introduced her. "I've loved the time I spent there. So many women with such varied interests."

"And all with the brains and confidence to pursue them," he added.

"But Emilia has been elusive lately," she said. "In fact, I believe she's been avoiding me."

"Emilia is a flighty creature, for all that she's the head of the place. She's likely fallen in love again and has no thought of anything or anyone else. I wouldn't worry."

She did worry, though. She had no real experience at having friends. She didn't want to put a foot wrong.

There was no time to indulge her worries now, however, as a man dressed like a crowned prince came to ask about her automaton, and others gathered to compliment her and listen as well.

She was kept busy for a time. Everyone was kind. While she did hear some whispered conjectures about Miss Ottridge, no one discussed the fellow initiate with her directly.

It was a relief, however, when Mr. Towland called for attention. "Let's proceed with the unmasking, shall we?"

Somewhere, a gong sounded. As everyone reached to remove their masks, footmen with champagne and trays of food streamed into the room. Kara noticed that the servers kept their masks on, though they were all alike and far simpler than those of the guests.

Mrs. Berringer approached, a footman trailing in her wake. "Do try the cream pastries," she urged them. "They go well with the sweet wine."

After Kara and Niall had sampled and agreed, the widow took Kara's arm. "Will you allow me to show you a bit of the Grove that is close to my heart?"

"Of course. Niall, would you care to come along?"

They followed Mrs. Berringer toward the back of the Grove and up to one of the highest terraces. She led them toward a curved section of the wall. Here, lights had been set up to highlight three carved figures, all in a row. Each was an exquisite relief of a stone woman, and at each figure's feet had been built planters, all filled with different specimens. The lights filtered through the plants, casting varied shadows on the stone figures and shrouding them in mystery.

"I mentioned that I was interested in the study of the Triple Goddesses," Mrs. Berringer said as she stopped before the figures.

"Ah, like the Norns?" asked Niall.

"Indeed. The Triple Goddesses are found in several cultures." She stepped forward, then turned to face them. "The Norns, of course, from the Nordic stories," she said with a nod. "They are the Moirae in Greek mythology, and there are several versions of the Morrigan in the Celtic legends." She waved a hand toward the stone figures. "For this piece, I commissioned three figures of the Fates from the Greek stories."

She looked past Kara and smiled. "I had help with this project."

She beckoned, and a woman of about the widow's age came

around them and stood, smiling pleasantly at Mrs. Berringer's side.

"Lady Flora Copely, may I introduce Miss Levett? And I believe you know Mr. Kier?"

Greetings were exchanged, and the widow smiled at her friend. "Lady Flora is the mastermind behind these gardens," she said, indicating all the different levels and their unique designs. "I was very fortunate that she agreed to join me in creating this display."

"Judging by your costume, I might have guessed you were a devoted gardener," Kara said. "And I would hazard a guess that you selected the plants for the boxes?" She indicated the woman's gown, trailing vines and blossoms, and the garland of flowers in her hair.

"I did." Lady Flora looked with satisfaction over all the parts that together made such an impressive display. "We think it turned out beautifully, but we do take care to warn newcomers to the Grove."

"Warn?" Niall raised a brow. "Clearly, I have not spent much time here in the Grove of late."

"Then we must warn you, as well." Mrs. Berringer moved to the first figure. "Here we have Clotho, the maiden, who spins the thread of life for everyone born into the world."

"We planted symbols of rebirth and new life at her feet," Lady Flora explained. "Anemone, daisies, and daffodils."

"Next is Lachesis, the matron," continued Mrs. Berringer. "She measures and allots the length of each life."

"For her we have planted symbols of fertility—poppies and hollyhocks and basket flowers," Lady Flora said. "As we unfortunately could not use orchids or lotus here in the Grove."

"Oh, I love hollyhocks," Kara said. She laid aside her mask, bent down to run a finger over the tall, vivid blooms, and inhaled deeply. "My gardener tells me that they came to England with the Crusaders, who used bits of the plant to make a salve to heal their horses."

"Oh, I hadn't heard about the horses," Lady Flora said, interested.

"If you've seen the pods they produce, filled with a great many seeds, you'll know why they represent fertility," Niall said.

Mrs. Berringer, though, had heard enough of hollyhocks. She moved on and beckoned them to come with her. "And last we have Atropos, the crone who severs the thread and ends a life." The widow stopped in front of the last figure.

"And you chose the poisonous blooms to plant for her?" Niall asked.

"Indeed," Lady Flora agreed. "Belladonna and oleander, both attractive enough to use in any garden, but both deadly."

"Thus the warning," Mrs. Berringer intoned.

"Thank you for explaining and for showing us your work. Your project is both lovely and fascinating." Kara paused. "I trust someone will warn Miss Ottridge?" She looked back and over the Grove, spotting the woman below. She was surprised. Without her mask, Miss Ottridge definitely looked older than Kara had expected.

"Oh, Miss Ottridge will be warned off," Mrs. Berringer said wryly.

Lady Flora had followed Kara's gaze and was staring intently at the other initiate.

"Lady Flora?" Kara asked.

"Oh, yes, of course. We must warn everyone not to touch the more dangerous plants." The lady's slight frown disappeared as she looked between Kara and Niall. "Be sure to show Miss Levett all the other interesting bits spread throughout the Grove. Others have created projects to showcase their interests," she told Kara. "And they are not all from antiquity like ours," she added with a smile.

"As a group, we have determined that if the bards still existed, they would be instrumental in sharing and spreading new knowledge, skills, and industry," Mrs. Berringer said.

Lady Flora leaned closer to speak low near Kara's ear. "Mr.

Chambers has an electricity machine set up in a closet in the summerhouse. Don't let him persuade you to wear the belt he has attached to it, despite his claims of all the ills it can cure."

"I was fool enough to fall for that gambit once, madam," Niall said with a laugh. "I swear, I can still feel the sizzle. I won't allow Miss Levett to make the same mistake."

But Kara had been distracted by a line of embroidery on Lady Flora's gown. "Forgive me, but I studied with Mr. Towland, and I thought I knew most of the Celtic knots. But I don't recognize this one." She pointed to the lighter green embroidery on the lady's long sleeves. "Although I can see it is related to the triquetra."

Lady Flora flushed a little. "Oh, it is one I designed myself."

Kara frowned as she studied it. "Motherhood?"

The other woman looked surprised at her insight—and suddenly intense. "Yes. It depicts the eternal bond of devotion between mother and child." She straightened and gave Kara a shrug and a small smile, waving a hand to encompass her gown. "Of course, I never married, myself, but I can still envision the love that Mother Nature herself must feel for all of her creations. She gives of herself endlessly to sustain us, to give us conditions to thrive. She provides food and drink, companionship and beauty, even music. Her care for us all is clear. Plants, animals, and even mankind."

Mrs. Berringer snorted. "No doubt some of us are more difficult to love than others."

"No doubt," Niall agreed with a grin.

Kara raised her brows at the pair of ladies. "As you've shared your work, perhaps you won't mind if I urge you both to attend the Great Exhibition before it draws to an end? Mr. Kier and I would both love to return the favor and show you our exhibitions. And there is no better place to discover new art, skills, and industry."

"I have been through several times, in fact, accompanying the queen," Lady Flora replied. "She is much intrigued, and I confess I am, as well."

"I thought for sure you must find something to interest you. Have you seen the white terracotta urns sent from Paris?" Kara asked with enthusiasm. "Those would look fine in any garden."

"I have seen them, but I was also much captured by Mr. Wilson's beehive. Have you seen it? I am struck by the idea of making a piece of art from such a common object. I would dearly love to have one in my own garden."

"You'll be accompanying Her Majesty to the closing ceremony, won't you, Lady Flora?" Mrs. Berringer asked. "I am trying to convince Arthur to escort me."

"I shall be happy to have you as my guest, should Mr. Towland prove otherwise occupied," Niall offered.

"Such gallantry." The widow smiled. "I may take you up on that, sir. But now, we will allow you young people to circulate. Remember to stay away from the dangerous blooms." She nodded. "Good evening."

The two women wandered off, and just as Kara turned to Niall, her stomach let out an embarrassing rumble. "I'm afraid I'm going to need more than a cream pastry," she said in apology.

"Let's go, then." Niall was always agreeable when it came to food. "I think I saw a footman with grilled oysters."

"I thought I spotted stuffed bits of venison," she countered. Her stomach grumbled again, and, laughing, they headed downward.

They did manage to track down the stuffed venison, as well as some lemon-flavored tarts. Thus fortified, Kara managed to smile and answer a great many idle questions and genuine welcomes over the next hours.

Niall was correct—she met quite an assortment of interesting characters. One gentleman, with the most enormous of mustaches, quizzed her about the phase of the moon on the night of her birth, insisting that should she find it out, he could use the information to predict her future. Escaping him, she found refuge beneath a spreading oak with a frail older woman who sat strumming a lyre. They had a delightful conversation about ancient music, and the lady proved to know a number of lively, rather risqué songs that soon drew a crowd around them.

After a bit, Kara slipped away. She thought she might actually enjoy growing to know quite a few of the Order's members, but she would definitely prefer to do it in smaller groups.

As the evening drew to a close, she went looking for Niall once more. She was wending her way through the thinning crowd when a woman abruptly collided with her.

"Oh, do forgive me," the woman said with a rush. Plainly dressed, she wore her hair scraped back into a severe bun and one of the plain servant's masks. "Excuse me." She glanced hurriedly over her shoulder as she tried to move around Kara.

"Hold a moment," Kara said, noticing her odd gait. "Have you hurt yourself?"

"No. No. An old injury." The woman looked back again. "Thank you, miss. I must go."

Turning, Kara saw Miss Ottridge approaching, her eye on the fleeing woman.

"Do you know her?" the other initiate demanded as she grew closer.

Kara stiffened. "No. Do you?"

"She looks familiar."

"She looks frightened."

"Yes, she does, doesn't she?" Evidently giving up the pursuit, Miss Ottridge took a step back and ran a measuring eye over her.

Kara had never been truly comfortable around others, but no one had ever made her feel such a flare of instant annoyance. Just standing next to the woman made her feel like a cat whose fur had been rubbed the wrong way.

Breathing deeply, she reached for patience. "I suppose we must both feel relieved," she began. "I wonder if they have ever turned anyone away at their initiation ceremony?"

"An interesting question." Miss Ottridge's gaze scrolled all around them. With a sudden smile, she snapped it back to Kara.

"Although my own acceptance was never in doubt." She nodded. "I wish you a good evening, then. I'm sure we'll see each other here again."

Yes, annoyance. It was honestly the right word. "So irritating," Kara breathed, watching Miss Ottridge go.

"Who? Me?" Niall appeared at her side, seemingly out of thin air.

"No, not you." She grinned at him. "Not presently, at any rate."

"Come, let's head for the summerhouse. Taking leave of these things goes in stages. We'll have to maneuver our way through there to get to the main house, and then work our way out of there, too."

"The sooner, the better. I'm growing tired."

They followed the flow of guests moving in that direction and had made it halfway through the open room when Niall accidentally grazed her with the beak of his mask. She suddenly realized she didn't have her own.

"Oh! That should have been part of the training," she said, indicating the loop on his belt to which he'd hooked his mask. "I must have set mine down somewhere." Kara thought back over the evening, retracing her steps. "I think I must have left it sitting on one of the planters before the Three Fates. Stay here," she ordered him. "I'll run and fetch it and be right back."

She wended through the diminishing crowd, then stopped in surprise when she stepped out onto the patio. The Grove was deserted. The servants had already snuffed out quite a few of the lights. She started across anyway. She could see well enough, and although the lights highlighting the figures of the Fates had been doused, she could see one light left on that particular high terrace.

Kara hurried. She didn't want to keep Niall waiting. That was all that was in her mind as she climbed the last, short set of stairs between terraces. When she reached the top level, though, she froze and gasped.

A small figure, her back toward Kara, was bent over the dead-

ly poison plants before Atropos, carefully picking berries and
leaves and depositing them into a little basket over her arm. She
stilled when she heard Kara's gasp, then deliberately reached out
and tipped over the lantern at her feet.

The light went out. For a moment, Kara could see nothing
but the abrupt darkness. By the time her eyes adjusted, the figure
was gone, rushing to the other side of the long terrace and
hurrying down the short stairs that led to the next level, a
different one from the level Kara had just climbed past.

Kara's ears worked just fine, though. She noticed the sound of
the hitched, uneven gait of the figure's hasty retreat.

Her mind awhirl, Kara inched forward and found her mask
right where she'd thought it would be. Turning, she made her
careful way back to the summerhouse, encountering not a soul
on the way.

Chapter Two

MR. NIALL KIER gazed out across the crowds from behind the large, Scottish-themed gate he'd created—the one that had clinched his position as an exhibitor here in the Crystal Palace. It felt as if there were as many visitors here on the last day of the Great Exhibition as there had been every day over the life of the event. Thousands, each and every day.

It had been a risk, to be sure, setting himself up as an exhibitor. Queen Victoria had visited thirty-four times. Her approval had meant that nearly everyone in Society followed in her wake. But he'd been careful. He'd made himself scarce when he had to. Made himself invisible when he must. He did not believe he'd caught the attention of anyone he should not, save for that of the all-knowing Lord Stayme—and there would have been no hiding his presence from that one, in any case.

And he'd been right. The benefits had far outweighed the risks. His reputation as an artist was growing—and no one questioned his name or background. His business was booming. He had more commissions than he could keep up with and more consultations waiting in the wings. He'd been invited to Paris, Vienna, and Oslo. He had several projects underway already, at his new forge at Bluefield Park.

Bluefield Park—and his friendship with the great estate's

mistress, Kara Levett. Therein lay the greatest change wrought by his time here at the Great Exhibition. A change that provided both benefit and risk.

"Niall? Niall? Are you listening?"

He turned a blank stare on his assistant. "I'm sorry, Gyda. What was that?"

"Kara's coming." She made an unobtrusive motion. "And look who is with her."

He came out from behind the gate to look.

"Can you scarcely believe it?" Kara asked, approaching. "It doesn't feel real, that this should be the end."

"Two more days," Niall reminded her. "Inspector Wooten." He greeted her companion with a bow. "I am surprised to find you here."

The inspector raised his hands, as if in surrender. "All hands on deck for the closing ceremonies. Prince Albert will be speaking. Other members of the court and the royal family are here today. We cannot be too careful." He frowned. "What was that you said about two more days, though? I thought this was to be the last day?"

"Today is the last open to the public, but the exhibitions will stay in place for two days so that the families and friends of the exhibitors may all visit, free of charge." Niall glanced at the man expectantly. "You mentioned, once, that your wife was hoping to come. We should be glad to welcome her, if she has not made it."

"Oh, no. She's been twice already," the inspector said, shaking his head. "But I thank you for thinking of her."

"Lady Flora sent the inspector to bring us along," Kara told him. "She means to make sure we have a good view of the proceedings."

"How kind," Niall remarked. He aimed a raised brow at Wooten. "Are you well acquainted with Lady Flora Copely, sir?"

The man reddened slightly. "I am, but recently. You will recall that I was involved with the court when we were investigating that thwarted case of espionage. Afterward, the prince thought it wise to maintain multiple lines of communication between Scotland Yard and the court. Her Majesty, of course, is briefed by the home secretary, who is kept informed by the commissioners. The prince wished to also keep a relationship with someone with boots on the street."

"And his ear to the ground?" asked Niall.

"Just so. Just so," Wooten answered. "Won't you come along? Lady Flora invited you both, specifically."

"Of course," Kara replied. "It's a kind invitation."

Niall looked to Gyda. "Will you join us?"

"Nay." She shook her head. "I've lived the Exhibition. I've no need hear anyone natter on about it, not even your Prince Albert."

"Turner holds the same opinion," Kara told her. "He stayed home today to do inventory of the wine cellars."

"Well, perhaps later I'll return and convince him to do a bit of tasting, eh?" Gyda grinned. "Good day to you. I have a friend to meet."

"Do try not to have too much of a good time," Niall cautioned her with a grin.

"Ah, Niall, my lad," Gyda said sadly. "So long we've known each other, and I still haven't managed to teach you the truth. There is no such thing as *too much* of a good time." Shaking her head at him, she smiled at Kara, nodded to Wooten, and slipped into the crowd.

Laughing, Niall turned to the others. "Shall we?"

They moved into the stream of visitors heading toward the barrel vault, where the perfumed fountain stood and where the prince meant to make his remarks. Niall's mind was churning, trying to devise a way to avoid the illustrious group they'd been asked to join.

Inspector Wooten was worrying about something else. "Speaking of having my ear to the ground," he began, "I've heard a rumor or two about you moving into the young lady's home, Mr. Kier. Is it true, then?"

He did not sound approving.

In front of him, Niall saw Kara's spine stiffen. "No. It is not," she answered tartly.

"Well, I should tell you what I've heard—"

"Oh, I know what you've heard, sir," she snapped. "And none of it good. Well, I give you leave to correct anyone else who might mention it. You can tell them that it is Miss Gyda Winther who has taken up residence in my home."

"Oh, that is good to hear, but—"

"To be fair, sir, Miss Levett has kindly set up a forge for me in one of her outbuildings," Niall interrupted. "I have a cot in the loft above it, and do occasionally sleep there, if I have worked into the night."

"He would not take a room in the house," Kara said sourly.

"I have not given up my rooms in London," Niall added.

"And well you have not," Wooten said with approval. "And you should thank the lad, young lady. The things I've heard! No one in your proper sphere will hold with Mr. Kier staying in your home—and you with no family nor proper chaperone."

"I have a house full of the most prudish servants, sir. It is guaranteed that nothing untoward would happen under their watch—indeed, under Turner's!"

"Well, there is that," Wooten mumbled. "Turner's reputation is polished amongst those at Scotland Yard, but it won't hold with the matrons of Society."

"How well I know it. My people, in fact, are being kept very busy denying such rumors to the gossipy servants' network."

"And I shall set straight those I speak to," the inspector assured her.

"I would appreciate it, sir."

Niall feared the damage had already been done, but that worry was for another day. Right now, he needed to concentrate on avoiding the esteemed personages they were headed toward.

He didn't have to worry, in the end. Lady Flora stood on an elevated platform with the rest of the court and the royal party.

When she saw them leave the British nave, she hurried down and over to join them.

"Mr. Kier. Miss Levett."

Greetings were exchanged. Inspector Wooten was called over to the platform.

Lady Flora smiled and took one of Kara's hands and one of Niall's into her own. "My dears. There are a great many awards to be given today, but so many more deserving exhibitors. Mr. Towland, Mrs. Berringer, and I all agreed that you have done great credit to the Order, with your experiences and conduct during this Great Exhibition. We gathered the council together, and all are agreed. Therefore, we are happy to present you these medals of merit, to honor your achievements here and to let you know how much we value them."

Niall exchanged glances with Kara as the lady rummaged in her reticule and pulled out two small boxes. Each contained a lovely bronze medal. One side of each was carved with a harp, and the other a stag's head.

He was touched, quite honestly, and he could see Kara was as well. "Thank you, ma'am. This is indeed an honor."

Lady Flora fussed a little, helping Kara pin her medal to her bodice. "Mr. Towland wished to be here to make the presentation, but he was called to court," she explained.

"Oh, that is too bad," Niall said, recalling his promise. "I know Mrs. Berringer wished to accompany him here today."

"Oh, she is here." She waved a hand toward the growing crowd around the fountain. "Somewhere. She convinced several of the council members to join her."

"Good."

"There, now." Lady Flora laid the medal flat against the fabric of Kara's bodice. "I am glad you have become a member of the Order, dear. I urge you to make the most of it." She sighed. "I have been a member since the beginning, and I'm so grateful for the chance to be a part of such a lovely, lively, and curious group." Her smile flattened a little. "You don't find many ladies of the court interested in growing things or learning about ancient tales, or the history and development of music."

"I daresay the ladies of the court are interested in the same things as other ladies in Society," Kara ventured.

"Gossip and husbands?" Niall asked.

"And lovers' intrigues," Lady Flora added. "Someone is always looking for a bit of spice to add to the tittle-tattle." She shook her head. "I should not complain. I've been honored to have been appointed as a Woman of the Bedchamber for several terms, but in my free days, I do cherish the chance to explore my interests in the Grove."

"Have you always been interested in plants and gardening?" Kara asked her.

"Oh, yes. Since I was a young girl. And the more I learn, the more interested I become in how the Druids regarded nature and I realize how vast and wonderful and powerful it is." She squeezed Kara's hand. "Do take advantage of everything the Grove has to offer, dear, but be careful as you go. The bards and the Druids studied the wheel of life, and they understood that nature requires a balance. There is much light to absorb, but there must be darkness in measure."

Niall was surprised by her warning. "I admit, there are eccentrics aplenty to be found in the Order, ma'am. But darkness?"

Lady Flora nodded but didn't get the chance to speak further, as Inspector Wooten returned. Kara showed him her medal. He made his compliments and was just suggesting that they all join the larger party when a disturbance arose in the crowd.

A low murmur of distress moved out from a fixed point near the fountain. There was a surge away from the spot. Niall seized upon the opportunity. "Something is amiss." He craned to see, then looked to Kara. "Stay with Lady Flora. I'll go and investigate."

"Hold a moment." Wooten was gazing up at the upper gallery, where one of his officers was at the rail.

"It's a woman, sir," the policeman called down. "It looks as if she's collapsed."

"Probably the heat and the close crowd," Wooten muttered. He motioned to two of his blue-coated officers standing watch nearby. "Clear the way," he ordered them. "Go back to the platform, ladies. I'll return shortly."

Niall followed.

Kara jumped to the end of their line, too. "I'm coming," she declared.

He didn't bother to argue.

It took a few moments to push through. People had surged back in, and a wall of gathered onlookers stood around a woman stretched out on the floor. She lay on her back. As the officers herded the crowd back a few steps, Niall approached and saw dark hair showing where her bonnet had been knocked askew. A man still crouched beside her. He alternated between patting her cheek and feeling at her throat for a pulse.

"What's this, then?" Wooten said, walking around to her feet.

The man looked up, his eyes wide. "She was in some distress, sir. Having trouble breathing, clutching her chest."

"She shot the cat," a young voice called from the crowd.

"Yes, so I can see," Wooten said, looking away from a spray of vomit.

"She collapsed," the gentleman said. "Taken by a fit."

Niall knelt down beside him. Kara did as well, and touched her fingers to the woman's wrist.

"Her heart was racing," the man said. "But now ... I think she's gone."

"She drank something," a woman called. "I was right next to her. She snatched up a drink from a girl's hand and drank it right down. Soon after, she started to choke."

Niall stood. "Drank what?" he asked. "Where is the drink?" He scanned the floor around the body, trying to see past a sea of skirts, shoes, and boots.

"Someone took it up," another man called out. "The lady dropped it. I saw it, right there." He pointed. "But we were all watching her when she had her fit, and when I looked back, the cup was gone."

"It looked like the bubbling water. The sort they are selling at the refreshment rooms." The woman sounded confident. "But it had berries in it." She frowned. "The girl carried two cups, but I don't see her laid out, dead."

"The drink had leaves in it, too," the man added. "I saw them, spilling out as the cup rolled. They are gone, too."

Niall heard Kara's indrawn breath.

"Who is she?" Wooten said, his voice ringing out. "Who came here with this poor soul?"

No one spoke.

"Well?" Wooten asked the man who had knelt beside her.

"I've no notion," he replied, getting to his feet. "I never saw her before today."

"We have," Kara said quietly. "Look, Niall." Gently, she closed the woman's staring eyes. "It's Miss Ottridge."

Chapter Three

INSPECTOR WOOTEN SET his men to scrambling, and soon enough Miss Ottridge's body was carried away. Order was restored.

"Poor woman suffered a fit," the inspector said soothingly to those who asked. As the crowd quieted, he moved back toward the platform, where the royal party milled about, waiting. Kara was surprised when Niall took her arm and inclined his head toward the exit, a question in his eye.

"Oh, yes, please," she answered. "Let's find a private place to talk."

First, they had to break free of the growing crowd, then they were forced to maneuver through those gathered outside, shopping among the souvenir vendors. Moving around to the side of the Crystal Palace, they found it much less busy. Taking a bench beneath a tree, they sat silently for several long moments, each absorbed in their own thoughts.

Abruptly, they both spoke at once.

"It cannot be a coincidence, can it?" Kara asked.

"How long until he considers Towland a suspect?" Niall said, sounding worried.

They stared at each other.

"Which coincidence?" Niall demanded.

"Berries and leaves, what else? Belladonna and oleander?" She blew an exasperated breath as he continued to look distracted. "Niall! Several days ago, I told you I saw someone gathering berries and leaves from the poisonous plants in the Grove—"

"Someone," he interrupted. "A woman."

"Someone in skirts," she corrected him. "It might have been a disguise." She thought about it. "But I did hear an uneven gait as they ran across the level below. That one is paved with flagstones." She told him about her encounter with the serving girl who had a limp, and had appeared to be fleeing Jane Ottridge.

He nodded absently.

"And now, here that same woman is poisoned by berries and leaves?" Kara said.

"The woman in the crowd said she snatched the drink from the girl who carried it. What if it wasn't meant for her at all? What if the girl was carrying it to someone else?"

"She was a self-proclaimed blackmailer. What are the odds that she was accidentally poisoned? After her performance the other night, it seems impossible that whoever did it wouldn't be someone connected with the Order."

"And with all the gossip about Jane Ottridge blackmailing Towland to allow her in, my question stands. How long until Wooten names him a suspect?"

"Not long," she answered grimly. "But you know he did not do it. Arthur Towland is no murderer."

"Absolutely not." His solemn gaze met hers. "But he is a police court magistrate. Even the suggestion of it could ruin him."

She felt the truth of that like a stab in her side. It hadn't been so long since she had been in the same frightening, frustrating state. "We will not allow that to happen."

"No," he agreed.

"You don't think that might be a motive for murder? To destroy Towland? Who would wish him such ill?"

"Perhaps we should—"

"There you are!"

They both turned to find Inspector Wooten had come around the corner. He waved his hat before his face as he advanced on them. "One of my men spotted you two out here." He leaned against the tree as Niall stood. "Good heavens, but it is growing warm in there."

"Are the ceremonies complete, then?" Kara asked.

"No. The awards are still going on, but I wanted to catch you before you'd gone." He replaced his hat and stood straight. "The coroner's officer has taken the body."

"He has decided it was foul play?"

"Of course he did. There will be an inquest. You two will likely be called as witnesses."

"I shall gladly stand as witness," Kara said blandly. "But I expect that this time my name will not be bandied about as a suspect. I trust the fact that I was standing next to you, Inspector, at the moment of the crime, will see me clear."

The man flushed a little, but Niall took pity on him.

"You got the names and directions of those who were near the lady when she ... went down?" Niall asked.

"I did." Wooten cleared his throat. "I also retrieved this." He held out a small notebook. "From her skirt pocket."

Niall took it and sat next to her again so they could examine it together. The pages were closely filled in two columns.

"Names. More precisely, surnames," Niall corrected himself. "And numbers."

"In pounds and pence," she said quietly.

"She's nearly filled it halfway," Wooten said with a sigh. "Look to the last page she used, if you will."

Niall riffled through. He saw it before Kara did. She felt him stiffen beside her. Silently, he pointed. It was the next-to-last entry.

"Towland," she read. "Five hundred pounds."

"Just thumbing through, I picked out several prominent names. And several very large numbers." Wooten switched into his Inspector-Detective-Asking-Questions tone. "You knew them both, Mr. Kier. How is the dead woman associated with the magistrate of the Marylebone Police Court?"

"She is—was—a new member of the Order," Kara replied. "If there is more than that, I am unaware of it."

"One of his Druids?" The inspector flicked a glance toward her. "Until today, I did not know that he admitted women."

Kara bristled. "Do you take issue with it, sir?"

"Not at all. It's his club. He has every right to run it as he sees fit." He frowned. "But not to go about murdering people. Druids or otherwise."

She pointed a finger. "You know Towland. As we do. We all know he did not murder the woman."

"If that book is what I think it is, it will prove to be a strong motive." Wooten sighed. "Others will see this. There will be talk. His name will be connected. I would like to speak with him before word gets out. If I have answers ready to the questions that will arise, then it will help keep his reputation clean."

"I think we all want that," she agreed.

"And you wish, as well, to also protect the reputation of the police and their court system," Niall said shrewdly.

"You cannot blame me for that!" Wooten said. "You know the mistrust people still hold for us, and the harassment our officers often suffer. We cannot allow any further doubts to fester. I don't believe the magistrate is a killer, but I must look into the possibility. I would prefer to handle the matter myself and do it quickly and quietly." He fixed Niall with a look. "I thought you might help."

"How?"

"You know the man. Come with me to speak with him, so it might not be construed as—"

"The questioning it is?" Kara asked.

"Precisely. And perhaps also …"

She suddenly understood. "You would like to speak with him in an out-of-the-way location, perhaps?"

"It would be best if we did it away from the court, and I would rather not be seen in his home or anyplace he might be associated with. Keep the talk to a minimum."

"Done," Kara stated. "I invite you to Bluefield Park, sir. After dinner tonight? A friendly gathering for … cards and conversation, perhaps? I am sure we can persuade Mr. Towland to attend."

"Thank you, Miss Levett," the inspector said with obvious relief. "I appreciate your help."

⇒⇒⇒≪≪≪

HOURS LATER, KARA emerged from her rooms with Turner by her side.

"Set up a card table in the green parlor. We should at least make the attempt to make this look like a social call. But also be sure to group enough chairs around the settee to make conversation easy."

Her butler—and friend, confidant, and lab manager—nodded. "The fire has been lit to drive out the chill. Cook is assembling a tea tray. She made a fig and apple tart and whipped fresh cream." His mouth twisted a bit as he relayed that last bit of information.

Kara bit back a smile. "I did hear Niall ask for his compliments to be sent after she served the same sweet last week. Another conquest." She grinned. "Well, I won't object, as I happen to enjoy her apple tart as well. And though I know she won't be the last Bluefield woman to develop a *tendre* for him, I do hope she doesn't join the pack of maids and laundresses who dredge up any excuse to stroll past the forge. Something in the kitchens will be sure to burn, should she join in the parade."

"I had a word with Mrs. Bolt about it, but she says it will not stop—not as long as Mr. Kier wears a kilt to work in and little else."

"Well, I am not going to tell him how to work," Kara said. "We will all adjust, I'm sure."

She started down the stairs. Before they reached the first landing, one of the housemaids came hurrying up.

"Begging your pardon, Mr. Turner." The maid dipped her head. "Miss Levett." She handed a card on a tray to Turner. "There is a visitor below."

"So soon?" Kara asked. "Is it Mr. Towland or the inspector?"

"Neither, miss," the maid breathed. "'Tis something else altogether. A *viscount!*"

"A what?" Kara said as Turner lifted the card, examined it, and passed it over.

"He's got the most chilling eyes I ever saw on a man," the girl said, giving a little shudder. At Turner's sharp look, she straightened. "Sorry, sir. I put him in the ivory sitting room, miss, as I didn't know if you wanted him mixing with your other guests."

"Thank you, Prudence."

The maid curtsied and continued upstairs, while Kara and Turner went down. "The Viscount Stayme? I don't believe we are acquainted. Why on earth would he come calling? And at this hour?" She frowned at Turner. "How long until the others arrive?"

"Just past an hour until they are due," he reminded her.

"Very well. I shall see him. But don't send tea," she warned.

He nodded, and Kara felt the comfort of knowing he would keep watch. Continuing on down a passageway, she went to the sitting room, a small, cozy spot where she spent many mornings when she was in the design phase of her work or attending to her correspondence. A footman stood outside the door. She nodded to him as she approached. He opened the door, and she swept in to meet her guest.

"Lord Stayme, what an unexpected pleasure. Welcome to Bluefield Park."

The gentleman stood at her bookcase, examining the contents. He turned to greet her, bowed, and then gave her an appraising look that made her glad she'd given in to her maid's urgings to don her tighter, more uncomfortable evening corset and a very fashionable, deep green silk damask.

"Good evening, Miss Levett. It is very good of you to see me when I have arrived unannounced." The viscount was older, thin, and very stylish, from his slick, coiffed hair to his smooth, manicured hands, and right down to the shine of his dress shoes. He gave her a practiced smile. "I knew your parents, you know. You look very like your mother."

She took it as a compliment. Her mother had been a renowned beauty. "Thank you."

He looked around. "This is a charming room. I confess, I've always harbored a wish to see Bluefield."

"If you were friends with my parents, then I am surprised you have not seen it already. I've heard they dearly loved to entertain, while my mother still lived."

His brow rose. "I said I knew them, but we were not friends. Not precisely. Your father found me too free with my opinions, I believe." He gave her a friendly smile. "I daresay you will come to feel the same."

She laughed. "Sir, my father was called many things. A radical, a socialist, a madman. After all, what man with a title and a fortune fouled himself with the running of an industrial empire?"

"He did, as all of your quite eccentric family did, before him, I believe."

"Exactly. I don't have the title, but that is a small difference, as I have the estate, the fortune, the iron and coal works, and other manufactories. But there is a bigger difference between my father and me."

"Oh?" He sounded truly interested.

"Yes. I am a woman. I am very much accustomed to anyone and everyone making free with their opinions."

Stayme laughed. "And I daresay you make the same use of them as he did."

"None at all. So, you may feel free to share your opinions, and I will feel free to ignore them, just as I do all the rest." She moved to one of the seats before the cold hearth and gestured.

"Now, won't you sit and tell me why you've come?"

He sat across from her but turned his head back to the book-case. "You have quite an eclectic collection here."

She nodded. "We have a lovely library, of course, but this is where I keep my particular favorites."

"And varied they are—and quite a few matches with my own favorites, I confess."

"Well, that bodes well for our friendship, doesn't it?"

"It might, at that." He gestured. "I noticed the well-thumbed copy of *Vanity Fair*. A tale like that, I suppose it is catnip to girls your age."

"And to a great many others, as well. Have you read it, sir?"

"Every word. Everyone I know has read it exhaustively, look-ing for signs of themselves in it."

She laughed, then raised a brow. "Well, now that you bring it up, there is a certain closeness between your name and the manipulative Lord Steyne. Are you saying that he is modeled after yourself?"

"Gracious, no." The viscount made a face. "Thackeray's Steyne doesn't come close to my own wickedness."

"Duly noted, sir."

"Well, that didn't put you out of countenance, did it, young lady? Do you know, my neighbor Lady Redman was also a devoted fan of the story, until she found her daughter was just as caught up in it. That changed her tune."

"What did she do?"

"She took the novel from the girl and called in the vicar to explain just why the story was so unsuitable."

Kara made a face.

Stayme tilted his head. "Are you not, then, one of those who is disappointed that the author does not use his characters to give us a moral or social prescription for reformation?"

"Not at all."

"Tell me, then, what did you take away from our *Novel Without a Hero*?"

She considered before answering. "A conviction that Mr. Thackeray is a great observer of human nature, but also that he does not actually like people very much."

Snorting, he gave her a long, critical look that lasted much longer than politeness dictated.

"We share a similar taste in friends, as well as in literature, Miss Levett," he said abruptly. "I have come to see Mr. Niall Kier."

"Oh, how nice," she said placidly. "I am afraid you won't find him in the house, though. Not unless it's one of the rare occasions we can tempt him in to dine with us. If he's at Bluefield, you will find him in his forge."

"He told me as much, but I have been more than curious to meet you, my dear."

"And now you have, sir." Kara stood. "I have a bit of time. I would be happy to take you through the house. We can go out the back, and I will walk you to the forge."

"That sounds delightful. How accommodating you are."

Her smile was as sharp as his look had been. "I am, sir. When I wish to be."

His eyes glittered as he offered his arm.

Kara took it and guided him out. She took him through the house and allowed the beauty of Bluefield to speak for her. She would hold it up against any estate of any nobleman in the country.

The viscount let his appreciation show as they made their way. He breathed deeply as they stepped outside, but held quiet as they strolled through the garden and out into the grounds. The moon still hid behind the trees, and the stars overhead shone bright. Wind rustled the leaves, still full, though their lovely autumn colors were hidden in the dark.

"One forgets," Stayme said, taking another deep breath. "It reminds me I have spent too much time, of late, in the city."

They approached the forge, coming toward a solid wall. The two perpendicular walls were set with large sliding doors, both now standing open and sending flickering light out into the darkness. As they made their way to the opening, they caught sight of Niall, pounding furiously at something on his anvil.

Yes. One does forget.

He looked magnificent. He'd tied his longish hair out of the way. Light and shadow moved across his face, highlighting then hiding the stark bones, the harsh lines of his brows, leading straight to the long line of an aquiline nose. He'd thrown off his shirt, and his long torso shone in the heat of the fire. His kilt swung as he hammered, and she found her gaze lingering on the long, muscled lines of his calves.

The viscount's grip on her arm tightened.

"Are you well?" she asked.

"Yes," he said softly. "I am just an old man caught in the imaginings of what might have been." He gave her a knowing look. "And you, my dear? What are you thinking?"

She looked back toward Niall's tall form. "That it is no wonder the maids keep sneaking out here."

Stayme laughed as she stepped forward.

"Niall!" She waved a hand to catch her friend's attention. "You have a visitor!"

The pounding stopped. Niall looked up, frowning. "Already?"

The viscount stepped out of the shadows. "It's me, I am afraid."

Niall blinked in surprise. "What are you doing here, old man?"

"I need a word."

Wiping a hand across his brow, Niall let his hammer drop and took up his shirt.

"I'll leave you to your visit," Kara said. "But I will remind you, Niall, that there will be visitors in the parlor within the hour, should you care to join us."

"I won't take up half so much time," the viscount assured her.

"I hadn't forgot," Niall told her. "I'll be there."

She turned to go.

"Miss Levett, a moment?" Lord Stayme called.

"Yes?" She turned back.

"Tell me, please. In *Vanity Fair*, after they reconcile at the end, are you of the opinion that Becky Sharpe killed Mr. Joseph Sedley?"

"What?" The question startled her. "No."

"It is not made absolutely clear in the narrative, just how he dies," the viscount pressed.

"No." She shook her head. "Becky Sharpe is a manipulative character, it is true. And utterly focused on finding her way to financial stability. But a killer? And after she obtains her ultimate goal? Absolutely not."

Niall gave her a look. "I'll see you inside, Kara."

"Very well. Goodnight, Lord Stayme. It was a pleasure to meet you." To her surprise, she meant it.

"Good evening, young lady. I do believe it was a pleasure to meet you, as well." He paused. "If ever you find yourself in need, my dear, you may call upon me."

She paused. It was an odd way to part. "Thank you, sir. I shall extend you the same offer."

He laughed. "Yes," he said, nodding in approval. "It has indeed been a pleasure."

With a smile for both men, she slipped out and headed for the house.

Chapter Four

NIALL TOOK UP a towel to wipe the sweat from his brow and the back of his neck. He stared wordlessly at his debonair old friend. For a man with a reputation for a reportedly wild and varied life, Stayme certainly did not look like he was familiar with the inside of a working forge.

"What? No words of welcome?" the viscount demanded.

"They are coming, old man. But just now, I am trying to recall the last time *you* came to *me*."

Stayme snorted. "You were small enough to dandle on my knee."

"That's what I thought. So, what is it that's brought you here now? It must be dire. And don't try to tell me you only came to meet Miss Levett."

"Well, I certainly have been wanting to meet her." Stayme paused, considering. "She is remarkably self-possessed for such a young lady."

"She is." Niall tossed aside the towel and fetched a wooden chair from the corner. He moved it a comfortable distance from the fire. "She's earned every bit of the confidence she possesses, too."

"So, it's true, then? The rumors of all the various lessons and trainings?"

"True."

"All of it? The fighting? The escapes? The high-wire walking?"

Niall paused. "The first two? Definitely. But this is first I've heard of the high wire." He grinned. "Wouldn't surprise me, though." He nodded for the old man to sit, then perched upon a nearby crate. "What is it, my lord? Tell me straight out."

"Nobody has died, you young fool." Stayme's tone hardened. "But there is trouble. Just a whisper."

"A whisper no one has heard but you?"

"Naturally."

Niall waited.

"It's Marston. He's been crawling about the city, into every pawn shop and secondhand store. He's even approached some of the better-known criminal fences. He's asking after a particular miniature. A portrait locket."

Niall breathed deeply.

"A portrait of a lady with her infant," Stayme said. "I need to know if she's seen it." He leaned forward. "Were you so foolish as to let her see it?"

The old man's words, his accusation, the worry and fear behind it all—they were lockpicks that worked inside of Niall to swing open a door he'd closed years ago. A hundred memories and feelings rushed out to swirl around him and obscure everything else. Hope turned to despair. Love to hate. Anger. Wariness. Betrayal. There were reasons he kept it all locked away.

"Yes," he said harshly. "But I caught her before she saw more than a glimpse." How many years ago had it been? He'd only just realized that things had begun to disappear. Silver candlesticks, a glass vase, a carved frame. He'd no more than had the thought than he went to check, and he'd found her with the bed pushed aside and her fingers in the secret compartment beneath the floor. "I doubt she saw enough for an accurate description. She cannot know anything."

"Then why is Marston looking?"

"I don't know." But it was worrying. "You cannot ask him or warn him off. You will only convince him of the rightness of whatever maggoty suspicions he has in his head. He's an ass, but a tenacious one."

"Do you think I am new to this?" Stayme said, aghast. "Where is it now?"

"Safe." Niall gave the old man a pointed look. "They are both safe."

"Both?" The viscount stilled. "You have them both?"

Niall nodded. "Both safely tucked away where they will never be found."

"I hope that you are right. I don't have to tell you—"

"No. You don't. Just ignore Marston."

"Easier to do now. He's just taken himself off to Paris."

"Following a wrong track? Good. Let him keep on."

"And you keep your head down. After the risks you've taken at the Exhibition, you need to lie low."

Niall gestured toward the forge. "I have enough work to last me a year or more. Perhaps two."

Stayme stood. Somehow, the flickering light aged him even more. "I am serious, my boy. One murder investigation was bad. Two will get you noticed in places you've no wish to be thought of."

Niall sighed. Of course the viscount knew. He knew everything. "I'm just speaking up for a friend. I'll keep out of sight."

"Good."

Niall smiled. "I assume you came in your carriage?"

"I did. You know how I feel about the railway."

"Send Wilson my best." The giant of a coachman would keep the old man safe. He'd done so for a good while now.

Stayme nodded, his distant dignity wrapping about him like a cloak once more. "Keep well, Niall."

"You do the same, sir."

Niall watched him go, lost in memories for a moment, before he looked at the clock and headed up to his loft to clean up.

>>><<<

KARA STOOD AS the parlor door opened, a greeting on her lips. It died away in surprise. "Mrs. Berringer! How ..." *Unexpected.* "How delightful to see you."

"Good evening, Miss Levett. I am aware of my unpardonably bad manners, pushing in where I was not invited, but if it is confessions you are after, you might as well hear all of it."

"Oh. Yes." Kara waved her in. "I have heard of your admirable efficiency, ma'am. Do come in."

Behind her, Mr. Towland was speaking quietly with Turner. The knocker sounded and her butler turned away, leaving the magistrate to drift into the room. He looked pale. A shadow of the vibrant man she was used to.

When he saw Kara, he began to shake his head. "Dead," he said woodenly. "I can scarcely believe it. She was a dreadful woman, to be sure, but who would have thought it would come to this?" He took Kara's hand and patted it. "Whatever the outcome, I have heard of your gallant defense, and I appreciate it. I thank you, too, for the chance to tell my side in relative privacy." He shuddered. "Anyone but Wooten would have cornered me at the court and made a spectacle of the thing."

"Of course, sir. You know Niall and I will do anything to help."

He sat down next to Mrs. Berringer on the settee. "One small mistake," he said, looking mournful. "The merest step off the path—and it all culminates in a mess like this." He sighed. "It is a lesson to us all."

His melancholy words struck Kara. She recalled the inspector's words about her reputation and hoped there were not too many parallels between their missteps.

But then the door opened and Niall came in, still damp at the edges. Her heart lightened immediately, and she knew she could not regret her decisions.

She'd just called for the tea tray when Inspector Wooten entered. He bowed to Mr. Towland and spoke kindly to everyone else. Kara dispensed tea all around, but no one had the stomach for apple tart. The room fell quiet until the inspector cleared his throat.

"Mr. Towland, sir. You must know I offer you the utmost respect. Your work, your way of fairly interpreting the law and balancing it with a keen sense of mercy, your reputation—"

"I thank you, Inspector," Towland interrupted him. He had retrieved some of his natural air of authority. "But I assume you have found evidence of Miss Ottridge's blackmail, and thus I find my reputation, my career, and everything else at risk."

Wooten's eyes widened in surprise. "That is the case, sir."

Towland sighed. He glanced over at Mrs. Berringer and spoke bluntly. "Well, it's true. The woman did blackmail me. I paid her price and considered the matter at an end. She'd already moved on to someone else." He looked around at them all. "I had no reason to kill her, you see."

Wooten took up his notebook and pencil. "I'm afraid we are going to need more than that, sir."

Mr. Towland closed his eyes. After a moment, he nodded.

"Whenever you are ready, sir. I will need the whole story, though," the inspector warned. "Start at the beginning. When did you first come in contact with Miss Ottridge?"

"I saw her for the first time about two months ago. She might have been studying me for longer, but if so, I had not noticed her. However, she obviously knew things about me."

"What sort of things?" asked Wooten.

"On my days as a sitting magistrate, rather than the presiding officer of the court, I often go around the corner to Stedd's Chop House for my dinner."

"Ah, yes." Wooten nodded. "His wife's oyster chowder."

"Divine," Towland said with a sigh. "And perhaps my undoing. For it was just outside Stedd's that I first set eyes on Janet Ottridge. She was speaking excitedly to a man just outside the place, rhapsodizing about a work of art. I would have passed her by without noticing, had she not mentioned the name of the piece. *Cerridwyn's Lament.*"

Niall leaned forward. "Then she did, indeed, target you specifically, sir?"

"I see it clearly now, but I was just a damned fool at that point."

Wooten paused in his note taking. "I'm afraid I don't follow."

Kara was trying to piece it together. Cerridwyn ... the Welsh goddess of wisdom ... "Ah!" she said suddenly. "I see. Taliesin."

"Yes. I'm glad to know you were paying attention when I spoke of Druid lore," Towland said. He looked to the inspector. "Cerridwyn is the goddess who keeps the cauldron of knowledge and brews the potion of wisdom and inspiration. It takes a year and a day to prepare. Legend says she set her serving boy, Gwion, to watch it. The boy accidentally touched the hot cauldron, stuck his fingers in his mouth, and ingested the potion, absorbing great wisdom, knowledge, and power."

"To shorten the story, for Arthur could go on for hours," Mrs. Berringer said, shooting Towland a look of affectionate exasperation, "the goddess was furious. Gwion led her on an epic chase in which they both transformed numerous times, always trying to escape or destroy each other. In the end, she swallowed the boy and, in nine months, gave birth to the child who would become the great bard, Taliesin."

"Taliesin the Bard is a figure of history and myth," Kara added. "It is well known how interested—"

"Fascinated. Absorbed," Mrs. Berringer corrected her.

"Mr. Towland's interest in Taliesin is well known," Kara finished.

"I see." Wooten looked to the magistrate. "Did you speak to the lady, then, sir?"

"No," Towland replied. "I paused and pretended to clean out my pipe on the other side of the doorway, all while listening to her rapturous description. The boy, the fiery goddess, the look in his eye as he absorbs all the light and music and wisdom of the world. I went into the chophouse, but I do not recall eating a meal. My mind was caught up in the images she spoke of." He glanced around. "The ladies are correct, of course. Taliesin is a passion of mine. I knew I had to have the painting for my collection."

"*Then* you spoke to the lady?"

"No. She was gone by the time I made up my mind. Still, I was utterly determined to find her and find out more about that painting."

Mrs. Berringer gave a nod of agreement.

"I went back by the chophouse. Several times a day. For several days. I was hoping to see the lady again. Finally, late on the third day, I caught a glimpse of her walking down the street."

Niall gave Kara a look, and she nodded. The woman had been knowledgeable and wily. She'd waited long enough for Towland to be desperately disappointed, but not so long that he'd given up.

Wooten raised a brow.

"Yes. Then I spoke to her," Towland said.

"Arthur! You just walked up to the woman on the street and began to speak to her?" Mrs. Berringer clearly did not approve of such a breach of manners.

"You know what a state I was in by then, Imogen. I conducted myself in an utterly respectful manner, but yes, I introduced myself and told her I'd heard her speaking of the painting. She was friendly and didn't seem at all offended. She said it was such an unusual piece, she could not forget it. She did say it was beyond her, however, as it was to be sold at an auction house and would likely be priced at more than she could spare."

"She gave you the name of the auction house?" Wooten's pencil was poised.

Towland color rose. "She did."

Everyone waited.

"It was to be sold off by Banks and Burroughs," the magistrate said quietly.

Wooten's pencil dropped. "Oh, sir. You didn't."

"I did." Towland straightened his shoulders.

"I warned him against it," declared Mrs. Berringer.

"I don't understand?" said Kara.

Wooten was scribbling again. "It's not a respectable business," he explained. "Banks and Burroughs are known to accept stolen goods. It's hinted that they sometimes orchestrate burglaries themselves. They seem to be always just a step ahead of the police. They set up their auctions in taverns or in empty stores or warehouses in disreputable areas. They circulate word of the date and location, host a day's sale, then move on."

"I know I should not have gone," Towland said. "They held this particular auction in a back room at the Hare and the Dog."

Even Kara had heard of the place. It was a particularly notorious tavern located in the warren around Covent Garden.

"I thought I would just see the painting, perhaps discover the name of the artist. But of course, once I was there, I had to have it." Towland's expression grew grim. "I bid on the painting, and someone in the back bid against me, again and again. I was triumphant when I won." He scowled. "Until the end of the auction, when I went to make my payment, I spotted the same woman. Miss Ottridge. She was in a dark corner, arguing with Mr. Banks. They were face to face, hissing insults at each other as she demanded payment for luring me in and for running up the price I paid. I realized what a fool I'd been." He covered his eyes with a hand. "I paid my fee, took the painting, and got out of there."

"But it didn't end there?" Niall prompted him.

"No. A week later, Miss Ottridge called at my home. She said she could only imagine what would happen if it were known that a police court magistrate had made a purchase from a criminal receiver of stolen goods."

"I'm sure you could imagine it," Wooten said.

"Yes," Towland answered curtly. "I know I might be censured. I could lose my appointment. Not to mention the damage it would do to the reputation of the magistrates and the police courts."

The inspector made a noise in the back of his throat and moved on. "So, she asked for money to keep quiet?"

"No. She demanded to be inducted into the Order of Druidic Bards." Towland straightened. "Of course, I had no wish to let her loose amongst my friends and fellow members."

"I absolutely forbade it," Mrs. Berringer said. "The wicked jade had no place in our group."

"I managed to convince her it was impossible. She didn't possess the interests, knowledge, or skill to warrant a membership."

"I met her with him," Mrs. Berringer said. "I explained that Arthur could not circumvent the rules to shove her in."

"I convinced her to take a sum of money, instead."

"Five hundred pounds," Wooten stated.

"Yes." The magistrate looked surprised. "I see you do have detailed knowledge of her activities."

"But how, then, was she inducted the other evening?" Kara asked.

"We thought the matter handled. But about a month after she took the payment, Miss Ottridge was nominated by another Order member."

"A member of the council," Mrs. Berringer clarified.

"Who?" asked Niall.

"Lady Madge Simmons."

Kara started. "What? That sweet old lady with the lyre?"

Mrs. Berringer snorted. "That sweet old lady has been a hellraiser since her youth. She's smart, fearless, and wields a cutting wit. She's not afraid to use it, either. She's had many adventures—and misadventures—and she has as many powerful enemies as she does powerful friends."

"Simmons?" The inspector frowned. "How do I know that name?" He shook his head. "In any case, she sounds like a subject for blackmail."

"If you do not fear the consequences," Mrs. Berringer said wryly.

"Lady Madge came to the council with a claim that Miss Ottridge had discovered a long-sought-after copy of a ballad, one written by the great Elizabethan composer William Byrd," Towland explained.

"A likely story. I think we can all agree that Miss Ottridge's performance the other night proves that lie." Mrs. Berringer's tone had gone distinctly catty. "Clearly the woman had not even a passing familiarity with poetry or music."

"I dared not contradict Lady Madge, though," Towland confessed.

"No one on the council will cross her," Mrs. Berringer added. "She's old, but still retains a powerful voice in Society. Worse, she's relentless if she decides to count you a foe. She will raze the field to remove a weed, as my old nursemaid used to say."

"I did fear to refuse her," Towland continued. "But it was more than the usual attempt to keep the lady appeased. I couldn't help but wonder what Miss Ottridge could have held over her head. It must have been daunting for Lady Madge to capitulate. What if something happened to the old girl?"

"I rather think you got that backwards," Niall said. "Something *did* happen to Miss Ottridge."

"You honestly think that frail old woman might have had Miss Ottridge murdered?" Kara was aghast.

"I think we must consider the possibility."

"Well, I certainly wasn't involved in her death," Towland insisted. "I swear it."

Mrs. Berringer sat straighter. "I did warn the grasping Ottridge woman. We exchanged terse words. I told her she had best not view the Grove as her hunting ground."

Kara guessed a few well-placed references to poisonous plants and electric belts might have been involved.

As if he'd heard her, Wooten cleared his throat. "And what's this whispering I hear of poisonous plants in the garden? In your place outside Shoreditch? Leaves and berries were said to be in the drink that killed Miss Ottridge."

Mrs. Berringer paled, but answered stoutly. "Those plants were part of a project I developed in the garden. I've had them torn out and replaced, just in case."

"Not before someone helped themselves," Kara said. She told them what she'd seen the night of the ceremony.

"So now, in addition to a notebook full of blackmailed men, I must question all the members of your Order?" Wooten asked.

"Perhaps just the members in attendance that evening," Niall replied.

"It was not a member of the Order!" Mr. Towland insisted.

"We had extra servants in for the night, as the ceremony was so well attended," Mrs. Berringer said. "You should question them, as well."

Wooten groaned.

"Clearly this must be a case of someone using the leaves and berries to point their finger toward the Order and away from themselves," Towland said.

"You might be right, but we cannot leave such a stone un-turned," Wooten replied. "We'll have to speak with your people."

"Someone really must question Lady Madge," Mrs. Berringer said with the conviction of a woman who knew the job would not fall to her. "She is the one who nominated Miss Ottridge."

"Madge. Madge. Simmons." Wooten's tapping pencil suddenly stilled. "Oh, no. Short for Lady *Margaret* Simmons?" He jumped up. "By my great-grannie's undergarments—no! I knew I recognized that name." He looked around at them all, wild-eyed. "Do you know who she is? She's the police commissioner's grandmother!"

"Oh dear," said Towland.

"Question her as a suspect for murder?" The inspector groaned. "I might as well toss my career in the sewers."

"Neither Arthur nor I can do it. It would cause utter chaos in the council." Mrs. Berringer eyed Niall. "But she does like a strapping young man."

"No." Towland sounded thoughtful. "She can smell a scheme—or imagine one—quicker than a matron sniffing out a fortune hunter. She pays attention to connections, alliances. Niall is known as my friend and ally. We do have another alternative, though."

Kara realized the magistrate was looking at her.

"Yes," the widow agreed. "She will think you as yet unconnected with any of the Order's schemes or rivalries. You can come upon her innocently in the music room. She spends a great deal of time there. You can engage her in conversation and lead it to Janet Ottridge."

"It was not Lady Madge collecting those bits of plants, but someone younger. Someone who moved swiftly, but with a strange gait," Kara said.

"Nevertheless." Mrs. Berringer was resolved.

"I ... I ..." Kara didn't know what to say. "I can scarcely believe that kind old lady is a killer."

"Even better," declared Towland. "The old girl can spot a lie at thirty paces."

Kara looked into his hopeful face. He'd helped her once. She could do no less now. "Very well."

"You are a *brick*, Miss Levett." The inspector was clearly relieved. "Do not worry. I will see you prepared."

She nodded.

Niall spoke up suddenly. "Mr. Towland, you said that Mr. Banks was arguing with Miss Ottridge at the auction?"

"Indeed, and it did not appear to be the first time." Towland's gaze unfocused as he sought the memory. "I would say there were long-held animosities at play. He was throwing old grievances at her, even as he was denying he owed her anything for bringing me in."

Niall looked to the inspector. "Surely he must be someone else you might question, sir?"

"Yes. As if I need another," Wooten grumbled in reply. "But

you are right."

"This is enough to exonerate Arthur, though, is it not?" For the first time, Mrs. Berringer sounded anxious. "We've told you all that we know. You must see that he has had nothing to do with this murder."

"You should be clear for now, sir." Wooten looked troubled. "I will have to explain your story to my superiors. I do not know what will come of it, but there will be no men knocking on your door to ask questions, and no informants to the press."

The magistrate bowed his head. "I understand. Thank you, sir." Towland stood. "And I thank you, Niall. And Miss Levett. You are both true friends."

Mrs. Berringer also stood to take her leave. Kara saw the couple out, then came back to the parlor to find both Niall and the inspector partaking of the fig and apple tart. "Thank goodness," she said, resuming her seat. "I was afraid of sending the untouched tart back to the kitchen. Pass me that serving knife, Niall?"

Niall handed it over and looked to the inspector. "You know you need to add one more question to the many already surrounding this case?"

"What's that?" Wooten nodded his thanks as Kara offered another piece of the tart.

"You have another suspect to search out."

Wooten stopped chewing.

"The last person in Miss Ottridge's notebook. It wasn't Lady Madge."

The inspector's eyes widened as he thought back. "By George, it wasn't. Simmons wasn't a name listed at all, that I recall."

"Why would Miss Ottridge not list Lady Madge, if she blackmailed her after Mr. Towland?" Kara asked. "She seemed most organized in keeping track of her nefarious activities." She thought a moment. "But perhaps that is the answer to the question. She did not take money from Lady Madge, but a favor.

Perhaps Janet Ottridge has a separate notebook for forced favors?"

Wooten groaned.

"It was not a name in the last spot, but initials. And a question mark. I recall it because it was a departure from the other entries." Niall set down his plate. "I have a feeling we will want to discover who WW is before we are done."

Kara made a face. "Not initials. Not again. You know they led to nothing but trouble the last time."

"They did allow Scotland Yard to stop a troublesome bit of industrial espionage," Niall reminded her.

"Let's hope nothing so complicated turns up here," the inspector said, hopefully, as he took another bite.

Chapter Five

"GOD'S TEETH, NIALL. I was cursing your name when your messenger banged on my door before dawn had barely cracked the sky, but now I must thank you for arranging my attendance today."

"Ansel." Niall was glad—and relieved—to see his friend. "I'm so glad you made it."

"Yes, well, sorry it's so late now, but I suspected you wished to ask for something in return, so I wandered the whole Exhibition before coming to find you."

Niall laughed. Perhaps he should have cringed. For Ansel Wells was correct—Lord Stayme's warnings had crawled under his skin. He had to do something, even it was just to stay as informed as possible, and Ansel could help with that.

"No wonder everyone has been so caught up with the Crystal Palace and all it holds. I could spend days here. So much artistry." His friend's eyes widened. "Did you see the collection of Froment-Meurice's work at the French exhibition?" Ansel, always dramatic, clapped his hands to his head. "That vanity table, so exquisitely carved, and all done in silver!"

"Yes, it's stunning. That gold casket, too. One of the most beautiful pieces here. I've studied it several times." Niall tilted his head. "I know you are fond of a bit of whimsy." He pointed.

"Head over to the British furniture and check out Mr. Stevens's cabinet."

"I will, by God."

Niall went back to writing out the detailed instructions for packing and shipping the pieces from his exhibit that would make their way out into the world—including the screen he'd promised to gift to Prince Albert, via the selection committee, back in the spring. He paused when Ansel came back, grinning.

"Whimsy? That thing is genius. Legs of manly torsos, garlands, scrolls, and lion's feet? I hope whoever ends up with it places it where it may be exclaimed over. Magnificent." Ansel shook his head. "Sometimes I wonder if I might have a go at sculpting or carving, but I'd miss the colors." He grinned. "And I don't know if I can create without the smell of linseed oil up my nose."

Niall laughed.

Ansel sighed. "I envy you, spending months amongst all this. So much beauty."

"It has been an honor and a privilege."

Ansel shrugged. "But I have enjoyed a spate of portrait commissions lately, and I would not have missed out on those. I do have a bit of free time now, though ..."

"I could arrange for you to have one more day ..."

He eyed Niall closely. "I knew it. I knew you wanted something. Very well, you've caught me up. Out with it!"

"Come. I'll buy you a drink at the refreshment court and we'll talk."

Once they were settled, Niall raised a brow at his friend. "Your cousin, Rupert. Is he still in Paris?"

"Aye. He'll never leave." Ansel took a long sip of his ginger beer. "He's formed too great an attachment to both French pastries and French women."

"Is he still open to the odd job? For a few extra sous?"

"Of course. French women are expensive."

"Aren't they all?" Niall said.

"Not all of them are as demanding as the French ladies."

"I'll take your word for it." He leaned in. "I need Rupert to keep an eye on a fellow. A visitor to Paris. I do not want him interfered with," Niall cautioned. "I just want to know where he goes, whom he speaks with—and as much of what he says that Rupert can manage to hear without alerting the man to his presence."

Ansel snapped his fingers. "Easy as that, for that scoundrel. Have you something to write on? I'll give you his address."

Niall pulled paper and pencil from his coat pocket.

"Came prepared, didn't you?" Ansel scribbled down the information. Taking another drink, he gave Niall an expectant look. "And for the second day?"

"You can have the second day, my friend. But if you wouldn't mind, I would like to ask a few questions. For a different matter altogether."

His friend waved his hand in a rolling motion. "Out with it, man."

Niall sat back. "How does it work amongst painters? Are you familiar with most of the working artists in London?"

Ansel looked surprised. "Well, I certainly know most of the important artists—or know *of* them." His mouth quirked. "We are a competitive lot and like to keep an eye on each other."

"You might have an idea, then, who might have created a certain painting, done recently?"

"I suppose it would depend on the painting."

"A mythological theme, rich in color. Welsh story. Entitled *Cerridwyn's Lament*. It depicts the goddess of wisdom—"

Ansel threw up his hands. "Yes, yes! The cauldron and the boy and the knowledge of the ages. I have heard of it, yes. More than I ever cared to." He frowned. "How do you know of it, though?"

"A friend of mine bought it. Clearly, you know the artist?"

"We drink at the same pub."

"What can you tell me of him?"

He eyed Niall curiously. "Michael Bowen. He's not well known. Not yet. He has the talent for it, I'll give him that, if he can stay sober long enough. He does babble on when he's drunk, though, and lately he's been nattering on about nothing but this work."

"Do you think he'd be interested in doing a companion piece?"

"I should say so. He got caught up in the story of it. Keeps talking about wanting to paint the next bit. Something about a mad, magical chase?"

Niall was surprised. "My friend would likely be thrilled to hear it. But if Bowen wanted to do a series, why sell the first to an auction house? Why not keep it until he could show them together?"

"Wasn't his idea, at first, you see. It was a commission. But the patron was late coming for it, and Bowen was out of funds."

Niall tensed, but let none of it show. "Who commissioned the piece?"

"Well, there's a character, now that you ask. A woman, no less. I can't recall her name ... Cotter or something?"

Close enough. "Is that unusual? A lady patron?"

"Somewhat unusual, but she's no proper patron, that one. She comes 'round the pub three, maybe four times a year. Always looking for a painter or sculptor to create something for her. She is always very specific about what she wants."

"Work for hire," Niall said with an artist's prejudice—and resignation.

"Aye, but a bloke has got to pay rent. And his bar bill. There's always someone willing to take on the projects she proposes."

"Have you ever done a commission for her?"

"Nay." Ansel shook his head. "I'm not that far up River Tick."

Niall gestured. "And yet you never forked over the shilling to see all this?"

Ansel lifted a shoulder.

Niall lowered his tone. "Have you also ever had to sell a piece to Banks and Burroughs? Just to make ends meet?"

Ansel blinked, then flushed. "How did you know where—"
He looked away. "Ah, your friend bought the painting there."

"Yes. And I think he'll be thrilled at the idea of purchasing
related works—directly from your friend and at full price." Niall
paused. "Ansel, you'll hear no judgment from me. I've told you of
my forge in Scotland. You'd be hard-pressed to find a place
smaller or more isolated. I've made hard choices, at times, to
survive. To make my way here. But now I rather urgently need
to speak to Mr. Banks. And you know how to find him."

"You don't understand," his friend whispered. "Scant few
know the address. If it were found out that I—"

"It will not be found out."

"These men. They are ..." Ansel looked at him pleadingly.
"Unscrupulous."

"I know. That's why you may be sure they will never know
how I found them." Niall stopped. "Does anyone know I
arranged your attendance here today?"

"No. You sent word too bloody early for anyone in that set to
be up."

He looked around. "Tell me you haven't been inspired by all
of this."

"Of course I have. Anyone with an ounce of art in their soul
must be." Ansel cursed. "Damn you, I've had ten ideas just this
afternoon."

"There you are, then. Finish out the day. Make notes of your
ideas. Come back tomorrow, wallow in it all, and find ten more.
No one need know where your inspiration comes from, nor will
they ask when you emerge with ideas and pieces underway."

Ansel looked tempted.

Niall pushed the paper back toward him. "Just write down
the address. You and I can both say neither their names nor any
details ever crossed your lips."

Ansel gave him a dark look before he grabbed up the pencil
and scribbled on the paper again. "Very well, but I am trusting

you to keep me out of it."

"On my honor, I absolutely will, my friend. Thank you."

"I don't want to know what business you have with such characters." Ansel stood. "There is still time before the exhibit closes. I am going to explore some more and calm my nerves."

Niall thanked him again and watched him go. Perhaps he'd pushed his friend a bit hard, but he didn't feel too guilty. Ansel had led him into more than one scrape, and their bond was too tight to hold room for grudges.

And Ansel had been incredibly helpful. More so than he'd expected. Niall felt lighter after doing something about Lord Stayme's unwelcome news. The odds that Marston could know anything of importance were low. But he didn't like the man's interest. At all.

Frowning, Niall looked around at the crowd. The Great Exhibition was nearly over. The wise thing would be for him to move on. Go back to Scotland and bury himself in his work. Or accept one of those invitations and travel to the Continent. Drink in new sights, new settings, and new stories.

Stepping out into the flow of attendees, he wandered down the aisle of the British nave, stopping well back from Kara's exhibit. She had a group of young people gathered around her workbench and was giving them a lesson on how she created her elaborate automatons.

Kara. He had to be honest and admit that she was the reason he was hesitating. Lingering. An anomaly for him, as he was usually quick to cut and move on, especially when old questions began to resurface.

He sighed, watching her laugh with her rapt audience. Odin's arse, but she was worth the risk.

Niall could see that at least one of the young men in the group had been caught by her spell. No. Not a spell. Just ... herself. That was one of the things about Kara that bemused but fascinated him. She had many gifts. Dark beauty. Intelligence. An easy charm that beguiled, but a vibrant, intense personality that one only discovered after boring through her protective walls.

That was the thing, really. She was candid. Utterly forthright in her dealings with others. No calculation. No maneuvering or manipulation. It was unusual in a female, in his experience. Most of the time, she appeared entirely unaware of her effect on people. Somehow, that doubled the devasting impact she made.

Or perhaps that was just how she affected him.

Truthfully, it was his reluctance that should be setting all the alarms in his head to clanging. The bond of their friendship was strong and grew warmer and more comfortable as they spent time together. But it couldn't lead to anything more. It was a fundamental truth he had to accept. He should go now, before anyone got hurt.

He would go. Soon.

But this killing … it made him uneasy. Murder itself was unsettling, of course. But he could feel the dark undertones swirling about this situation. Blackmail. Anger. Money. Reputations at risk. It could quickly grow dangerous.

The Order was full of unique and impressive people. They had welcomed him and made him one of their own. He had enough experience of the world to know how rare that was. He'd brought Kara into their fold—just in time for darkness to roll in like fog. And she was already caught up in it.

He would stay, then, to see the thing solved.

And then he would go.

THE AFTERNOON LIGHT was still bright in the Crystal Palace when Kara looked up to find Niall approaching.

"Why do I feel so unaccountably nervous?" she asked.

"Because Wooten has infected you with his anxieties. Don't allow it, Kara. You are not one of his officers. You are seeking out a conversation, not conducting an interrogation."

How did he know exactly how to calm her nerves? She didn't know, but she continued to appreciate it. "You don't think Lady Madge is involved in Miss Ottridge's death?"

"No more than you do. Trust your instincts. They are sound."

She tried not to flush with pleasure at the compliment. It wasn't always easy for her to read people, but she was trying to improve.

"I trust what I know of Lady Madge, as well," he continued. "The lady is smart. Cagey. Witty. She's quick to stand up to a rival, but though she might ruin their social life, I cannot see her resorting to murder."

"You agreed she should be questioned," she reminded him.

"Lady Madge nominated the woman as a candidate for the Order. How? Why? Even if she didn't know Miss Ottridge beforehand, she must have had several conversations with her. Who knows what we might learn from her, should she decide to cooperate."

"*If* I can convince her to cooperate."

"I doubt anyone could sway the old girl to do anything she had no inclination for." He grinned, and her dread lessened a little more. "All you can do is give her the opportunity. Come." He cast a glance over her empty workbench. "I see you are ready? I'll ride with you to Shoreditch, but you should talk to Lady Madge alone."

Traffic was surprisingly light for the afternoon hour and grew lighter still as they traveled east. Kara watched the theater district roll by, but didn't really grow alert until they moved beyond the high street to less crowded territory. Soon they turned through a tall gate onto a long drive.

"Towland didn't spare any expense, did he?" she said. "It's hard to believe he purchased this entire place for the use of the Order."

"It's one of the signs that show how important the Order is to him," Niall replied. "He believes in the work, the preservation and study, as well as the dissemination of knowledge. Having a place to collect all of that, as well as for members to gather … well, it's been both useful and enjoyable."

"I heard that some members keep a set of rooms in the house as well."

"Towland does, although he spends most of his time at his home in the city, as it's closer to the court. Several other council members have a place here, as well."

"Mrs. Berringer?"

"Yes."

The gossips had said as much. Her face flared hot. "I've heard the whispers. Now people are talking about us in the same way."

"They are trying." He shrugged. "We have the truth on our side."

Because he had refused to accept a room at Bluefield. And because their affection for each other had remained strictly platonic. Suddenly, her blood heated. "To hell with the gossips. If it wasn't our friendship, it would be something else. Some other difference the Society matrons would use to tear me down, make me feel as if I'm not one of them. Do they think this is the way to bring me to heel? Why should I worry about they think?"

He frowned. "Because someday their good opinion might matter to you."

"I find that hard to imagine."

"They are your cohort, Kara."

She stared at him blankly for a moment. Then she understood—and gave a stunned laugh. "So I am to fit myself into their mold so that someday one of their lordlings will deign to marry me?" She scowled. "I have no idea if or when I will be ready to marry. It seems a bad bargain to me. And that's the problem, isn't it? It's the real issue they all have with me. I have so much to lose in a marriage—and I have not given in to the notion that I am helpless and unable to manage it all without one of their golden sons to lift the burden from my shoulders."

He blinked. "Your bloodline is old and venerable," he began.

"I am no longer the daughter of a baron, but the cousin to one. It's not my bloodline that makes me attractive to them, but my businesses, factories, and the old money that comes with them—and that sort of liaison, I am not interested in." She shot him a dark look. "Is that what you see as my future, Niall? Married to a blooded fortune hunter?"

He didn't answer. The carriage had slowed, and an attentive footman had the door open almost before it drew to a halt. "Welcome to the Druid's Grove," he intoned.

She held her silence as Niall disembarked then handed her out. He turned toward the house without resuming their conversation.

"Does Lady Madge have rooms here?" she asked as they ascended the stairs to the porticoed entrance.

"No. She spends many afternoons in the music library, though. She is curating a collection of instruments and as much documentation on old music and poetry as she can find."

An opening, perhaps. Something she could use.

Niall drifted toward the stairs, and Kara let the idea bloom as she followed a servant toward the back of the house.

Halfway back a long passage, she encountered Lady Flora, who sat on a bench, stomping her feet into tall boots. "Oh, good morning, dear," she said as the last one popped on.

"Good morning, my lady." Kara nodded to the maid who stood nearby, holding a rough coat.

"Last night's rain is going to make this a messy business, but I must tear out the planters from the Triple Goddesses display." Sadness lined Lady Flora's face. "Such a terrible thing to have happened, so close."

"It is, indeed."

The lady sighed. "I suppose we should have known better, but who would have thought word of a few dangerous plants would spread beyond these walls?" She shook her head. "For I just cannot believe any of our own people would have done such a thing. Turned beauty and life to death." She stood and turned so that the maid could help her into the jacket. "Thank you, Mary, dear. Why don't you go spend some time in the kitchens? I'll send for you when I'm ready to depart."

The maid nodded, but stood, head down, until Lady Flora bade Kara a good day and moved out toward the gardens.

Kara watched her go, gave the maid a nod, then went on, following the waiting footman to the musical library.

She sighed in appreciation as she entered.

A wall of long-case windows. Two more of bookshelves. Everything done in dark walnut and varying shades of blue. She moved toward the nearest bookcase—and stopped as if in surprise when she caught sight of Lady Madge Simmons seated at a carved desk.

"Pardon me. But is it ... allowed?" Dropping a curtsy, she gave the old woman a quizzical look. "Is anyone allowed to use the musical references?"

"Anyone in the Order, though few enough avail themselves of it." Lady Madge waved a hand. "Help yourself, young lady." She turned back to her papers.

"Thank you."

Kara leaned in to examine the collection of books, manuscripts, and folders of music. Everything appeared to be ordered chronologically. She followed the timeline, moving backward, and stopped to inspect the earliest works. Lingering, fascinated, she looked over a booklet describing the early musical notations developed by Benedictine monks, a treatise on old ballads of highwaymen and gentlemen thieves, and songs of ancient Irish battles. Nothing to support the idea she'd just formed, though.

Standing to straighten out her back, she gave a sigh.

"Didn't find what you are looking for, girl?"

She turned her head to find Lady Madge watching her closely. "I was hoping to find something on music the Vikings played."

The old woman's gaze sharpened. "Why?"

"I'm working on a project."

"One of your automatons?"

"This one will only be a sculpture, or at least I thought so. She's to be a Valkyrie."

Lady Madge grinned. "A self-portrait, eh?"

Kara's brow rose. Not many people knew Kara had been the name of one of the Valkyries of legend. "More of an idea who I might be," she admitted. Valkyries were strong. Powerful. At home in different worlds. "I hadn't meant to include more, but as I've been working on her, I keep imagining a song."

The noblewoman's expression changed. "What does it sound like?"

Kara turned and moved closer. "It begins slowly. A mournful dirge as I imagine her starting out, walking onto the field of death. It quickens, though, becoming almost martial as she makes her choices, collects her warriors. And it rises to a crescendo, triumphant, as she takes them to their reward in Valhalla."

"I like it. I can almost hear it myself. Perhaps we will take it up as a project ourselves. We can collaborate. Compose something for you."

"I …" Kara was stunned at the generous offer. "We?"

"The Bardic Tradition. It's the official name of our musical group, although most everyone calls us the Merry Minstrels. We play the old instruments, keep the skills alive. Lyre, harp, bone whistle, lute, bodhran. We train up recruits, too, if you are interested."

"I am not musical, alas," Kara confessed. "I can craft a music box, copying notes to accompany my figures, but I cannot carry a tune myself."

"Not everyone can. Ah, well. We need apprentices, students to pass the old songs along. That's how it was done, in ages past, you see. No musical notation, so the master must pass his store of songs on to his pupils. Otherwise, they were lost to time. Although we do, of course, write them down now." Lady Madge cast a look at Kara. "It's why you will find no Viking music on those shelves. We know they played instruments. Lyre and harp, bone flute and cow horn, even pan pipes. Yet they died without passing their music on. Their songs are lost to us."

"How tragic." Kara dropped into a chair near the old woman's desk.

"It is. So much lost to the ages. And so you see how important our work here becomes."

"I do." She sat silent a moment. "I heard that is why you nominated Miss Ottridge for membership into the Order. She found a long-lost piece of music?"

"She did," Lady Madge answered curtly.

"Was she to join your group? Become an apprentice?"

"No. Her talents did not take a musical bent, any more than yours."

"How did the two of you meet?" Kara held her breath, waiting to see if the other woman would answer.

Lady Madge looked at her a long moment. Shrewdness lived in that gaze.

"Now I see where your allegiances lie, young miss, but I will give you what you came after, because I don't believe Arthur Towland has a vicious bone in his body, let alone a capacity to kill."

"Nor do I," agreed Kara.

The noblewoman sat back in her chair. "Very well." Another long look, and then she began to speak. "The girl approached me in the park. She wanted to know how she could nab an invitation to join the Order. I brushed her off, but she came back. Several times. Persistent, but not pushy about it, you see. I respected that."

Kara nodded.

"I gave in, finally, and told her all the musical world wished to find a rumored ballad of love written by Queen Elizabeth's pet composer, William Byrd. It's a missing part of his lexicon, long rumored to exist and long sought. Find that, and she would be in." She closed her eyes a moment. "I thought that would be the end of the matter."

"It wasn't, though."

"No. A mere three weeks later, while I was at breakfast, Miss Ottridge knocked on my door, waltzed in, cool as a breeze, and laid that missing ballad right onto my dining table. You could have bowled me over with a feather."

Kara straightened. "Then she didn't blackmail you to gain her nomination?"

"No." Lady Madge laughed. "And there's no lack of scandal in my past, either. The girl might have dug up any one of several old hidden sins to use against me, but she didn't. Instead, she found something generations have looked for. I thought a woman with a talent for finding missing or lost things would be an asset to the Order, so I nominated her." She paused. "I thought I might have made a mistake when she spouted off that dreadful poem at the initiation ceremony." Her fierce expression fell a little. "And I suppose I did. She must have approached someone in the group with her scheming." She sighed. "Killed with bits of Imogen and Flora's plants. A quick bit of flummery, that."

"Then you don't believe the ladies were involved, either?"

"Nary a bit of it—and don't you believe those sharp-tongued biddies who will try to whisper that Imogen did it to keep the girl away from her man. Arthur Towland hasn't looked at another woman since Imogen Berringer stood in the Grove and recited Taliesin's 'Ode to King Urien Rheged.'"

"I won't," Kara said wryly. "I've only known her a short while, but I wouldn't have believed it, in any case. If Mrs. Berringer had arranged it, it would have looked like an accident and there would be no investigation."

Lady Madge gave a sharp crack of laughter. "That's true enough."

"Did you speak with Miss Ottridge again, after the initiation?"

"Only that very evening. I pulled her aside and asked if she'd approached me only to gain access to our members, for her scheming's sake." The older woman breathed deeply. "She was a cold one, I tell you. She admitted it, out loud, without a blink of an eye. Said the Order was rich ground. She assured me, though, that she would not tease out any of my secrets, as I'd helped her get in."

"What did you say to her?"

"I warned her that this lot might be eccentric, but that didn't make them easy marks. I warned her—and I'll do you the same favor. Someone killed that woman, and whoever it was, I doubt they'll hesitate to do the same to you, should your snooping alarm them."

"So you *do* think the killer is someone in the Order?"

"Could the leaves in the drink have been a smokescreen? Yes, they might have been meant to send all the attention our way. But I have a feeling." She paused. "There's something else. I'd nearly forgotten ..."

Kara waited.

"I saw Miss Ottridge with one of the maids. It was near the end of the night, when I went to find the woman, to accuse her of the scheming she was happy to admit. They were huddled, whispering, near the summerhouse. They looked ... intimate, if you know what I mean. Like they knew each other. When I called out, the maid slipped inside."

"Do you know which maid it was?"

Lady Madge shook her head. "You can't tell them apart, not on ceremony nights. They all wear somber clothes and the same mask. But she was young, I'd say, and whichever one she was, I'd wager she knows something about what Miss Janet Ottridge was up to."

Kara drew a deep breath, thinking.

"Listen, girl. Something's stirring. I feel it in my bones. You go carefully."

Kara stood. "I will. I promise. Thank you for answering my questions."

"You are welcome, child. And I am indeed going to talk to my group about your song, too." Lady Madge's eyes unfocused a bit. "The Valkyrie's song. Yes. I can almost hear it."

"I don't wish to impose," Kara said. "But I also cannot wait to hear it."

Lady Madge laughed. "Go on with you, girl."

With a grin and squeeze of the old woman's veined hand, Kara obeyed. She didn't search out Niall right away, though. Instead, she found her way to the green baize door and down to the servants' hall.

Chapter Six

THEY WAITED UNTIL the last moment, on the last day, before joining the flow of exhibitioners leaving the Crystal Palace for the last time.

They indulged in fond goodbyes and leave-takings, then Niall and Kara left the Great Exhibition the way they'd gained entrance—together. They traveled to Bluefield Park in silence, both lost in contemplation of the grand experience and the changes it had wrought.

They shed their stillness once they reached Bluefield, however. The evening was spent in celebration, with Gyda and Turner in attendance, as well as all the assistants and hirelings that had helped see them through such an intense undertaking. An undeniable feeling of accomplishment flowed through the room, along with plenty of food and drink. Gyda was in her element. Kara smiled unceasingly, and even Turner unbent enough to crack a smile or two.

Niall let himself indulge a little in the fine wine Turner had chosen for the evening. "To Prince Albert's vision," he called, lifting his glass. "And to the opportunities it has awakened in the world—and in us."

Everyone drank enthusiastically. Kara raised her glass as well. "To new friendships. To all of us."

Gyda, not to be outdone, came next. "To Turner's greatest rival—Mrs. Canning of Wood Rose Abbey, across the river. May he forever outshine her in orderliness, organization, and superiority of staff—at least until he acknowledges that the woman is also an object of his affection."

Shocked silence fell, and all turned to Turner, whose mouth had fallen open. He blinked, then raised his own glass. "To Gyda Winther. May she wreak her havoc amongst Mrs. Canning's staff and leave Bluefield's in peace."

Utter silence again, then someone giggled. Someone else snorted, and then everyone dissolved in laughter, and the evening came to a close on a light note.

The next morning, Niall woke in his loft, his head too tender to think of starting up the forge right away. He searched a bit and found Kara in her laboratory. He nearly missed her, as her great, supremely organized worktable sat empty. If she hadn't moved to cover what she was working on in a corner spot, he might have turned and kept searching.

"There you are." He headed for the corner just as she stepped away from it. "I didn't think you worked on two projects at a time."

"It's not my usual habit." She lifted a shoulder and headed for her main workbench. "But I need a small, special piece for the turtle, in order to make the right sort of movement." He knew a wealthy merchant had commissioned her to create a large, lifelike automaton of a sea turtle. The man had regaled them all with the tale of one he swore had saved his life. "I constructed a cast and mold of what I need, but I'm waiting for the factory in Sussex to send the finished parts. I started something else while I wait."

"May I see it?" Niall gestured toward the covered piece.

"Yes. Eventually," she said, raising a hand to keep him from moving directly over there. "This one is ... different. I'll be ready to show it soon enough, and I promise, you'll be the first."

"I'll be content to wait until you are ready," he assured her, surprised.

"I did wish to consult with you, though, on the movements I'm building into the turtle. You've spent time enough at sea—I suppose you've seen sea turtles?"

"Yes, but you don't often see them at the surface. I did see a big one, once, in a lovely, still bay just off Jersey." He shook his head. "It was so clear I could see it as if I was right there. I swear, it didn't swim, it *flew*, so smoothly did it move through the water."

Her brows rose. "Small movements, then?"

"Almost languid," he recalled.

They spoke at length, and she showed him what she meant for her mechanical turtle to do, and they plotted together how to make it all more fluid. She scribbled a few notes and at last looked up. "Thank you. That was indeed helpful." She hesitated. "There was something, though, I wished to discuss with you."

He grinned. "I was just going to say the same thing."

Neither got to speak, however, as the door opened and Turner entered, carrying a tray. "Cook said neither of you has eaten. I've brought something to soak up last night's wine."

Niall went to move a large, wheeled rack full of various cables out of the way as Turner headed for the fire at the end of the lab. Comfortable seats and a decent-sized table were arranged before it.

Turner set down the tray and pulled out an envelope. "Today's post has something addressed to you both."

He handed it to Kara as she took a seat. Niall was more interested in the contents of the tray. Warm, soft rolls, fresh butter, and—

"Parritch!" he said happily. "You are a wonder, Turner."

"Cook does turn her nose up at such *peasant food*, but I convinced her that today, it would be just the thing."

"Thank you." Niall ladled out a bowl with a sigh of bliss.

"I'll return for the tray." Turner inclined his head and left.

Kara had opened the letter and was scanning the contents. "It's from Wooten. He thanks me for speaking with Lady Madge and says they have eliminated several suspects from the note-book." She looked up. "Nothing about talking to anyone in the Order. He seems to be concentrating all of his energy on the blackmail victims."

"I think it is a mistake. But likely his superiors are more inter-ested in the failings of those men than the eccentricities of those in the Order." Niall nodded toward the tray. "Eat first. Then we'll discuss."

He laughed as her stomach rumbled in response.

They ate in companionable silence. The tray held a pot of chocolate for her and one of strong coffee for him. Kara poured for them both, then rose and went to a locked drawer nearby. She had the key at her waist and pulled out a bottle of whisky—a good one. After adding a dollop to their respective cups, she sat back to savor hers with a sigh.

Niall took a long drink and leaned his head against the high chair back. Ah, these were his favorite mornings—even more than the hearty breakfasts and loud camaraderie he found at the White Hart, where he kept rooms. He loved a late night—although he usually filled it with work instead of a party, a fuzzy wakening that sharpened with talk of art and angles and the sheen of refracted light on metal, a quiet meal with just the two of them and Kara smiling at him over her cup—

He went still. Too comfortable. Too content. And all new. He rarely let himself feel so much for a woman—and never one he wasn't dallying with. In those uncommon instances, he'd always heard the alarm bells begin before such feelings of contentment set in. The worry of danger. For him. For her. It poked him with the urge to go. To pick up and move on.

But here? Now? With Kara? He just wanted to sink deeper into the chair and stay.

"So, this murder," Kara began.

He sat up. "Wait. How did this happen?"

"What?"

"How have we created a world in which those words—"

"*So, this murder?*"

"Yes. Those. How can that be a casual start to a breakfast conversation?"

She considered. "Because we are ... interesting?"

"Is that what you call it?"

"Well, I'm interested."

"Well, I'm dismayed." He waved a hand. "But do carry on. This murder ... are we getting involved? Is that what you meant to ask?"

"We are already involved. The question must be, will we stay involved?"

"Honestly? We shouldn't. Towland is clear. We will have to testify, but we've done our part."

"One murder investigation is indeed interesting," she mused. "Two seems excessive."

"It does. It also would likely behoove us both to keep our names out of the spotlight."

She made a face. He always found her twisted expressions endearing. "True. We've stirred up enough gossip."

"It would be better for our respective professional reputations. I wish to be known for my art, not my involvement in scandal and murder."

"And yet ... I hear the hesitation in your tone."

"Wooten does seem to be slightly overwhelmed," he said slowly.

"There are a great number of individuals that need questioning in this matter," she agreed.

"We could speak to the Order members. Quietly. Unofficially. No need for our involvement to be known by anyone save the inspector."

"Would he appreciate our interference?"

"He certainly did the last time we brought him all the pertinent information."

"We should tread carefully," she warned. "Lady Madge has a feeling."

"As well she should."

"You did say it was a mistake for the police to focus only on the blackmail victims."

"The coroner's medical man was of the opinion that Miss Ottridge's symptoms were in line with those caused by oleander, but he has no way of knowing if she might already have been suffering heart palpitations or seizures beforehand or if it might have been caused by something else entirely." He paused and looked at her seriously. "But even if someone did use the plants as a distraction, they would have had to know of the poisonous plants in the Grove."

"My thought exactly. But think, what if we could connect someone at the Grove with another, a known enemy of Janet Ottridge?"

A charge of interest—and grudging appreciation—ran down his spine. "What do you mean?"

"After my interview with Lady Madge, I spoke with a trio of maids employed at the Grove." The corner of her mouth twitched. "They already knew you and I had helped to exonerate Arthur Towland."

"Servants," he said wryly.

"Their knowledge stood me in good stead, though. They were happy to gossip with me about who just might have had a hand in the nasty business."

"And their theory was …?"

"Very helpful indeed. They had also noticed Miss Ottridge's familiarity with one of the women usually brought in as extra help for bigger events."

"The maid Lady Madge spotted?"

"It would seem so. And have a guess at where she is more regularly employed?"

He sensed the excitement in her. "Don't tease."

"The Hare and the Dog!" she said, triumphant.

He straightened. "Well done, Kara." He felt it, too. The familiar tightening, the thrill of the hunt. "A connection with that maid could very well be how Miss Ottridge came to set her sights on the Order in the first place. It explains how she would have known about Arthur's interest in all things Taliesin."

"It explains how someone outside the Order would have known about the poisonous plants. Someone who also held ill feelings towards Jane Ottridge."

"Banks." Niall stood. His mind was turning and his feet needed to move as well. He paced to the fire and back. "He and this maid have both been recently connected with the tavern. If this was the woman you saw picking the leaves and berries—"

"She wasn't," she interrupted.

He pulled up. "How do you know she wasn't?"

She drew a deep breath. "I spoke to her. It wasn't her. She is entirely too tall to be the woman I saw."

"You spoke to her?" Alarm set his pulse to pounding. "Where? When?"

"The maids named her, and I had Turner deliver a message. I convinced her to meet me yesterday outside the Crystal Palace, in the park."

"Why didn't you tell me?"

"She was skittish. It was difficult enough to get her to speak with me alone."

He blinked at her. "How?"

"I told her I merely wanted to ask some questions, but if she chose not to answer me, then I would give her name to the police. I warned her they might be prone to taking her up as an accessory to blackmail and possibly murder."

"Damnation, Kara! She might have arrived with a bully boy in tow, ready to remove you as a threat."

"Turner warned her I was only after a bit of information. And that I was not the only one to know of her involvement, and our appointment."

"You shouldn't have taken such a chance!" Shaking his head, he leaned on the mantel. "What did you learn?"

"Your instincts were right. She was the source of Janet Ottridge's interest in the Order. She had known the woman for years, knew of her occupation as a blackmailer, and, indeed, had helped set up Janet's victims more than once."

"Odin's arse," he swore.

"And one more thing."

He lifted his head.

"I told her we needed to speak to Mr. Banks. She didn't know where exactly to find him, but she gave me Mr. Burroughs's direction." She pulled a strip of paper from her bosom and laid it on the table.

He threw back his head and laughed.

"What is amusing?" she demanded. "That is a closely held secret!"

"This." He drew out the folded sheet Ansel had scribbled on from his waistcoat pocket. "I obtained Banks's direction."

Surprised, she looked at both lying in front of her ... and then they were both laughing.

"If I recall correctly, we began our partnership on our last investigation in a very similar fashion," Niall said.

"We did find the same sort of crucial information, separately," she agreed. "I assume this means we are proceeding?"

He ran a look of fond exasperation over her. Even if he hadn't wanted the matter cleared before he left, the odds of her quitting now were damned low. "I suppose we are."

"And I suppose your find was more directly pertinent. Banks is the one who was seen arguing with the woman." She unfolded his paper, then blinked up at him in surprise.

"What?"

"They are the same."

"Hmmm." Possibilities were tumbling over themselves in his head.

"It is interesting," she said with a twinkle in her eye.

"Yes. But in which way?"

Kara stood. "It's a good day to find out."

Chapter Seven

K ARA TOOK NIALL'S hand and emerged from the hack. She saw
when he glanced again at her new day gown. He hadn't
mentioned it, but he possessed an artist's eye, and she knew he'd
noticed.

Attractive in garnet shot silk, the gown had a neckline and
cuffs that were trimmed in black ribbon applique and beads. The
end of the long bodice also bore the black trim. She'd had another
version of her favorite bonnet—adorned with a drafter's
compass—made to match. It was all lovely, but it was the skirt
that was truly special, and not even Niall's sharp gaze could
detect the adaptations she'd requested. She'd made sure of that.

"It's a far nicer neighborhood than I expected." She swept a
discreet glance around the well-kept corner.

"It's not what I expected either. I thought we'd find them in a
warehouse or in the back of a tavern. They must be doing well
for themselves." Niall lifted a shoulder. "Ah well. Easier on our
watchers." He gave a nod to someone behind her.

She spun in surprise. "Harold!" she exclaimed in delight.
"How lovely to see you!" She gave the boy a quick squeeze, then
grasped him by the shoulders. "And how well you look! You've
grown an inch since I saw you last, at the least! Maisie must be
feeding you well."

"Aye, miss. Thank ye, miss." The youngling, who had been her champion when she was being investigated, flushed bright red with pleasure.

"But what brings you to Cheapside? Has Maisie sent you so far afield?" She raised a brow at him. "I don't see any pies."

"No, miss! I left young Rarebit to deliver pies today. He's trustworthy, I promise. I had to come once I knew Mr. Kier needed a good set of eyes."

"Does he, indeed?" She glanced askance at Niall, then back to the boy. "And what are you watching with your good eyes?"

"The 'ouse, miss, just like Mr. Kier said." He looked eagerly to Niall. "Been little enough to see, though, sir. A man went in, early, just after sunrise. A big 'un, 'e was. Wild 'air that stuck out all over his head, and a bushy beard, too. No one in or out, since, sir."

"Excellent. And you recruited a friend to watch the back?" Niall asked.

"Aye, sir. No one in or out there, either." The boy shifted. "Odd thing, though, sir. I don't think there's any servants in there."

"No?"

"Leastways, no one came out this morning to sweep the step. And no one at the back, either, to take deliveries. No footman sneaking a smoke out the back door or stealing a bit of time with a maid. No movement in the windows."

Niall tossed him one coin, then another. "Good job, Harold. Both of you. Nicely done." He gazed up the street toward the house in question. "Keep to your post a little longer, would you? Miss Levett and I mean to make a call there. If we are not out in thirty minutes, then come to the front door and knock. Loudly. Relentlessly. Keep knocking until someone answers. But don't go in."

The boy straightened. "Yes, sir."

"If you cannot get an answer, then get yourself straight off to Inspector Wooten at the Yard and bring him and his men back here. Tell him we were looking into Banks."

Harold blinked. "Yes, sir."

"Thank you, Harold." Niall offered his arm, and Kara took it.

They set off, and she leaned in to speak low. "The maid at the Hare and the Dog told me a little about each of the auctioneers. Harold's description sounds like Burroughs—a large head of wayward hair and a bushy beard. He's reputed to be the one to enforce the rules, to deal with unruly tavern owners, customers who don't want to pay, or anyone who tries to betray them to the authorities or otherwise thwart them. He also has a bit of a Scots accent."

"And Banks?" Niall asked.

"He's said to be quite a dandy. He's the businessman. Negotiates the contracts and runs the auctions. Hair slicked back, always neat and dressed in the height of fashion. And apparently, smells like a dream."

Niall's mouth twitched as they turned to approach the house. "Be sure to get a good whiff, then."

He knocked briskly, and they waited. Several long moments passed. Glancing at her, he knocked again.

A muffled shout sounded from within.

"Someone is annoyed," she whispered.

Niall knocked yet again, and the door was roughly yanked open. A man stood there, with short, ruffled hair, no coat, and a waistcoat that hung unbuttoned. "What is it?" he demanded.

"Good day to you, sir." Niall bowed. "We seek to speak with Mr. Banks."

"On what topic?" The fellow didn't frown, but he wore a look of … dissatisfaction. Kara guessed it was habitual, based on the lines on his face.

"We wish to discuss art with the gentleman," she answered.

"Buying or selling?" He sounded interested now. He let his gaze run down over her fine new gown, and suddenly he looked interested, too.

"Selling," Niall answered.

At the same time, she said, "Buying."

Niall closed his eyes. "Both, actually. But we should like to do the selling first."

The man looked disappointed. "Ah, well. You'll want my cousin, then. The other Mr. Banks. You'll have to come back. He's not here."

"He is the Mr. Banks who curates works of art and other items of décor for his own auction house?" Niall asked.

"Indeed."

"And his partner? Mr. Burroughs? Is he out as well?"

"He is. They are busy men."

Then they did indeed dwell at the same address. Kara drew a deep breath, drawing the gentleman's attention back to her. She fixed her gaze on his cuff, which showed several splotches of paint. "Are you an artist yourself, sir?" she asked, widening her eyes.

"I am."

The splotches were in shades of green and brown. "Dare I ask if you paint landscapes?"

"I do, in fact. I am known for them." He preened a little.

"Oh," she breathed. "I adore landscapes."

The gentleman paused, looked between them, and shrugged. "Would you care to see a bit of my work?"

"Oh, heavens, yes!" Kara enthused. "That is, if my brother does not object."

"Of course not," Niall said easily. "Perhaps the other Mr. Banks will return while we have a look."

Banks stood back and held the door open. Kara smiled as she passed him and caught a wisp of a strong, distinctive scent. She blinked, startled. This Mr. Banks did not wear the dreamy smell the maid had described. But the strong scent tickled at her brain. She knew she'd encountered it before, but she could not place it.

"This way." Banks led them to a parlor decked out in masculine browns, beiges, and dark wood. Kara eyed the dusty surfaces, stray cobwebs, and crooked carpet and silently agreed with

Harold's assessment about the lack of servants.

Banks swept an arm toward a wall dominated by a large landscape. It was a lovely scene, depicting a lush valley with a stone manor house nestled in amongst the hills, and a vibrant sky overhead.

"Ooh," she sighed. "It's beautiful."

It truly was. Like all good art, it tugged at her emotions. In this case, it called forth the urge to stroll down from the artist's high vantage point and get closer, to explore the flower-bedecked fieldstone walls and the wooded lane that led to the inviting house. To enter and be welcomed.

Niall stood next to her, his head tilted. "Would your cousin sell it, do you think?"

"Never," Banks declared. "It was a particular commission. The house is special to him."

"He felt at home there," Kara ventured.

"Indeed." The man's gaze softened as he faced her. "You are perceptive indeed, Miss ...?"

"Williams," she said absently. "You have captured that feeling of ... belonging. I feel the tug of it." She laughed a little. "Forgive me. It's all very bad manners, isn't it? Arriving unannounced, without an introduction." She turned back to the painting. "And yet, in the face of such loveliness, the need for conventions fades, does it not?"

"So it does," he agreed.

"Are there others, perhaps?"

"There are. Upstairs in my studio." He paused. "I could show you, should you care to see them?"

"See a true artist's studio?" Kara widened her eyes again. Acting the enthusiastic innocent didn't come naturally. "Come, brother! Can you believe our luck? Let us go and see!"

"You go on," Niall said, standing before a portrait of a lady sitting in a garden. "I see another room through there with more art to see." He gestured. "I should like to stay and examine the pieces your cousin chose to keep for himself, rather than pass on through his auctions. I might learn something," he said humbly.

Banks hesitated. "I'm not sure I can leave a stranger loose in my cousin's house ..."

Niall threw his hands up. "On my honor, I shall only look and not touch a thing." He raised a brow. "Or, if you would care to leave a footman to watch over me, I assure you, I won't be offended."

Banks frowned. His gaze darted between them. "No. No, of course, you may stay. You are entrusting me with your sister, after all."

It was said quite blandly, but the meaning was clear. Niall did a thorough job of acting the brother who should have been thinking of his sister's reputation. "I will only catch a quick look," he added. "And then I shall be right up behind you."

Banks nodded. "This way to the stairwell, Miss Williams."

He let Kara go ahead of him, and she once again caught that scent as she passed by. Not linseed oil or turpentine ... yet so distinctive. She knew she'd encountered it before. Perhaps another solvent?

"To the left," Banks directed her as she reached the first landing. He came up beside her and guided her to the end of the hallway, where he opened the last door. "Welcome to my studio."

Her eyes widened again. The room was large and bright, with several windows to let in the north-facing light. A long table against one wall held brushes, jars of pigments, and tubes of paint. A large washtub sat next to it. The corner beyond was stacked with finished canvases. In the center of the room stood an easel with a half-finished image upon it. Next to it sat a palette, still wet with paint. Here were the smells she'd expected—linseed oil and turpentine.

"What a lovely room." She walked further in. "Your cousin is generous indeed." Clearly, this must be one of the best rooms in the house.

"He is. This room outdoes all the others put together."

She studied the work on the easel, a view of a stone bridge with a party of young people upon and around it. "This is a pretty spot. Do you paint it from memory?"

"From memory. From dreams." He stood next to her, his gaze fixed upon the painting. "And from sketches, of course."

Just past the easel, still in the midst of the room, sat a small table. It held a worn frame and a smattering of tools—a thick pad, a broad stiff-haired brush, a long, narrow knife with a blunt end, and an agate burnisher. The tools of a gilder and framer. "You do restoration work, as well, Mr. Banks?"

He nodded. "Whenever my cousin has need of it. I can spruce up the goods to get a better price."

"How lucky he is to have you, then." She looked toward the canvases in the corner. "May I?"

"Of course."

He didn't follow her, but moved toward a table on the other side of the room. From the corner of her eye, she saw him toss a stretch of tarp over it.

Taking her time, hoping to give Niall the chance to look for whatever he hoped to find downstairs, she examined each canvas, making noises of admiration and asking questions as she went.

The landscapes mostly varied between views of country houses or mountains. She found several seascapes and two portraits. One was a sweet image of a smiling young lady in a riding habit, sitting atop a stone wall. The other was of Janet Ottridge.

Kara kept her movements easy and was careful not to react when the dead woman's face appeared beneath her hand. Banks had moved closer, a little off to the side.

"Portraits are not my strength," he said.

He'd definitely caught Miss Ottridge. Her smirk shone from the canvas, and she looked as if she'd been a little younger when she sat for the portrait.

"I prefer nature," she said. "Have you shown at the Royal Academy? I imagine your work must have generated much enthusiasm."

"No." Bitterness colored his tone. "I was not deemed talented enough for that august institution."

"Not connected enough, seems more likely. I've heard that an artist needs the right friendships to gain admittance." She moved toward the easel again, making sure to cross on the side of the covered table. With Banks behind her, she cast her eye over it, trying to make out the shape of the objects he'd covered. But it was what peeked out from beneath the tarp that struck her—and solidified her suspicions.

"There is some truth to that," he said. "Unfortunately, I have found no patron or art critic willing to sponsor me."

Turning, she gave him a sympathetic smile. "Is that why you first decided to set up your own roving auction house?"

He stilled.

"I imagine it was a good avenue in which to sell your own work? Perhaps you hoped to find a discerning patron?"

Scowling, he took a step toward her. "I don't know what you mean."

"I mean only to ask a few questions." She gestured. "There's no use in denying it. I can see a bit of the false hair and beard you tried to cover up, poking from beneath that tarp. Just exactly the color of Mr. Burroughs's wild hair, as it was described to me. And I smelled the spirit gum on you—I just did not recognize the scent until I saw the hair. You use it to fix the false hair and beard in place, yes?" She narrowed her eyes at him. "But now I see you've left a bit on your face, just there." She pointed.

Absently, he scratched the spot and peeled away the adhesive. "How very clever you are."

"I see the sense in the creation of the auction house, though I'm unclear why you didn't just make an honest enterprise of it."

"Do you think I didn't try?" The bitterness crept back as he again moved toward her, his steps slow and deliberate.

Kara edged toward the door.

"No one is interested in a new, small auction house." He

sounded aggrieved. "Not when the older, established places can offer up expensive or renowned objects and art. I needed something to make mine stand out."

"And stolen goods fit the bill," she said disapprovingly, hoping he wouldn't notice how close she was to the door.

"They do. Suddenly, my auctions were all the rage. You would be surprised at how interested some upstanding men become when they think they can get their hands on something that once belonged to the upper crust. Especially at a good price."

She hadn't distracted him from her position. He moved quickly and pressed his large hand flat against the panel above her head, closing the door firmly.

She slumped, wondering where Niall had got to and determined to find out all she could before he showed up.

"But why the masquerade?" She looked up into Banks's face. "Why risk playing different roles?"

"Because I discovered, the hard way, that a man alone is too easy to cheat, especially when I am dealing with sordid, back-alley tavern owners or crooked warehouse tenants."

"You needed Burroughs to be the bully?"

"He has proved useful. Odd enough to cause anyone to hesitate, and he does have a reputation as merciless and cruel," he agreed.

"And you play the debonair Mr. Banks as well, I must conclude. What purpose does he serve?"

"He's the Society connection. Friend to the rich. Entrée into the best houses. A knowledge of who owns something worth … having." He grasped her wrist firmly and began to pull her back into the room.

She dug in and tried to drag her heels, but the floor was smooth, and she slid along behind him. "Leaving you free to pursue your art?" she bit out.

"Yes. And to gossip about my 'cousin' and his 'partner.' In my own role I can speak to their successes—and to their formidable reputations." He opened a door set halfway down the inside of the room, revealing a supply closet. "Any other questions?" he asked with sarcasm as he shoved her inside.

Kara stumbled, but straightened and turned to face him. "Just one. Why did you kill Janet Ottridge?"

He ceased moving. His color faded, and she could swear he didn't breathe. He stared at her for a moment, then slowly closed the door.

She heard the key turn in the lock. It was utterly dark in the small space. She reached out, in all directions, feeling the dimensions of the closet and ensuring she was alone.

Quickly, then, she unhooked the special clasp at the side of her skirt waist. The panel she'd designed fell back, and by hand she sorted along the small pockets she'd had inserted into the folds of the skirt. A tiny vial. A packet of powder. *There.* Her lockpicks, thin and elegant even in the dark. She relished the feel of them. She'd undergone extensive training with them when she was young and had recently begun to brush up her skills.

A good thing, it turned out. This would take a little longer without any sort of light to go by, and she quite desperately wanted to see what Niall and Banks would make of each other.

NIALL HADN'T WASTED much time downstairs. Banks's willingness to leave him there told him there wasn't likely much to find. He searched through the desk in the study attached to the parlor. He found a box of trinkets and figurines, along with a list of their features and possible values, but little else, until the last drawer. There he found a thick roll of bank notes and a stack of tradesman's ads for a pawn shop in Great Earl Street.

Slipping one into his pocket, he closed the drawer again, left the study, and trod carefully up the stairs. He kept to the side, near the wall, hoping to avoid squeaking boards. Kara's voice floated down the passage from the studio as he reached the first landing. He turned to the right, away from it.

The first door he tried led to a bedroom, with a rumpled bed and clothes strewn about on the floor. The second was a linen closet. The third held more interest, full as it was of boxes and crates and stacks of books and canvases. He spotted a half-open crate full of candlesticks and another of fine porcelain. He didn't go in to examine the goods. He just closed the door and went on to be sure the other rooms were empty.

Once he'd determined the floor was deserted, he crept up to the next to be sure the attic rooms and servants' quarters were empty as well. He found no signs of life or occupation anywhere. It was as if Banks lived here entirely alone.

Quickly descending back to the floor below, Niall approached the studio door. It stood closed now, the voices cut off. Pressing his ear to it, he listened.

There. Kara's tone sounded strained. He lifted the latch, slowly, slowly. Peering through the merest crack, he saw Banks push her into a closet.

On silent feet, Niall squeezed into the room and came up close behind the man. Banks stood for a long moment, shoulders stooped, breathing deeply, facing the closet. When he turned at last, Niall swung hard. Banks stepped right into the blow of his fist.

Niall felt the crunch of the man's nose giving way. Blood flowed. Banks staggered back, but recovered quickly and dove for Niall's legs. He managed to step back, but not quickly enough. Banks had a hold of one of his feet.

Shifting his balance to his one free foot, Niall kicked out at the man with the foot he held, fast and hard. Banks reared back and lost hold. He lunged again, but missed. The man's hand landed near a table pushed up against the wall. He gripped the leg and heaved, sliding it hard into Niall's side. It wasn't much of a blow, but the table tilted and the contents slid off. Niall jumped back, startled, as something hairy slid down the front of him.

Banks used the spare seconds to begin to rise. Niall stepped back and found himself nearly in the center of the room. He snatched the painting off an easel and slammed it over Banks's head. The canvas tore. The frame was too large and loose to hold the man, but the blow had stunned him a little. Niall took the moment to reach a nearby table and grab a long, narrow gilder's knife.

He held it before the other man's face, pressing into his flesh. "The end may be blunt, but it will take out your eye, just the same."

Banks started to snarl a reply, but they were both startled into silence when a loud pounding echoed up from below.

Niall pressed again with the blade. "We didn't come unprepared. If I don't show my face at that door, the Metropolitan Police will invade the place within the next thirty minutes. Let me reassure the messenger, though, and if you agree to answer our questions, you will be left alone."

Banks eyed him suspiciously. "You don't mean to turn me in?"

Niall shook his head. "We've come to ask you about Janet Ottridge."

The man slumped. "She truly is dead, then?"

"She is, I'm sorry to say."

The pounding started up again.

All of the fight went out of the man. "Go, then. Call off the blue bellies. I'll tell you about her."

Niall pulled out a pair of snaps he'd begged off Inspector Wooten. "Over here, then." He hooked one metal ring to Banks's wrist and the other to the plumbing of the wash tub. "I'll only be a moment."

He left Banks slumped against the wall, raced downstairs, and opened the door.

"Oh, thanks be," Harold muttered, clutching his chest. "I was about to run off and fetch the inspector."

"Good lad, Harold. Keep watch, will you? Until Miss Levett and I come out?"

"Aye, sir."

Niall raced back upstairs, intending to free Kara. But when he threw open the studio door, he found her emerging from the closet, lockpicks in hand.

"That took longer than expected," she said calmly. "Apologies. I must begin to practice blindfolded."

Niall grinned. "Well, fetch that chair for Banks first, will you?" He opened the snaps with a key and gave the man a questioning look. "Do we need these now?"

"No. I said I would answer you, and so I will." Banks lifted the frame over his head and dropped into the chair.

Niall slid the stool near the easel over to Kara and perched himself on the table. He looked expectantly to Banks. "Janet Ottridge," he said.

Banks gave a short, sharp laugh. "Don't know much, do you? Janet Ottridge, indeed. Janet Ott, that's her name." He looked suddenly bleak. "Or, at least, that's what I have believed."

Niall exchanged a glance with Kara. "Tell us about Janet Ott, then."

Banks sighed. "Lord, but she's a ..." He stopped himself. "She *was* a saucy one. Sneaky, too, and with a sharp tongue on her. Pretty," he mused. "Especially in her younger days. She kept several of us on the hook and we fought and snarled over her like a pack of lap dogs looking for the best spot to lay our heads." He frowned. "Her prettiness soured, though, as she grew older and cagier."

"You've known her a good while, then."

"Since my first days in London." He snorted. "I was green as grass, and she knew it. She might have exploited it, but she took pity on me and taught me how to get by in Town."

"You were close?" Kara asked delicately.

"Close as a body could get to that girl." He'd grown bleak again. "She let me stay with her. Over a year, we were together. It took me that long to figure out she had other men at the same time." His mouth turned down. "And my own brother counted among them."

Silent and scowling, he sat for a moment, clearly looking inward. "How did she die?" he asked gruffly.

"Poison," Niall answered. "It wasn't easy. Or pretty."

Banks closed his eyes. Niall let him alone for a minute before he cleared his throat. He hated to admit it, but he felt a certain amount of empathy for the man. For any man who had loved the wrong woman and still felt the echoes of it, sounding in his ear, in his life, when he least expected it. "How much did you know about her ... occupations?"

"The blackmail, you mean? I knew of it, although it used to be on a smaller, safer scale. She grew cocky, though. Aimed too high. Took risks. I had to withdraw. I banned her from working in and around my auctions because she was drawing the wrong sort of attention."

"Did she blackmail you, to keep your secrets?" Kara asked. "She must have known about your various roles."

"She did know. She helped me establish the different reputations. She wouldn't tell. It wasn't like that between us."

"When did you turn her away?" Niall asked.

Banks thought back. "Over a year ago. I knew she was bound to get herself in trouble, the way she was operating. I couldn't let her drag me down with her."

"And yet she lured a man to your auction just last month," Niall remarked.

"Yes. I was furious. What did she think she was doing, mucking about with a police court magistrate?" He snorted. "A clerk? A whore? A shopkeeper? That's one thing. But you strike at a blue blood or a magistrate, and they will hit back." He passed a sardonic look between them. "And so, here you sit."

"We didn't come to harm you, sir," Kara said. "But we do know you had quite a row with the lady—and you were heard threatening to kill her."

He grew shamefaced. "I said terrible things to her that day. I went too far. But you don't understand. She could rile me up with just a look. She's the only one who ever brought my temper out like that."

"You cared for her," Kara suggested softly.

"God help me, but I did. She was so clever. Full of wit and fun, at times. She made me laugh like no one before or since." He drew a deep breath. "It was hard to get close to her. She grew up rough. She'd been hurt. A lot. Badly. She wore a shell around her, strong and thick. But I got under it. For a while." His visage darkened. "But then she took my heart in her hand and squeezed it dead and dry. She left me behind. When she finally came back, she brought along someone who could destroy me."

"You were angry enough to threaten her," Niall reminded him. "Perhaps you were angry enough to arrange her death, so that she could never again hurt you, involve you in her scheming, or put your business at risk."

"No." Banks shook his head emphatically. "I could not harm her. I just ... couldn't." His eyes narrowed. "In fact, if it was one of those nobs she was putting the screws to, then I hope you find him and hang him." He straightened suddenly. "She kept a notebook, you must know. With all of their names in it. If you find that—"

"We have it," Niall told him.

"Well, there's your list of suspects, then. Any of them could have gone after her. For revenge, if naught else. Or, should you find who she was pinning to the wall now ... mayhap they decided to kill rather than pay."

"You could be correct," Niall admitted. "Do you know where she was staying now? Her rooms might yield some evidence to support your theory."

"No. After she left me, I had no desire to hear from her or about her. I knew, though, I would someday hear tidings like this." Banks slumped again. "I warned her, over and over."

"I concede the possibility of your idea," Kara said. "But none of those blackmail victims were heard shouting at her that they would kill her. You did that. And one thing we've learned is that murder is often a crime of strong emotion."

Her words hit Banks almost palpably. He abruptly paled.

Niall leaned toward him. "The names in the notebook are being investigated, but we are appraising the matter from other angles. I see it in your face, Banks. You've only just thought of someone. Someone who might feel strongly enough to murder her."

"No." The other man stood. "I've answered your questions. Now I have to start packing." He shot Niall a hard glance. "You say you didn't come to expose me, but once someone knows, word will get out." He stood a moment, looking around at the bright studio with regret. "I hate to lose this place." He shrugged. "I always knew Janet Ott would cost me. I suppose it could have been worse."

Kara stood as well and stepped directly into his path. She looked up into his face. "Your brother. Was it he you thought of?"

Banks flinched.

"If you suspect something ..."

"No." He stepped away. "I said I would answer your questions about Janet. I've done so. There's nothing more to say."

"Nothing more you *will* say," she corrected him.

"Take my words as you like, young miss. Just take them and go."

Banks turned away, and Niall shared a look with Kara. "Let's go, then."

They were nearly to the studio door when Banks spoke again. Niall looked back to see him in the far corner of the room, holding a canvas and gazing down at it. "She didn't deserve it, you know. The saints knew she had her faults, but she didn't deserve to go out that way."

"No," Niall agreed. "She didn't."

Chapter Eight

A FTER REASSURING HAROLD and his friend—and tossing them both a bit of extra coin—Kara promised to visit him soon at Maisie Dobbs's bakery, before she and Niall set off in search of a hack. They discussed their destination as they walked.

"It's growing late," Niall said, looking at the sun's descent in the sky.

"We owe it to the inspector to see him quickly," she argued. "We should report Janet Ott's true name. And we can also relieve him of one interview off his list."

"And add another," Niall said with a sigh. "We need to direct resources to find Banks's brother."

"I doubt that's his true name," Kara said glumly. "Perhaps we should ask Wooten to set men to watching this place. Banks is going to disappear quickly and thoroughly, I suspect."

"He is," Niall agreed. "He had a stash of goods in there, but I doubt it's his only one. I believe him innocent—at least of Janet Ott's murder. What were your thoughts?"

"I don't think he killed her. His surprise about her death was genuine. I shocked him when I first mentioned it. But I've no doubt he's guilty of the other crimes we've heard laid at his door."

"Yes."

"Wooten is bound to ask where we encountered him. I suppose we should answer, but we did tell Banks we weren't there for such reasons."

"I daresay we should disclose his location." Niall glanced back along the street. "But perhaps not right away."

"It's a thin line, but it sounds a logical compromise between duty and sympathy."

They walked in silence then, until Niall waved down a hack and they set off, heading west.

Kara's mind kept going back to that last glimpse of Banks. It had been Janet Ott's portrait he'd held, she felt sure. "It won't seem real to him," she said quietly. "Her death. Not for a while."

Niall only nodded in agreement.

"I kept forgetting, after my father died. For a bit, it was all I could think about, of course. But then life went on. I'd get caught up in my lessons or my work. I'd come up with an idea I couldn't wait to share with him, or I'd make some ridiculous mistake in training. I'd trip over my own feet or drop a blade at a crucial moment, and I'd think how he'd laugh when I told him. And then I would remember. And it would hurt. Like a literal stab of grief, stealing my breath."

"I think it's always a slow adjustment, losing someone you love."

They rode in silence for a bit, each watching the city go by and thinking their own thoughts. It was a companionable silence, and Kara was grateful again at having found someone it was so easy to be with, in nearly any circumstance.

Suddenly, Niall spoke. "It's rosewater for me."

She held her breath. He so rarely spoke of his past.

He said nothing else for a moment, and she thought perhaps he hadn't meant to speak at all.

"My mother wore rosewater. Every day. She adored the scent, and on those rare times when I could get close and she would embrace me, I would be enveloped in it. I always think of her when I smell roses." He sighed and gave her half a smile.

"When she grew older, she would have days when she was a bit ... addled. She would forget she'd already applied it and douse herself again. The smell could knock you back a step, on those days. Still, I breathed it in, gladly. And I think of her still when I catch a whiff of it, even all these years later."

Kara reached over and pressed his hand, but said nothing. He was so careful not to speak of his past. She knew there were reasons for it. Secrets that weighed on him and he dared not share. She'd privately vowed never to press him, and she'd kept that promise. But to have him offer up a memory like that ... she accepted it as the gift it was.

It was not much longer before they were set down in Whitehall Place. Kara glanced around, curious, as they passed through a stone archway into the cobbled yard. All the times they had consulted or met with Inspector Wooten, and this was the first time she'd been to his offices in Scotland Yard.

They entered to find a sergeant standing behind a desk just inside. Niall spoke quietly to him, and the policeman passed them through into a large, desk-filled room and then to a connected passage. He stopped to open an office door. Kara was pleased to find Wooten inside, seated in a tidy little office at an oak desk.

He frowned down at a stack of papers. Nearby sat a small table, covered with a doily and holding a hinged pair of frames. One side held a portrait of Wooten, the other of a woman with a tiny smile tucked into the side of her mouth. Though the walls of the space were painted an institutional gray, they held a print of the queen and one of Green Park, complete with cows and dairy maids.

"Good day, Inspector," she said brightly as Niall held the door for her. "How charming your office is."

Wooten rose, his face flushed. "Good day, Miss Levett. Mr. Kier." He nodded. "I thank you, miss. My wife likes for me to have a few homey touches here."

"Quite right she is, too," Kara said. He indicated the seat across from him, and she took it as Niall leaned against a wall.

"We've come bearing news."

"Good news, I hope. I'm glad you've come. I was just considering writing to request your assistance, Miss Levett."

Niall shut the door behind her. "Again?" he asked in surprise.

"Well, she did a fine job with Lady Madge," Wooten said. "You've a delicate touch, my dear, and I'm beginning to see how such a thing can be helpful, in certain ... unusual situations."

"Let us fill you in," she suggested. "And then you can explain the difficulty."

"Very well."

She and Niall took turns relating their encounter with Banks.

"What on earth made you go haring off after a dangerous man like that?" the inspector demanded.

"Your note made it clear that you and your men are concentrating on the names in Janet Ott's notebook," Kara said.

"Orders from above," Wooten mumbled.

"I suspected as much." Niall had taken on his stubborn look. "Still, it's not wise to ignore the possibility of a connection with the Druidic Order. It should be looked into, even if only to exonerate them. When Kara discovered the connection between the maid and Banks and Burroughs, it made sense to follow up on it." He hesitated a moment. "I'll be leaving London soon, and I can't be comfortable going until I know the Order is safe, especially now that Kara is a member."

Kara blinked. "Leaving?"

But the inspector was responding. "Yes, yes. I meant to investigate that trail. I should be thanking you for looking into it, but I cannot encourage such interference. You might have run into the partner, Burroughs." He shook his head. "That one is reputed to be a loose cannon."

Niall began to explain about the "partners," but Kara scarcely heard him. She was quietly reeling. Leaving? Where was he going? And when? Why hadn't he answered her? And why was this the first she was hearing of it?

"It sounds as if you were lucky to escape unscathed," Wooten said when the story was done. "It was good work, though, both of you. And I think you are right—it sounds as if this brother bears looking into. Anyone with an axe to grind against the woman ..." He made a face. "And speaking of which, you've come in time this afternoon. If you wouldn't mind accompanying me, Miss Levett, we should be able to conduct this interview today."

She was started out of her reverie. "Oh, yes. Of course. I'm happy to help."

"What interview?" asked Niall.

"Well!" Wooten reached into a drawer and pulled out Janet Ott's notebook. "We've found an anomaly in the woman's records." He thumbed back from the last marked page. "Look there!" He slid it over so that they could see.

Kara looked to where he pointed toward a name close to the end of the page, and immediately noted that the usual accompanying number—the amount of blackmail money paid—was missing.

"Someone didn't pay the blackmail," she breathed.

"*Refused* to pay," Wooten corrected her.

"J. Riley," she said, reading the name out loud.

"Mrs. Joy Riley. Widow. And one not too happy with the Metropolitan Police." He pressed his lips together. "It seems she lodged a complaint about Janet Ottridge two months ago. She was brushed aside."

"So she has an axe to grind against Janet Ott and against you as well," Niall said with a grin.

"Yes." The inspector sighed. "She has no wish to talk to us. I thought she might be more comfortable if a woman came along when I try to speak with her." He looked expectantly at Kara. "A woman in charity with the police ..."

"Yes. I'll do what I can."

"And I'll poke about a bit, see if I can drum up anything on Banks's brother," Niall stated.

Which effectively gave him an escape from her questions,

Kara thought. She stood. A temporary reprieve only, she vowed.

⟫⟩⟨⟨⟨

NIALL LEFT WHITEHALL and took an omnibus, then another, all the way to Shoreditch. It let him off in the main street, and he set out, walking the last bit to the Druid's Grove. He didn't mind. His mind was moving faster than his feet.

He hadn't meant to mention his leaving to Kara. He'd thought to keep it to himself until his departure was imminent. Easier to avoid the questions, the explanations. Past experience had proved the wisdom of such a course.

But he hadn't meant to speak of his mother, either. He *never* spoke of her. He hadn't, not even with—

Pausing on a short stone bridge, he stared down at the water running beneath. They had just slipped out—the memories of his mother. Naturally. As if he were just anyone and free to speak of his life, of his formative years, his relationships.

He pushed away from the stone wall and resumed walking. It was another way in which his association with Kara differed from—everything else. No alarm bells. No telltale signs that she was growing fonder of him than he could allow himself to feel for her. A hundred times worse, this dangerous feeling of freedom. This slip into easy, comfortable revelation. It had spooked him, and he'd tossed out the notion of his leaving to keep it from happening again.

"Good afternoon, Mr. Kier."

He gave a start and realized he'd reached the gates of the Grove—and nearly walked past them.

"Meant to come in, then, did you?" the gate watchman asked.

"Indeed. I was merely lost in thought. Thank you."

The servant shrugged, and Niall thought his distraction would scarcely be the oddest thing the man had witnessed in his post.

He strode up the drive and into the house. No one was about, but he asked a footman for Mrs. Berringer and was directed to the summerhouse.

A good many of the windows had been opened to let in the unusual October sun, he found as he entered. He also found Lady Flora Copely sitting at one of the long tables, a pile of twisted wire and torn newspapers before her. A maid sat at a smaller table nearby, carefully measuring water into a thick mixture in a bowl.

"Good afternoon, Lady Flora. You certainly look busy."

"Good afternoon, young man. And yes, it seems I'm always making messes when I'm at the Grove, only this time it's flour and water instead of soil and fertilizer."

"I've come looking for Mrs. Berringer. I was told she was out here?"

"Indeed." She gestured toward a seat further down the table with a similar pile of materials before it. "She went to the kitchens to request a tea tray. She thought she'd fortify herself before we truly get messy." She held up a twisted wire form. "We are making papier mâché flowers, you see. We are forming safer versions of the blooms we had planted at the feet of our three Moirae. We will arrange them in a border at the bottom of the reliefs and have a thin layer of plaster applied over top. Then they can be painted to match the stone and we'll have a similar result, with no chance of anyone misusing our tribute for their own foul means."

"It must have been disturbing for you," he said softly.

"Indeed. Imogen says doing the job ourselves can serve as a sort of penance, but I don't feel that it can be enough." She glanced up at him with sad eyes. "Such a dreadful business. I never even met the woman, and still, I feel a sense of responsibility for her death." She sighed and tossed the form onto the pile. "That's the last lotus blossom. We can craft some of the blooms that were too exotic to plant, you see."

"An added benefit to the scheme," he said with a smile.

"Yes. And do you know, I do not feel the inclination to wait for tea before I begin. I'm inspired right now." She turned her head to the maid still stirring at another bowl of paste. "Mary, dear. Do you have that all mixed and ready?"

"Yes, my lady. One bowl is complete."

"You didn't forget the salt?"

"No, ma'am." The maid looked only slightly younger than her mistress. She gave Lady Flora a wry look. "How could I forget, with you so diligently reminding me?"

Lady Flora laughed. "Yes, I am an old nag, it's true, but Mary is used to me. Will you bring me over the bowl, my dear? I'm ready to begin."

The maid looked with dismay at her paste-covered hands, but dutifully began to rise.

"No, allow me." Niall waved her back into her seat. He took the first bowl of paste and set it beside Lady Flora. "I'll leave you to it, ma'am. I believe I'll try to intercept Mrs. Berringer on her way back." He grinned at the older lady. "I'll be sure to tell her that you are getting ahead of her."

"You do that, Mr. Kier. Imogen does like a competition." She smiled in glee as she dipped a strip of paper into the paste and squeezed the extra off. "I'll see how many I can get done while you detain her."

Niall laughed and gave her a bow before he set off back toward the house. As he'd hoped, he ran into Imogen Berringer just inside. "Good day to you, ma'am. I was hoping to have a private word with you."

The lady gave him a sharp look. "Of course. Come up to my sitting room, Mr. Kier. Shall I send for tea?"

"No, though I appreciate the offer. I won't keep you, as I know you are in the midst of a project."

"Oh, yes. Thank you."

She led the way upstairs and into a small parlor. It was bright, still decorated in the light blues and soft whites that had been popular years ago. She took a seat near the cold hearth and indicated the one across from her.

"Thank you. I wanted to ask you about the maid. The extra woman hired for larger events—the one associated with Janet Ott."

"Janet Ott?" she asked.

"Yes. We've found Ottridge was a false name. Probably just one of several."

Mrs. Berringer sighed.

"Arthur mentioned that you see to the household accounts for the Grove. I hoped you would have the woman's address on record? Perhaps a residence, not just the location of the Hare and the Dog?"

"I'm sure I do." She rose, and as he did too, she waved him back. "No. Stay there. I just need a look at my files." Crossing over, she sat at a desk in the corner. "Mr. Kier," she said pointedly as she opened a drawer. "Why are you continuing to stay involved in this woman's death? Arthur's name is clear now." She made it sound as if that should be the end of the matter.

"But the Order's name is not. Surely you cannot wish to leave such dark rumors and whispers hanging above our heads?"

She shrugged. "Perhaps it will not hurt. We are so often regarded as eccentrics and oddities. Perhaps a bit of dark mystique would do our reputation some good."

"Nonsense. What sort of element would that draw to us?" Niall shook his head. "No. We need to clear the Order's name—not to mention, we need to be sure we are not harboring a murderer in our midst."

She lifted a shoulder again. "The woman was a menace."

"Many would agree, but that doesn't mean she deserved an early, ugly death."

"Perhaps it was her predestined fate. Perhaps Atropos was meant to cut her life thread on that day."

Niall regarded her steadily. "We've both been in the Order long enough to understand one another. I know you for a learned and eminently practical woman. Were you a man, you would have made an effective and efficient general. I know you don't believe any such thing."

She pulled out a file and made a face. "You are correct, but sometimes, around here, I can say such things."

And get her way, he finished silently. "Mrs. Berringer. Imogen. I personally doubt the killer is a Druid, but we must know. And if they are, then we cannot let them go free."

"Can't we?"

"Perhaps Janet Ott did blackmail someone here and they did away with her. What will happen the next time someone crosses him?"

"Or her," she said sharply.

"Either," he agreed. "You know how the intrigues ebb and flow throughout the Grove. Will someone who has murdered freely think they might do it again? If threatened, irritated, or annoyed, will they attempt that which has worked before? The council could create a rule they didn't agree with. Or Arthur could invite someone they found undesirable. They could strike again, anywhere."

At Kara, perhaps.

"You are wise to use my fondness for Arthur against me." She stopped copying down information from the file long enough to look at him directly. "I thought you would look to me as a suspect next. Have you not listened to the whispers of my jealous rage? Others here have said as much."

He laughed. "As Miss Levett has said, if you had done it, the death would have looked like an entirely benign accident and there would be no inquest."

She looked gratified. "That's true enough. What a shambles the killer made of it. In a crowd, no less!" She set down her pen. "Here is the maid's name and address. Honestly, I don't think an Order member killed the woman. She hadn't really had time to get up to her tricks here yet."

"I hope you are right, but we have to know."

"Good luck in your hunt," she said, rising.

"And good luck with your project." He raised his brows at

her. "Lady Flora has likely got a good head start on you, by now."

"Oh, good heavens. And the tea is likely cooling, as well." She opened the door and made a shooing motion. "Off with you, then."

He tucked the paper in a pocket and left.

Chapter Nine

"**G**OOD HEAVENS, INSPECTOR. Where is your widow living?" Kara said as their hack took them a good ways past Hyde Park and toward Notting Hill.

"She's in Shepherd's Bush, which is still largely rural. It appears the lady likes it that way," Wooten replied. "She has a nice-sized house and a small bit of land. Enough for a grand garden. Her husband was an engineer, one of those who helped develop this section of London. He did well for himself and left her comfortably settled."

"How nice for her, although I'm sure she'd rather have her husband alive to share it with."

"In this case, I believe you are right. I think they truly cared for each other. She's quite fiercely protective of his memory. It's something Janet Ottridge—I mean, Ott—hoped to exploit. It backfired on her, though, from what I've heard."

"Good," Kara said fiercely. "I confess, I'm glad to hear someone thwarted the woman. Without killing her."

"This widowed lady reminds me of you, a little. Very independent, she is." He did not sound entirely approving. "I gather you and Mr. Kier went on your little adventure this morning quite alone."

"Actually, young Harold was on the scene, as well as one of

his friends." She arched a brow at him. "Even had they not been there, though, how would the situation have been different from *this* adventure, out alone with you, sir?"

"The situations are quite different," Wooten protested. "Not the same at all. I am both married and twice your age—literally old enough to be your father. Mr. Kier is young, handsome, virile—and known to gallivant about Town in a kilt."

"He does indeed work in a faded tartan, which has proved endlessly tempting to my maids, but as for gallivanting ... I've only seen him don his formal kilt for special occasions." She cocked her head. "Don't tell me that you disapprove of the kilt, Inspector? The queen herself has been vocal about her approval, and the men in the royal family all have worn them at times."

He shot her a look of censure. "You know that it is not the kilt that worries me, Miss Levett."

She sobered. "I do appreciate your concern."

He softened. "I don't believe you have enough people who have a concern for you, my dear."

"Oh, but the number is growing! I have Turner and Gyda Winther and my friend Elinor, on the rare occasions she is in Town, and Niall and now—you." She smiled warmly and then suddenly widened her eyes. "Oh, and Jenny, too! I cannot forget her."

"Who is Jenny?" he inquired mildly.

"She is a chambermaid at the White Hart. She and her sisters have been lovely, inviting me into their businesses and lives. They have taught me to make cold cream and to bake bannocks." She smiled. "That is another handful of friends. It feels like an embarrassment of riches, when compared to my life not so very long ago." She straightened. "Oh! And I forgot my cousin—Joseph! Though I admit, I have not seen much of him since his difficulties this past summer."

"That is a terribly short list for a young lady like you," Wooten said gently. "Not to mention, mildly inappropriate. Is there no older female in your family? One who could come and stay with you at Bluefield Park? Someone to guide you, as well as to lend you respectability."

"No. There is no one, I'm afraid. But I promise I am quite respectable and do not feel the lack." She paused. "Inspector, after last summer, I am sure that you must know and understand my history."

"Every man in the police force knows about your kidnapping," he said quietly. "And about your rescue, and the subsequent attempts to take you for ransom."

"I do believe I became somewhat of a Golden Fleece, a challenge for some of the lower elements of London," she said on a sigh. "They all wanted to take a stab at me." She pursed her lips. "The thing is, everyone in Society knows all about it, too. More, they know about my father's reaction to it all."

"The lessons," he said.

She laughed. "Ah, your tone says it all, sir. Yes. My lessons." She looked at him with curiosity. "May I ask what you have heard?"

"We've all heard that you have been taught to fight. To fight back and throw off an assailant." He raised a brow. "A skill I believe you demonstrated a few months ago, when that body was discovered in the Crystal Palace."

"Yes. I did learn all of that—and I use it when I must. That was the start of it, you see." She leaned in. "But there is so much more. I learned to fight *dirty*, Inspector. To take advantage of weakness. To escape." Sitting back, she smiled. "I can also scale most buildings and break a window with a minimum of sound. I can craft dozens of knots—"

"And I've seen what you can do with a rope and pulley," he interjected, shaking his head.

"There is even more, too," she said confidingly. "And none of it the usual round of watercolors and pianoforte recitals that so many Society girls pursue. So, if you, like Mr. Niall Kier, believe my future to be a marriage into the peerage, you can abandon such thoughts. I can never be the meek and quiet sort of wife that men of the *beau monde* expect to wed."

"But your family line ..."

She waved a hand. "I am the daughter of a baron, but my cousin holds the title now." She held up a finger. "That leaves me with an unusual—some say unfit—upbringing." Another finger went up. "And no direct line to the peerage. And you ask why no suitors have been lining up?"

He looked as if he might say something, but he stopped himself.

She grinned. "I can see what you are thinking. What of my fortune? What of Bluefield, one of the most beautiful estates in the south of England? What of my factories and businesses? Surely some blue-blooded man out there might look over my oddities for all of that." She shot him a scornful glance. "Do you think I want to be courted for my coin, sir? For my acreage or my ironworks? Do you think that a man who had to *overlook* all of the skills I've worked so hard for could make me happy? Or could be happy with me?"

"Perhaps you have a point," he conceded.

"Please, do not worry for me." She patted his hand. "I do not." She tossed her head. "Consider it, sir. There are changes afoot in England. New industries. New ways to travel. New ways of thinking. Perhaps I am a new sort of woman for a new age in Britain?"

"I might embrace that prospect with you, if you did not stand alone."

"I am scarcely alone." She sighed. "When I am routinely scolded for keeping a firm hand in the family businesses I inherited, I always point out Eleanor Coade, who ran her stone business for fifty years and produced statuary and architectural décor for St. George's, Carlton House, the Pavilion in Brighton, and Buckingham Palace."

"That was another age," he said.

"I remind them of the Countess of Jersey, who was the senior partner at Child's Bank, and Harriot Mellon Coutts, who ran

Coutts bank for years, even after she became the Duchess of St. Albans. Beyond business, England has famous women authoresses. Women played significant roles in the abolition of slavery. What of prison reformers such as Elizabeth Fry and Hannah Bevan? Surely you have read the books of Harriet Martineau—a social theorist who is both prolific and female. Women run taverns and fabric and modiste's shops across London. And you cannot forget the women serving as postmistresses and letter carriers for the General Post Office."

He frowned. "Even the vanguard can be a most dangerous place, Miss Levett."

"We have a queen on the throne," she reminded him. "I would call her the vanguard."

He looked worried. "Yes. And she judges herself equal to any task—but expects other woman to adhere to traditional roles. Insists on it. Especially women of standing and bloodline. A great many men feel the same way."

"Men who wish women to be coddled, soft, uneducated, and biddable? Men who don't wish to admire a female's accomplishments? Men who don't wish to work to match them?" She raised her chin. "There are plenty of us who see them for what they are."

"I hope you are right, my dear, or else I'm afraid you will have a difficult time of it." He heaved a sigh. "Do forgive me for meddling. I've grown fond of you. And I assure you, I appreciate your abilities. I merely wish to see you happy and settled."

"There is nothing to forgive. I do appreciate your concern, sir. And I value our friendship."

"As I value yours, even though I am about to take shameful advantage of it." He nodded ahead, and she saw the hack had begun to slow. A lane of cottages gave way to unattached homes of stone, surrounded by quaint fences and well-tended gardens. They rolled to a stop before the last one in line, a bit larger than the others. Its far edge abutted a pasture that gave way to woods.

Kara allowed the inspector to hand her down, her gaze fixed

upon the garden. "How lovely. Someone has poured a lot of work and tender care into this place."

A gate sat in the fence. A flagstone path to the house lay beyond it. Her eye on the carefully tended beds, the trimmed shrubbery, and the late-blooming roses, Kara absently let herself in.

Mrrrp.

She paused and turned to look. Under a large, lush hydrangea curled a pretty, little gray tabby, head lifted.

Kneeling, she held out a hand. "Good day to you. Aren't you a darling?" The cat trilled again, but before Kara could touch her, a great, echoing boom sounded behind her, above her, around her.

She ducked. Wooten threw himself on the flagstones just inside the gate. The cat, however, merely looked on, calm and curious.

"I told you I would blow your head off if you ever set foot on my property again!" It was a woman's voice, harsh and full of dark promise. "Begone! And don't touch my cat!"

Holding her hands out so that they might be clearly seen, Kara stood and turned to face the house. "I'm afraid there's been a mistake," she called out.

"Your mistake was in trying to besmirch my husband's good name." A woman in black stood on the stone portico, an old, long rifle raised and pointed at Kara. "I don't want to hear another word from your mouth. Go. Or I won't shoot over your head next time."

"I am not Janet Ottridge. My name is Miss Kara Levett."

The rifle lowered a bit as the woman peered at her.

"In fact, Janet Ottridge is dead."

"What?" The woman looked shocked. "Oh. Well." She lowered the rifle, resting the butt end on the floor and holding the barrel. "Good, then." She sighed, and her eyes narrowed as Inspector Wooten climbed to his feet. "Fine. Come inside if you must."

The inspector took Kara's arm as they approached. "Mrs. Riley, I cannot recommend greeting visitors with a rifle blast. Not even unwelcome guests."

"Yes, well, I daresay it's the welcome your sort deserves," the widow answered smartly. "Now I can see that the lady is not the vile blackmailer, but before all I could see was skirts and dark hair. You can understand my mistake." She stepped aside to invite them in. Following, she propped the rifle in the corner behind the door.

"That weapon is so old it's more likely to harm you than anyone else," Wooten said.

"You are wrong there, Inspector. Old Bess is clean and oiled and cared for. She's as ready and as good as when my grandfather carried her to war." She turned away from the gun and looked Kara over. "Well, then. Miss Levett, is it? Why has the inspector brought you to my door? Is he hoping to sweeten me up a bit? Get me to cooperate?"

"I believe he thought it might make you more comfortable to have a woman present as he asks his questions," Kara replied.

"Well, I believe a great many more people would be comfortable had the police cooperated when I first told them about that woman and her evil ways. But she'd dead now, you said? Tell me. Was she done in by one of her latest blackmail victims?"

"That's what we are hoping to discover," said Wooten.

"And you wish for my help?" The widow sounded incredulous.

Kara stepped closer. "Mrs. Riley, murder is a more vile crime than blackmail."

"Oh. Well, there is that." The widow threw up her hands. "Very well. Do sit down, the pair of you, and hold a moment. I've lemonade, and I've just baked shortbread this morning. Sit. Sit." She indicated a small parlor. "I won't be but a moment."

Kara took a spot on a settee, while Inspector Wooten took a chair. After a moment, the tabby sauntered in and jumped up onto the back of the furniture.

"Hello again. And how did you get in?" she asked the cat as it draped itself behind her.

"Kitchen door." Mrs. Riley entered with a tray. "I should be thankful, I suppose, since opening the door for her multiple times a day is sometimes the most constructive thing I manage, but then she goes and makes up sweet with a total stranger." Taking a seat on the settee, she gave the cat a dark look, then proceeded to serve all around. She took up her own lemonade, sat back, and looked between them. "Well? What is it you want?"

Kara sat straighter. "I should perhaps apologize, Mrs. Riley. I'm afraid I don't know the particulars of your run-in with Janet Ott—which was, we believe, her real name. I'm sorry to have to ask you to repeat it, but we might learn something useful." The woman's expression hardened, and Kara rushed to add, "Especially as you are the only person we know of who didn't give in to her scheming."

That clearly surprised the widow. "Am I, then? Well, I will count it among my accomplishments."

"As well you should," Kara told her.

"What is it you wish to know?"

Kara glanced at the inspector, but he waved her on.

"I'd like to hear it all, from the beginning. Where did you first meet Miss Ottridge, as you knew her?"

"About five months ago, at a dinner at the Sostratus Club."

Kara raised a brow at the inspector, who hurriedly clarified, "A gentlemen's club for engineers, architects, draftsmen, that sort of thing."

"Indeed. Sostratus of Cridus built the great Lighthouse of Alexandria. The only taller structures in ancient times were the pyramids at Giza. It was one of the Seven Wonders of the World. The gentlemen named their club after him, and my husband was proud to be counted a member."

"Ladies were welcome?" Kara asked in surprise. Certainly she'd never been asked to join any of the artists' or metal workers' guilds.

Mrs. Riley snorted. "Wives and female guests are tolerated at special dinners, once or twice a year," she replied. "Still, I did enjoy those evenings. It was nice to go out together, as a couple."

Kara leaned in. "Who brought Janet Ott as their guest?"

"Douglas Saunders," the widow replied. "He did not look happy about it, either. He spent the evening glaring at her and drinking too much."

"And how did she spend her evening?"

"Cozying up to everyone possible. I thought she was on the lookout for potential husbands." Her lip curled. "That would have been so much better."

"Was she looking to meet as many members as possible, looking for victims to blackmail?" Kara looked to the inspector. "Perhaps it's a pattern, then. Infiltrate a group and exploit the members, then move on to the next?"

"Twice is possibly the start of a pattern," Wooten mused. "We'll find out as we follow up on more of those names, I suppose."

"Do you have the list, sir? Perhaps Mrs. Riley would know some of them."

"Aye, I do." He took out a bundle of papers, searched through them, and handed one over to the widow. "Your name is just there, ma'am. Do you recognize any of the names around yours?"

Mrs. Riley studied the paper. "Yes. The two before mine. Hambleton and Martinson. Both are names of members of the club." Her eyes wandered over the page. "These are the amounts she was paid? Were they in single or multiple payments?"

"We do not know."

"Hmmph." She handed the list back. "I just wondered if she would have come back again, had I given in the first time." She raised her chin. "There's no question of any of the club's members coming after me, though. There wouldn't be any."

"Why not?" Wooten's tone was sharp.

"Because that evil woman made a large mistake when she

110

showed up here *four days* after I laid my husband to rest."

"Good heavens," Kara murmured.

"First I schooled her on the reality of my husband's behavior—the very same actions that she tried to twist into something as sordid and ugly as her soul."

Kara tried not to allow her curiosity to show. The details were not pertinent to why they had come. But Mrs. Riley was a perceptive creature.

"My husband went into London once a fortnight to visit his old nursemaid. The woman raised him, practically, after his mother's death. Mrs. Landers had a niece, a pretty, young girl who came to stay with her while the banns were read for her marriage to a young man from Cheapside. Miss Ottridge must have heard some gossip about my Alden's visits to the city, or perhaps she just followed him there, but she witnessed his welcome by the two ladies and drew all the worst conclusions."

"I'm so sorry," Kara said. "It must have been so difficult to hear such things, and so close after his passing. Even if you knew it to be false."

"It was horrid. Alden's death was a tragic accident, and I shall miss him every day of my life. My only consolation is that he never heard her erroneous claims." The widow sniffed. "I set her straight, then I told her what I thought of her. Old Bess and I sent her swiftly on her way. After that, I marched right down to the Sostratus, pushed my way past the porters, and spoke my piece right in the club's main room. I told them what she had done and said. I told them to prepare themselves, as she would be targeting one of them next."

"Good heavens. I'm sure they all looked askance at Mr. Saunders for bringing her in to their midst."

"They did. He was there that evening. He stood and confessed all. The woman had witnessed him indulge in some sort of dishonest or disgraceful behavior at a pawn shop. She must have followed him home, for she showed up later, threatening to expose him to his neighbors, family, and business contacts, just as she'd said she would do with poor Alden's reputation. Saunders paid her, but she'd also demanded an introduction to the club." She tossed the inspector a scornful look. "I tried to report her activities to the police, but I was patted on the head and sent home."

"Can you give us Mr. Saunders's address?" Inspector Wooten had his notebook out.

"I could, but it wouldn't be any help to you. The man couldn't hold up his head any longer. He left in disgrace, setting out on a long tour of the Continent."

"You should check that he did indeed set out before the woman was killed," Kara told him.

"Already noted." Wooten looked up again. "Did he mention the name of the pawn shop?"

Mrs. Riley frowned, thinking. "No."

"How many pawn shops in London?" asked Kara.

"Hundreds." He shook his head.

"His servants, perhaps? They might be familiar with his habits and haunts. A valet might have found a pawn ticket in a pocket."

"Already noted." The inspector looked to the widow. "Is there anything else you recall about Miss Ott? Anything odd or different? Something she might have let slip that might tell us more about her?"

"No." Mrs. Riley frowned. "When I think of her, I can only recall that treacly, sweet tone, acting like she would be doing me a favor taking my money, instead of ruining my dead husband's name." Tears filled her eyes.

Kara leaned over and pressed the widow's hand. "I'm sorry to have stirred it all up again, but you have been incredibly helpful. And I am inspired by your bravery in confronting and thwarting her. You must indeed have saved some of your husband's friends from her extortion."

"Thank you." Mrs. Riley wiped her eyes. She gave Wooten another scornful look. "You were wise to bring the young lady along. She's almost made me forget how annoyed I've been with your lot."

The inspector stood. "Then I will thank you for your help, ma'am, and I'll leave while I am still in your good graces."

She stood as well and reached out to stay him with a hand on his arm. "You'll stay in my good graces if you will but make me a promise."

He waited.

"Teach your men to listen," she pleaded. "Even if it seems as if a woman, a child, or someone else has come to you with a silly complaint or a frivolous story. Teach them to listen. There might be more there, if they do but consider."

"I give you my word, madam." It sounded like a vow.

Kara bade both the cat and the widow a good day. She waited until they were on their way back to Town before she turned to the inspector. "You knew she needed someone else to share her story with."

Wooten nodded. "She was treated badly. A shameful thing for us all. I just thought about how my own wife might feel." He gave her a little smile. "And I have noticed that you are very easy to talk to, Miss Levett."

"And you are very skilled at your job, sir."

He blinked. "Thank you. It's a compliment that means something, coming from you."

She grinned. "Do you know what this feels like?"

He looked baffled.

"It feels like a lesson," she confided.

He looked horrified. "It is no such thing."

"And yet it feels so." She laughed a little. "Even worse, sir. It feels like I am good at this, too."

Chapter Ten

T HE INSPECTOR OFFERED to transport her all the way to Bluefield Park, but Kara declined. Bluefield was likely empty. The shift in Niall's demeanor had been swift and obvious. She would bet good money that he would be out and about somewhere. Perhaps avoiding her. The thought of sitting at home and awaiting his return ... it set her back up.

"Shall we set you down at your rooms near the park? Do you mean to keep them?" Wooten asked. "Now that the Exhibition is over?"

"I do. I think they will be useful for several purposes." She didn't bother to tell him that she owned the building the rooms were in, as well as the one next to it.

"Aye. I can see that you might not always wish to drive all the way out to Bluefield after an evening's entertainment." He paused. "Shall we take you to the Druid's Grove?"

"No." She recalled Gyda mentioning she would likely be at Lake Nemi today. She gave the inspector that address.

It didn't take long to arrive at New Street. She bade the inspector goodbye and gave him her thanks. As the hack moved away, she turned to face the nondescript townhouse.

Established at first as a defiant, feminine counterpart to the underground brothels and sex clubs enjoyed by so many gentlemen, the place still bore bits of décor from its early days as a safe place for women to explore their own proclivities. But though it might have begun its early life as an exotic playground, Lake Nemi had grown beyond its original purpose. Named after an ancient Roman temple to the Goddess Diana, it now acted as a true women's club, providing a haven for women to delve into pursuits that were not easily found or sanctioned elsewhere. There was a scientific laboratory, a well-stocked library, and a travel room full of globes, maps, travel guides, and diaries from all across the world, just to start.

This place, too, was a gift Niall had given her. He'd introduced her here, and she'd breathed a sigh of relief once she understood. Free moments had been scarce these last months. The Great Exhibition had consumed many of her waking moments, but she'd made the time to visit here. To meet and befriend women with clever minds and open spirits. She'd made friends who, like her, loved to learn. She'd learned new ways to pursue knowledge and embrace life. As the evening shadows deepened around her, she paused to breathe out her thanks for the place.

She'd only hesitated a moment, standing still on the pavement, but suddenly the hair at the back of her neck began to rise. She froze, casting her gaze about—and stopped when she discovered a woman a few feet away, staring at her intently.

Kara didn't know her. Had never seen her before. The woman was very pretty, with smooth ivory skin and a long, sharp blade of a nose. Her strawberry-blonde hair had been piled high atop her head, and perched on her curls was a small burgundy hat, trailing wine and gold ribbons. Her walking gown was obviously expensive and done in the same colors. The matching pelisse boasted exquisite gold embroidery.

There had been shock and surprise at first on the woman's face, as if she knew Kara somehow. But now her expression melted into a cool, measuring disdain. Her chin lifted.

The woman said nothing. Neither did Kara. They stared until

Kara gave a shrug, gathered her skirts, and unhurriedly climbed the stairs to enter the house.

"Miss Winther, is she here at present?" she asked the maid who admitted her.

"Upstairs in her studio, I believe, miss."

She hurried then. Rushing up, Kara burst through Gyda's door without knocking and ran to the window. Keeping hidden behind the curtain, she peered down into the street.

Gyda, busy at work, didn't notice her bad manners. "Kara, I'm glad you are here." She didn't look up. "I wanted to consult with you."

"I've just had the strangest encounter," Kara said. The woman had disappeared from the street below. She abandoned the curtain and pressed against the window, straining to see as far as she could, but there was no sign of her. "Are there any new women about the club?" she asked.

"There always are." Gyda was still bent over the design she was working on.

"Do any of them possess creamy skin, sharp noses, and red-gold hair?"

The description made Gyda look up, frowning. "I don't think so? Surely I would have noticed."

Kara described her brief encounter. "It was unsettling."

Gyda made a face. "Perhaps she recognized you from the Great Exhibition?"

"She looked like she *despised* me."

"Then perhaps she's one of those backward ladies who don't believe we women should be allowed to think about anything beyond planning dinners and popping out children?"

"Perhaps." Kara resolved to put the woman out of her mind. "Is Emilia around this evening?"

"I heard her say she meant to be out tonight. Why? Have you need of something?"

"No. It's just that she's been a bit … skittish, lately. At least in my company."

"I've barely seen her myself. I imagine she's either plotting something, or she's found a new lover. Either will distract her or set her to running about." Gyda at last set down her pencil. "In any case, I am glad you are here. I have questions for you regarding this design I'm working on."

"What is it?" Kara asked, curious.

"A knife. Small and dramatically curved." Gyda met Kara's eye. "We are having a ceremony in a few days."

Kara sat up straight. Ceremonies were serious business. "For whom?"

"For Beth."

"Oh. Is that a good idea?" Beth had only been coming around the club for six months or so. She was extremely timid. She barely spoke to anyone, and Kara had seen her start at a loud voice, a sneeze, the clatter of a pan, and, once, just the opening of a closed door.

"I think it is." Gyda had been gentle with the girl from the start. "I've heard her story, and it is not good."

Kara blinked, concerned.

"She's safe. Now." Gyda sounded bitter. "But she's having difficulty moving past it all. I think the ceremony will boost her confidence." Her gaze grew crafty. "As will the knife."

"May I see it?"

"Of course." She handed over the design, and Kara caught her breath. The blade was unique and beautiful. "I hope you are crafting a scabbard as well. That blade looks lethal."

"It will be. And yes, there's to be a scabbard. I don't want the girl harming herself." Gyda pointed to the corner of the paper, where some images were lightly drawn. "I want to have symbols of feminine power etched on the blade and into the scabbard. I think it will lend Beth courage to see them. I know you studied symbols with the Druids, and I thought you might be able to help."

"Oh, yes, of course. I see you have the triple spiral. That is perfect. It speaks of female power and transition and growth.

Also, there is a triple-moon symbol that reflects further aspects of the female—fertility, wisdom, and strength. It's also associated with the Triple Goddesses, the phases of a woman's life—maiden, mother, and crone." She motioned for Gyda to pass her a sheet of paper and drew the image.

"Excellent. I spoke to Magda, and she showed me this one—Zhiva, the Slavic goddess of life."

"Orchids and hollyhocks represent fertility," Kara said, recalling Mrs. Berringer's description in the Grove. "You could etch the blooms."

"Jane Ingram told me that seashells invoke feminine beauty and protection. I've never heard that, in all my travels, but she grew up on the coast, so I suppose she should know."

Kara shrugged. "As long as *Beth* believes it, what else would matter?"

"True enough."

Kara stood and began to explore the small room, straightening a small shelf of cups, saucers, and cutlery before moving on to papers and other bric-à-brac. "There was something I wished to discuss with you, as well."

Gyda looked up. "Yes?"

Kara hesitated, her fingers still busily smoothing folded cloths and tidying drafting tools.

Her friend sat back and gave her a direct stare. "What has Niall done now?"

"He's leaving," Kara blurted.

"Ah. I see." Gyda leaned back in her chair. "Honestly, I'm surprised he lasted this long."

Her eyes widened. "What does that mean?"

"It's nothing to do with you, my dear. It's just Niall. This is who he is. He's a nomad. He rarely stays anywhere long before his feet get the itch to wander again." Gyda straightened. "I truly don't think he would have made it through all the long months of the Exhibition were it not for you."

"What?"

"Oh, he would have left his work, the large pieces, at least, but had you not also been an exhibitor, he likely would have been stomping about new ground by the end of August."

"I can't tell whether you think I am a good influence or a bad one in this scenario."

"It is neither good nor bad, just curious. Niall has many friends, you see. He calls them friends, and they regard him so. But truly? He has acquaintances the world over. Friendly? Yes. Warm? Yes. Good for drinks, dinner, business, a bit of adventure. But the true bond of friendship? I have not seen him risk that in a very long time."

"Not since your friendship began," Kara hazarded.

Gyda nodded. "It's true. But our relationships with him, although both true and honest, are not the same."

"Because he knows not to view you ... romantically?" she asked.

Her friend laughed. "He does know better, and has from the first. In fact, there have been nights when we wagered over which of us would have the chance to pursue a comely female."

Kara swallowed. "Do you think that's why he and I get along so well? Because he doesn't view me in that way?"

Another laugh—and this one sounded more like a guffaw. "No, that's not it. He's interested in you, Kara. We've all seen how he looks at you when your attention is elsewhere." Gyda grinned. "And we see you sneaking the same sort of looks."

Kara flushed, fully red from scalp to toes, it felt like.

"Attraction is not the problem," Gyda continued. "If he were *only* attracted, he would flirt, dally, and then move on. It's all the other things that draw him up short."

"Other things?"

"Need I spell it out, girl? He looks beyond your beauty. He sees your intelligence, and he delights in it. He is interested in what you say, how you think. He's never encountered a problem like you before. It's why he has stayed—and why he must force himself to go."

"He's afraid I'll begin to ask about his secrets, isn't he?" Kara asked.

Gyda gaped. "What makes you say that? Has he told you he has secrets?"

Kara frowned. "No."

"Then how do you know?"

"It's there, isn't it? Obvious in his deflections, in the way he never speaks of his family or anything in his past. He'll mention his home, the way it smelled or what it felt like, but never a name or location, and never, ever the people there, then or now."

"No wonder he's running scared," Gyda whispered.

"What? Why?"

"Kara, Niall does not mention his past, his family, or his home. Ever."

"But ..."

"More importantly, no one ever notices the lack. Niall is smooth. Open. Easy. He makes them laugh, or flips the conversation, or asks them a question about something he knows they wish to talk about. And they follow his lead. Every time. They never even realize what he's done or that they have revealed far more of themselves than he has."

"Perhaps *they* are just too polite to remark on it," Kara said.

Gyda let out a bark of laughter. "No, apparently that is just *you*. But if he's suddenly understood how much of him you see—he'll have to run."

Kara stilled her restless hands, and all the rest of her along with them. "Will you go, too?"

Gyda thought about it. "I do, sometimes. Other times we go our separate ways for a bit before meeting up later." She looked down at her design, then turned to gaze out the window. "I'll think about it."

Kara headed back to the window. The street was dark now. "Perhaps he has the right idea. Perhaps a journey is exactly what's needed after spending so long in the Crystal Palace." She turned back to Gyda and saw the alarm on her face. "Oh! No, not with him. Not after him, either, if that's what you were about to ask. But after I finish the turtle, perhaps I'll take a journey. New faces. New places. Maybe it will make it easier." She lowered her voice. "Missing him. For I will, you know."

"Oh, I know. But you are wise to let him go. It's the only path to getting him back, you see."

"I hope you are right."

"I'll predict it right now. I doubt he'll be able to keep away for long."

They both paused as heavy footsteps sounded on the stair outside. A quick knock, the door opened, and Niall poked his head around it.

"Ah, there you are," he said to Kara. "The maid, Lizzie, Janet Ott's friend? She's not at the Hare and the Dog this evening, and I have her direction."

Kara shot Gyda a look.

"Just as I said." Gyda's mouth quirked.

"Well? Are you coming along?" Niall demanded. "I dared not go without you, and I hope to hear what happened with Wooten."

"Yes, I'm ready." Kara stood.

She was indeed. Ready to do what she must.

⟫⟫⟫⟪⟪⟪

NIALL COULD NOT dampen the tension that racked him as Kara gathered up her cloak and bade Gyda farewell. As they departed Lake Nemi, he offered her his arm. "We can walk, if you don't mind. It's not actually too far. The girl lives in a lane off Chandos Street."

"Not at all. I won't mind stretching my legs."

"Stay close. We're not that far from Covent Garden."

He braced himself for her questions as they set off. Perhaps she would lob a few thinly veiled admonitions as well. He would take it and give her back answers. Those he could. He owed her that much.

But she spoke at length about her afternoon's interview with Wooten. He asked questions, and they batted theories about like shuttlecocks.

"We need more information," Kara fretted. "I never thought to know a woman so many people have reason to see dead. Though perhaps some of them only feel relief at news of her death. But who hated her so much they would actually do the deed?"

"I keep thinking of Banks's face when you asked him if it was his brother," Niall said. "I have a feeling we must find him."

"I hope this Lizzie will give us something useful."

"They shared lodgings for a while. A girl in the taproom at the Hare and the Dog told me as much." He pulled her closer as a wagon rolled to a stop in the street and a pile of men hopped out. "I have a feeling she might know something that will help."

"I hope you are right."

They fell silent as they moved through the crowd of men, who had clustered around the door to a house and commenced knocking. They passed through without incident, though. Niall was relieved, until the silence stretched out, and his nerves did as well. At last, he could wait no longer. "I'm sorry I sprang the news of my leaving on you like that," he said abruptly. "It was not well done of me."

She frowned up at him. "You've nothing to apologize for."

"But I do. You've been a kind friend and a generous companion. I should have let you know what I was thinking."

She patted his arm. Her touch felt soft against the tension running through his frame. "Niall, it's fine." She took a deep breath and looked ahead as she spoke. "Do you remember what I told you about my father's reaction to my kidnapping, and to the subsequent attempts at abduction?"

"He began your lessons, teaching you avoidance and defense and escape," he said with a nod.

"You haven't even heard of them all. I learned so much," she said wistfully. "Anything he could think of to give me an advantage, a chance. One summer he decided I should learn games of chance, in case someone wagered over my well-being. I learned everything from the knucklebones the street urchins play in corners, to hazard and faro and the other games bored aristocrats play in the gaming hells."

Niall tried to imagine how those lessons might have been managed. He didn't like any of the mental images he called forth.

"Those were easy lessons," she said. "Logical and fun. I mastered them quickly." She sighed. "But it didn't satisfy my father."

"Why not?"

She lifted her free hand. "Nothing ever did. I could never learn fast enough, or even just *enough* to satisfy him. He was always afraid. Always looking for more, expecting more of me. Nothing I did was ever enough."

"He cared for you. He wanted to keep you safe." He hesitated. "Though his methods might have been … unconventional."

"It's true. That's all he wanted. And I was grateful. I had no wish to be captured, not after that first time. I actually enjoyed many of the lessons. Most of them, in fact. But I hated feeling like I was letting him down. That I wasn't doing enough."

She expelled a long breath and gave a bitter laugh at the end of it. "And then I was old enough to start going about in Society. He was nervous, of course, but I couldn't wait. But that was a shock in itself."

"Why?"

"Because it didn't take long for everyone to realize that I am quite a bit *too much* for them."

"Ridiculous," he muttered.

"You've seen it yourself," she reminded him. "None of them approve of my upbringing. They certainly don't enjoy my unfortunate tendency to talk of business, art, politics, science, or anything beyond fashion."

"And yet I'd wager you make a damned good whist partner,"

he said with a chuckle.

"Actually, I do." She grinned.

"Then I shall be glad to quickly claim you as my partner the next time we venture into Society."

Abruptly, she stopped walking, forcing him to turn to face her.

"That is why, Niall, you do not owe me any answers or explanations. I treasure our friendship, in so many ways. I don't think I can adequately explain what it has meant to me. I should have had blonde hair." She laughed. "I've been such a Goldilocks from the old tale."

Silently, he disagreed with her, his gaze locked on the thick, dark chestnut locks beneath her smart little hat.

"I'd been wandering about, always too much or not enough. Until, with you, for the first time, I don't feel that way. Finally, I can be ... just me. And you seem to be able to completely accept me and all of my strange and unusual ways."

"I'm not the only one," he replied.

"You were the first. The first to know me as a grown woman. A lady who fits nowhere, precisely. But at your side, in your company, I felt ..."

"Perfect," he said, low.

"No." She laughed. "But close enough." She shook her head and pressed her hand to his arm again. "Thank you. These months we've been spending time together have been easy and comfortable, and they've given me a soft landing, a place to pause and breathe and think about who I am. I will always be in your debt for that. I certainly will not repay you with questions or demands."

Even if I want to.

The words echoed at the end of her quiet sentence. Or perhaps he was the only one who heard them. For she started forward again, seemingly at ease. "Isn't that Chandos just ahead?"

"Yes." He cleared his throat. "Let's see what Lizzie Hartley can tell us."

The strain had leached out of him. There was only an odd tightness in his chest left behind. Had he judged her wrongly? She was different from the other women he'd known in so many ways. Why not this one as well?

But did that mean she didn't feel enough for him to make demands? Or did she not have softer feelings for him at all?

The thought should bring a rush of relief, a breath of freedom.

Instead, it made him feel unaccountably ruffled.

He didn't feel much better, either, once they stood in the decrepit entry of the building where Lizzie Hartley, the tavern wench and sometimes maid, kept rooms.

"Don't tell Wooten about this," he whispered into the dark, dank gloom.

"I won't." Kara pressed a hand to her face. "What is that smell?"

"It smells like someone is cooking something that has been dead for too long."

"In vinegar," she agreed with a shudder. A staircase lay ahead of them. "What floor does she live on?" Kara asked.

"Fourth."

"Of course she does," she said with a sigh. "Very well." She stepped up to the first stair. "Let's hope it holds until we make it up."

"And back down."

"That too."

The stairs did creak in protest as they climbed. Everything else in the old building lay eerily silent.

"I know my feet are climbing, and that we are rising," she said, whispering again. "But why does it feel as if we are descending into the rank bowels of the earth?"

"It's just our luck, it would seem."

"The unlucky are the poor souls who pay to live here."

They reached the fourth floor, and Niall led them to the correct door. Still, there was none of the noise one expected from a shared building. No crying babies or shouting children. No singing, no arguments or scolding, and nor did he hear anything from beyond the door.

With a look at Kara, he raised a fist and knocked.

The thuds echoed into the silent passages and down the stairs.

No answer. He knocked again.

"Yes, yes!"

He heard Kara's soft sigh of relief at the very human, slightly exasperated call from inside.

"I'm coming. Keep it quiet, will ye?" The door swung open. "I told ye and told ye to wait until the appointed hour, didn't I ...?" The woman's words trailed away as she looked at him and blinked in surprise. She wasn't fully dressed. A shift, corset, and petticoats were covered only in a voluminous shawl thrown over her shoulders. She let it fall a little as she looked him up and down. A smile of welcome spread over her face, only to fade away as Kara stepped up to his side.

"It's you, then. Again," she said to Kara. "I already answered yer questions."

"We've come up with a few more," Niall said with a smile. "We were hoping you would help us. We won't keep you long."

She hesitated.

"We are trying to find justice for your friend," he said, leaning in. "We rather thought you might wish to help."

The woman gave him another measuring glance and then leaned in to give a slow sniff. "Smoke," she said appreciatively. "Just a hint. Janet would have liked it. She liked a bit of subtlety about a man." She let the door swing open. "Come in, then, but ye cannot stay long. I am expecting company."

"Thank you." Niall allowed Kara to precede him, as he could detect no sign of anyone else in the rooms. It wasn't a large area. Just a small parlor and a bedroom beyond. A wall separated them, but there was a wide archway between instead of a regular doorway. The place was clean, and there were colorful, homey touches in the cloth over the small table, a tiny portrait on the wall, and a figurine of a pair of dancers on the mantel.

Niall strode over to the cold hearth, where a pair of wooden chairs sat. He spun one around and indicated Kara should take it, then turned the other for himself. Now they faced the well-worn chaise set under a window. Lizzie Hartley perched there and sat, waiting.

Kara made the opening salvo. "I was just remarking to Mr. Kier how sad this all seems to me. In trying to speak to those who knew Janet, we have encountered too many who feel satisfaction or relief at the news of her death."

"Ye've been talking to the people on her list, then, in her wee notebook," Lizzie said with a sniff. "No surprise there, that kind of attitude. She outsmarted them all, didn't she?"

"Manipulated them," Niall corrected her.

"Without hesitation or mercy," Kara added.

"Mercy?" The girl spoke the word as if it were so much mud in her mouth. "Whoever showed Janet Ott any bit of mercy?"

"It appears that you did," Kara said gently, looking around.

"We were friends. Associates. Partners, sometimes, although I was always the junior." Lizzie pulled the shawl tighter around her shoulders. "Janet was a hard woman, true enough. But 'twas the world that made her hard. It's a testament to her, the way she grew strong, instead of letting the weight of it all break her."

"It sounds as if you admired her," Niall remarked.

"And so I did. Janet was a canny one, I swear. She understood people. She knew which ones made a good mark and which would hit back." She paused. "Mostly."

"How did she learn to read people so well?" Kara sounded truly interested.

"How do ye think?" Lizzie pointed a finger toward the grimy window. "On the streets." She snorted. "Did you think she went to some fancy finishing school? No. She learned the same way we all did. Ye watch to see who will feel sorry fer ye and toss over a coin. Pick the ones who are too distracted to feel yer fingers slip into a pocket. Stay away from the ones who will hurt ye to take what's yours—or just fer the fun of it."

"I'm sorry." Kara's empathy rang true to Niall's ears. "You are not the first person to mention Janet's difficult past."

"Ah, ye'll have found Banks, then," the maid said with a nod. "He knows near as much as I do of the strange and dark things she saw."

"Strange?" asked Niall.

"Ye'll have seen some of the names on that list, eh? There's highly respected men on there, and they got up to some outlandish behavior." She shook her head. "Janet always had the best stories to tell over a pint. The fellows would line up to buy her a drink, just to hear the latest. But some of the most bizarre tales were just of the random people she met in the streets, or some of the jobs she took, early on, to get by." Lizzie's expression grew fierce. "But she did. She did get by. She survived. And she never had to resort to work on her back to do it. She found a way to get a bit of her own back and she made a success of it. A success of herself."

"A bit of her own?" Kara had begun to sound irritated. "I might agree, except she wasn't targeting those who had hurt her, was she? Just anyone who had a secret she could ferret out."

"Aye, and they weren't innocents, were they? They all had done or said or sold something they were ashamed of, hadn't they? Things they didn't want known. Or else they wouldn't have paid Janet."

"They didn't all pay her though, did they?"

"Ye spoke to the widow?" Lizzie asked derisively.

"I did."

"And you believed her, right off." Her lip curled in disgust. "Because she has a nice house and had a nice husband? What kind of nice woman keeps a gun like that? If anyone has a secret, it's that one—and that's what I told Janet."

Kara only looked flustered at the suggestion.

"In any case, they weren't all original sins, were they?" Niall reminded the woman. "Some of those mistakes were made because Janet engineered them." He was thinking of Arthur Towland, and of the art she'd commissioned for cheap from Ansel's artist friends. "She tempted some of her victims into their misdeeds."

"So what if she did? She created the opportunity to sin, and they took it."

"And she exploited it," Kara said.

"And if they hadn't taken up the temptation she presented, they wouldn't have had secrets to hide, would they?"

"If they had never crossed Janet Ott's path, they wouldn't have had secrets to hide, would they?" Kara countered.

"It's Janet's secrets we are interested in," Niall interrupted. "She seems to have been a genius at choosing her victims. Most of them have paid and been happy to put her and her blackmail behind them. They all seem to have trusted her to keep her silence—and she seems to have done so."

"She kept her part of her bargains," Lizzie insisted.

"Still, the sheer audacity of it tempts us to think it must have been one of her victims who killed her. But honestly, I wonder if it wasn't one of Janet's own secrets that got her killed."

"She kept those to herself," Lizzie muttered.

"Except that she seems to have shared a few with you and with Banks."

"And the fellows at the pub," Kara added.

"No, those were never her own," Lizzie protested. "And she never named names, even if she did share a few of the more outrageous details. And what about Banks?" She pointed her chin at Kara. "*She* said he was heard threatening Janet."

"We did speak to him," Kara answered. "He appeared to be genuinely shocked at the news of her death."

"And saddened. He seemed to still be harboring feelings for her." That twinge of empathy sounded a low note inside Niall again.

"Aye, he never could move past that soft spot he held for

her." Lizzie pressed her lips together. "Not that it would have done him any good. Janet would never let him too close."

"Him in particular?" asked Niall.

"No. No one got truly close," Lizzie said quietly. "Some folks walk alone, aye? Janet was one of them. I think she saw too much hurting, too young. It made her keep everyone at a distance. She felt safer that way, I think. But it left her sad, too. Empty."

Niall shifted in his seat. The picture she painted ... it hit too close.

"Did she keep Banks's brother at a distance, too?" asked Kara. She was watching the girl closely for a reaction.

"Banks told ye about him, did he?" Lizzie sounded surprised.

"He came up when I said that murder is often a crime of passion."

"Oh, well that would make sense, wouldn't it? Charlie Banks—that's the brother—he was powerful mad when she wouldn't choose him. Such a roaring fuss, straight up. I thought he might have murdered them both, had she picked his brother over him. Instead, she left them both behind, and Charlie stalked her for weeks after. Shouting and thundering. Getting drunk, then pleading and crying. Made a spectacle of them both. She hated it, Janet did. She hated folks talking about her like that. Finally, she paid off old Bull George the Second to make him stop."

"Bull George the Second?" Niall repeated, trying not to be amused.

"Heard of him?" Lizzie asked.

"No."

"He's a bully boy. A brute for hire. He'll crack heads or knees for a decent price, or give a thorough beating for more. Janet hired him, and it only took a couple of charges at Charlie for him to take the meaning of it." She sighed. "But that were long ago. Over a year since Charlie licked his wounds, retreated back to his pawn shop, and stayed there."

"His pawn shop?" Kara perked up. "The widow, Mrs. Riley—

she mentioned that Janet came to the Sostratus Club through an encounter with one of the members at a pawn shop." She met Niall's gaze. "And that was only four months ago."

Lizzie Hartley's eyes widened. "Four months ago?" she breathed. "She didn't." She gave a moan. "She wouldn't have been so stupid."

Another look exchanged with Kara. "Well, go on, then," Niall said.

"Four months ago, Janet moved in here. She'd hit a bad run. Nothing worked out. No secrets to turn to coin. She was getting desperate. She let her place go, moved in here. She said she might be forced to do something daft." Her hand drifted up to rub her brow. "Oh, but I never thought she'd go back."

"To Charlie Banks?"

"It was at his pawn shop that she first figured out her tricks. She would hang about there. Charlie would let her work, dusting or rearranging his stock sometimes. She saw the great men and women come in there, trading their trinkets or valuables for coin to cover their debts or their sins. She watched it happen, over and over. And then she got the notion to follow them after."

Kara frowned. "To rob them?"

But Niall understood. "No. She wanted to uncover their sins, see what they were trying to hide from the world."

"Yes. Poor folk pawn their things to survive. To feed their families or pay their rent. Rich folk do it to pay off debts or to keep up appearances or to fool someone into believing they are worth more—oh, she found a hundred different secrets."

"And she began to exploit them."

"Yes."

"But Charlie wouldn't have liked it," Niall surmised.

"No. It started affecting his business. Word started to spread that he was not discreet. That's a death knell to a pawn shop. He ordered her to stop."

"But she didn't."

"No. His anger climbed as high as his itch for her. Their affair started then, and I wondered if he bullied her into it. He thought she owed him."

"But wasn't she living with his brother at the time?" Niall asked.

"Yes, but he hadn't a care for it. At first. She had other men, too. After a while, it started to bother him. Charlie demanded she give up the others and marry him. He wanted a cut of the coin she was bringing in, as well. To make up for his losses, he said."

"And that's when the trouble started."

"Yes. She left them all behind. But it took so long and cost her so much, I can't believe she went back. It would have got him all stirred up again."

"She must have felt desperate," Kara mused.

Lizzie nodded, her gaze unfocused, clearly looking back.

"There is something else here. Something else going on that we are not seeing." Kara's tone forced the girl to look at her. "We've seen the notebook, Lizzie. We know how much money she was taking off the men and women she blackmailed. She should not have been desperate. She should have had plenty of cash."

Lizzie looked away again.

Kara continued, her face set, "What was Janet doing with the money?"

"She didn't want it known."

"It might have something to do with her murder," Niall added.

"It doesn't."

Kara's expression had taken on a strange look of understanding and perhaps a mix of hope and doubt. "She was doing something ... generous with it, wasn't she? Something good?"

Lizzie didn't answer, but her face said everything Kara needed for confirmation.

"What was it? Food for the hungry? Donations to a soup kitchen in a church in the stews? Support for a poorhouse? An orphanage?"

Niall saw the change in Lizzie's expression. "An orphanage." He shook his head in surprise.

Lizzie ducked her head. "Not an orphanage. They call it a school." When she looked back up, after a moment, her face was bleak. "It was the only time she were ever truly happy," she whispered. "Helping those girls. It was a place that took her in, off the streets, when she was younger. They tried to help her. Train her up. She was so clever, and they thought she would do well working in a shop. But it all went wrong. The shopkeeper's son ..." She let her voice trail away.

Kara heaved a long sigh.

"She went a little mad after that. Did some things. Terrible things with bad people. But she woke herself up after a while. Tried to straighten up. She couldn't go back to the school, but she never forgot what they did for her. And once she begun to make some real money, she started helping them."

Kara looked directly at Niall. "That's where they are," she said softly. "The ones who mourn her. I'm glad we found someone."

"I mourn her," Lizzie said.

Kara's eyes widened suddenly. "Did they know where the money came from?"

"No. She told them she had a good post with a merchant."

"I imagine they knew better, if she was donating that amount of money," Niall said. "But they weren't fool enough to question their good luck."

"It was more than just money," Lizzie replied. "She taught those girls things. Useful things. How to make the most of a job, how to handle difficult people, how to make change, that sort of thing." She blinked. "They cared for her, and she for them."

"No wonder you looked up to her," Kara said softly.

"She fancied herself a Robin Hood," Niall said, thinking out loud.

"I said so, too. But Janet insisted it was not quite the same," Lizzie said. "She wasn't robbing the rich to give to the poor. She said she was shifting the balance of misery. Making it a little more equal, she said."

Kara made a small, sad sound.

"It was another thing they fought about, Janet and Charlie Banks. He said she cost him money, ill using his customers. He didn't want her money going to help unwanted girls. He wanted what was owed him."

Grim possibility hung in the room between the three of them. Niall named it out loud. "Well, perhaps he finally decided to call in the debt."

"Where is Charlie Banks's pawn shop?" Kara demanded.

Lizzie Hartley's mouth pressed closed. He saw the fear in her eyes.

"We've spoken to multiple people who knew Janet Ott," Kara reminded her. "He wouldn't ever know who gave us his name and direction."

Lizzie did not look convinced.

"It doesn't matter," Niall told them. He thought back to the pile of tradesman's cards he'd found in the desk at the home of Banks and Burroughs, such as they were. "I know where he is."

Chapter Eleven

"**W**ELL, THAT FLATTENS one of my theories," Niall said as they left Lizzie's rooming house. "She had knowledge and access to the poisonous plants. I had entertained the notion that Lizzie might have done Janet in, for the chance to take over her enterprise. But that's clearly not the case."

"No, I knew she hadn't done it since I first spoke with her," Kara said absently. "She was quite fiercely angry about it and furiously sure no one would care enough to look for the killer."

Her head felt heavy, her mind abuzz. The girl had given her so much to think about, to reconcile. So many things that must be done and followed up on. It all grew to a roar inside her head as they finally reached a main thoroughfare and found a hack. She climbed in, resting her head against the side. Closing her eyes, she tried to sort through the noise and lower the clamor.

The next thing she knew, Turner was coaxing her out of the hack and onto the drive at Bluefield. She looked about, befuddled. The roaring returned as she stepped onto the gravel. It made her eyelids feel heavy and gritty, her limbs sluggish. So much to do. And yet she felt so tired.

Turner put an arm around her and began to lead her off, the same way he'd done when she was young and had read too late in the library or lingered too long at work in her laboratory. She let her head fall against him—but then she straightened. "Wait. Niall."

She turned to see her friend heading across the grounds, aiming for his forge and the loft above. He looked back, and she pointed a finger at him. "Breakfast. Early. We have much to discuss. And to plot."

He nodded and went on. She let Turner guide her to her bedroom. She had no memory of her maid undressing her, but she woke in her night rail, with the sun higher than usual and that sense of heaviness still with her.

She hurried through her morning preparations. "Has Mr. Kier arrived for breakfast yet?" she asked her maid.

"Not that I'm aware of." Elsie met her gaze in the mirror and grinned. "I'm sure we would have heard the sighs from here."

Kara laughed. "No doubt. Well, he'll arrive shortly, I'm sure. I think I'll wait in the ivory sitting room. Have them send word for me there."

She strode through the house and felt a little better when she reached the comfort of her retreat. Searching out a notepad and pen, she leaned over the desk to start making lists.

It didn't help. She still felt restless and uneasy, her mind full.

She had to go, to move. She strode out and passed a footman in the corridor. "Please tell them I'll be in my lab," she said as she flew by.

The staff was used to her odd behavior. He only inclined his head. "Very good, miss."

She rushed outside and through the grounds. After unlocking her laboratory, she went straight to the back, to the partially complete sculpture. The Valkyrie. It was supposed to represent her. A self-portrait. How could it, when every day she discovered more she didn't know about herself?

She stood, staring, lost again. She trailed her finger over the flaring skirts, but her mind was entirely occupied, far away.

She didn't come back until the door opened behind her. She threw the cover back over the piece and turned. Niall stood there.

Neither spoke for a moment, then her stomach let out a long, loud gurgle.

He laughed. "Breakfast is coming. I asked Turner to bring it out here once more. I hope you don't mind?" She didn't answer, and his gaze sharpened. "Are you all right?"

"Yes. No?"

His eye went past her to the shrouded sculpture. "What are you doing out here?"

She swallowed. "I'm afraid I'm indulging in a dreadful wallow at the moment."

"What? Why?"

"I'm trying to understand Janet Ott."

"No wonder you look lost, then."

"I had such a negative reaction to her at first," she confessed. "She seemed so blunt and so unconcerned with anyone else's feelings or opinions. She rubbed me the wrong way. She was an irritant to those she exploited, of course. But even the man who still reluctantly cares for her seemed entirely resigned to her fate. But then to find she was donating her ill-gotten gains to keep girls off the streets? I am quite gobsmacked."

"People are rarely one thing or another."

"It's true." She moved toward the cold hearth and the table before it.

He went to meet her there. "I was struck by Lizzie's remark about Janet trying to equalize the misery in the world."

"It hit me, too. It's such a cynical approach to doing something so kind. It's ... disturbing."

"It's a hard outlook." He looked thoughtful. "But perhaps it is more, as well. Janet obviously suffered. She obviously did wrong. But perhaps she was trying to find that sense of balance in herself."

"I had the same thought. And that's why I was in here. Perhaps I should turn the same lens upon myself."

"Only in so much as we all should."

She turned away, crossed to a shelf, and began to sort the

gears upon it. "I wonder. Because even though I'm appalled at myself for turning this into some strange competition, I'm even more dismayed at comparing myself to a woman who stole, manipulated, and blackmailed people—and coming up short."

"Nonsense. Is this about the girls at that school?"

"Mostly. A houseful of girls sheltered, fed, inspired, and *saved*."

He frowned. "Perhaps I am cynical as well, for I can only wonder what Janet Ott did in the past to make her feel as if she must make up for it in such a large fashion later."

She paused. "I hope you are not right in your thinking, for it must have been dreadful. But you cannot erase the fact that she did such good works." She hesitated, then blurted out, "I have had so many more advantages and haven't done half so much."

She turned back to her gears until she felt him approach. Gently, he reached out to stop her busy hands. He grasped them and turned her to face him. "I think you might be hearing the echo of your father's voice a little too loudly, Kara."

He did smell just slightly of smoke. She'd known just what Lizzie meant when she mentioned it. The tang of it lingered from the forge and blended with the citrus scent of his soap or cologne. She was never sure which. She breathed it in. "What do you mean?"

"This all sounds like a version of *not enough*."

Shocked by the truth of it, she looked up into his dark eyes.

"It's not a competition." He arched a brow. "But what of those apprenticeships you fund amongst the toolmakers and in your ironworks?"

Her mouth dropped. "Who told you of those?"

"Turner. Who else?"

She stepped away, pulling her hands from his. "That's just money." She snapped her fingers. "I don't miss it. And you heard Lizzie—Janet Ott gave a bit of herself to those girls."

"And what of Maisie Dobbs? Your interest in her and her bakery has certainly improved both her life and her business. And the life and prospects of her son. And for that matter, what of Harold? He was a starving street rat. Now, thanks to your patronage, he has a home and steady income."

He was right. Both points hit home. The ache in her heart eased a little. Gratitude swelled. "Thank you," she said, low. "Perhaps I just need to turn my attentions outward. Stop concentrating on my own worries."

"It's a lesson we can all make use of."

She would. Some of that crushing weight rolled off at the resolution. And as she considered how kindly he'd eased her fears, she realized something else. "You've already been pushing me in that direction. When you've encouraged me to find more friends."

"It can't hurt," he said lightly.

He'd been asking her to care, and she was going to listen. And she was going to start with him.

He'd told her what he needed—freedom. Not in so many words, but the message rang clear. Gyda had confirmed it.

She'd made him a promise, months ago, when she offered him the forge and asked him to stay. She'd vowed not to ask for what he could not—or would not—give.

Now she was at the sticking point, when she wanted more. When she was tentatively sure he did, too. But he still held back, and he must have his reasons.

I've never felt more my complete self than when I am with you. She'd said that to him, too, at the time. But now she had the chance to be more. To do better.

And so she would keep her vow.

No matter how much it hurt.

NIALL POPPED THE last bit of honeyed bannock into his mouth and leaned back in his chair. "This is by far my favorite place to breakfast." He stretched his feet out toward the fire he'd built up and patted his stomach.

"Mine as well." Kara stopped picking at her shirred eggs and took up her notepad again. "After talking with Lizzie Hartley, I have a long list of items to follow up on."

"Investigating Charlie Banks is at the top, I hope?"

"Of course. But there are others."

He rolled his head to watch her and waited.

"I need to send Inspector Wooten a note," she said. "We should speak with him, I think."

Niall straightened. "If we tell him about Charlie Banks, he'll probably wish for his men to interview him, if not himself."

Pressing her lips together, she nodded. "It might be best."

"Charlie owns a pawn shop. I think he would sooner speak to us than the police. His brother did."

"You might be right, but what if we miss something?" She made a face. "Lizzie's point struck home last night. I did just take Mrs. Riley's word about her husband's activities. Wooten should send his men to speak with the old nursemaid and her niece, to make sure the widow's story was true."

"I'd wager he's done it already."

"Then I need to hear what he found." She sighed. "I'm not as good at this as I thought."

"Nor should you be." He pointed back at her half-finished turtle. "You've plenty of commissions to keep you busy. As soon as we uncover Janet's killer, you'll be safe. You can go back to work and forget all about this sort of deviltry."

"I'm still waiting on that specialized joint for the turtle, but there are other jobs I could begin. And in any case, you also have plenty of work waiting, but instead you are taking off to parts unknown."

He had no answer for that. He couldn't tell her that he planned first to go back to his forge at home on Hilton Bay. He needed to think, and he did that best with the heat of the fire in his face and the burn of the hammer in his arm.

At first, he'd thought to go to Paris, straight off. A report had come from Ansel's cousin to change his mind, though. Rupert said he'd followed the Viscount Marston all over Paris, and he'd visited a number of high-society Parisians but had not once set foot in a pawn shop or jeweler's.

It had eased his fears. Not enough to stay, but enough for him to think of retreating, of hiding away while he sorted through his feelings—and how they conflicted with the rules by which he must live.

He was spared from answering Kara, though, by the dramatic swing of the door.

"There you are!" Gyda said on a huff. She looked as flushed and frenzied as the shield maiden he imagined lived in her soul.

"Good heavens, are you all right?" Kara asked. "Come and breakfast with us."

Gyda ignored the invitation. "I've been looking for you everywhere." She marched to the table and slapped down a folded bit of parchment before Kara.

"What's this?"

Her name was on the front. K. LEVETT. It had been crafted from individual letters cut from newspapers.

Kara went still and looked up at him.

"Open it," he urged.

The same crude cut-out letters spelled out the message inside.

THE WOMAN WAS EVIL. SHE SHOULD HAVE HANGED LONG AGO. STOP LOOKING OR THE SAME MIGHT HAPPEN TO YOU. SHE GOT THE JUSTICE SHE DESERVED.

"It was left at Lake Nemi this morning," Gyda told them. "A street urchin gave it over to the maid sweeping the step, just after dawn."

"Something else to share with Inspector Wooten," Kara said lightly, though he could see it had unsettled her. She passed it over to him, and he was impressed at the steadiness of her hand. Any other woman—besides Gyda—would have been set atremble.

"I think perhaps we might speak with Imogen Berringer first," he said grimly. He was thinking of the piles of newspaper strips on a table, and how Mrs. Berringer had left to fetch the tea tray, but returned without one.

"Wait!" Kara pulled the paper back and laid it out flat. "Do you know what this means? *Long ago!*" She stared up at him, eyes bright.

He understood at once. "Long ago. An old vendetta. Then we are on the right track. Wooten is not going to find the killer among the recent blackmail victims. It must be someone from Janet Ott's past."

She frowned. "But Charlie Banks ... his conflict with her was over a year ago. That's not exactly *long ago*."

"Their volatile parting was last year, but Lizzie made it sound as if they all knew each other for much longer. If it wasn't him who killed her over an old offense, he might have an idea who did."

Kara was clearly thinking. "Pawn shops are likely not open this early in the morning, are they?"

He thought about it. "Likely not."

She nodded. "Well, then. I have a couple of errands to run, but I'll meet you back at the house around noon?"

"Yes. I have some work I should be getting on with. I'll see you at noon and we'll be off."

She grinned. "I've always wanted to go into a pawn shop. How interesting."

Gyda looked back and forth between them, then dropped into the chair next to Kara. "You listen to me, Niall," she said fiercely. "It's *her* name on that ... warning. If you are going venturing into the stews of the city, then you keep her close and watch out for her, do you hear me?"

He met his friend's solemn look with one of his own. "I will. And if I require help, I'll ask for yours."

"See that you do," Gyda said, satisfied. "Now, pass me those bannocks."

Chapter Twelve

N OT THIRTY MINUTES later, Turner was handing Kara into her favorite gig—a one-horse chaise that was small, light, and a dream to drive. As soon as he settled in next to her, she snapped the reins and they were off.

"Where is it we're going?" he asked, holding on.

"You'll see." She wheeled them down the drive and onto the road that led to the village. Ambleburrow, nestled between Bluefield, Wood Rose Abbey, and several other large estates in the area, was a bustling place. She nodded to several acquaintances, but did not slow. They kept on going down the high street and took the main bridge across the river.

Turner said nothing as they passed the grand entrance to the abbey, but he watched it go by.

"Have you seen much of Mrs. Canning?" she asked gently.

"No. She's busy with the family all at home."

Kara kept quiet and drove on until they'd passed the bulk of the abbey's extensive estate. After a while, she pulled onto a small road, not really more than a track. She followed it to pull up before a good-sized pond that was overgrown and neglected.

They sat, enjoying the quiet, interrupted only by the chirping of busy birds and the humming of a few late-season insects. A splash sounded, and a crane flew suddenly out of the tall grasses before them.

"It's a lovely spot," she said. "Not in use, obviously. What are the chances that the Camleighs would sell it?"

"To you?"

She rolled her eyes at him.

He made a face.

"That bad? What have I done?"

"Not you, but Gyda may have taken my suggestion about causing an uproar among the abbey staff a little too much to heart."

"Oh dear."

He cleared his throat. "However, I do happen to know the family is punting a bit far on River Tick. Apparently the son and heir's gambling debts have become problematic. For the right price, they might be willing to part with a few acres."

Kara raised a brow. "Mrs. Canning never told you that!"

"No, but Gyda's friends among the maids are not so discreet."

"You and Gyda are quite a formidable pair." She chuckled. "May I ask what you mean to do with it?"

"I'm turning my attention onto others," she said, then flashed him a grin. "And I've been thinking that the maidens of Lake Nemi ought to have a real lake to retreat to, as did the Roman maidens of old."

He thought about it. "Ceremonies? That could be quite interesting."

"And more moving and meaningful, don't you think? Out here, in the night, alone with the stars and the sisters?"

"Pageantry," he said with approval. "We could do quite a lot with that."

"Will you set up a meeting with my solicitor? And find out who is handling the abbey's property?"

"Indeed. It shouldn't take long."

"You are a treasure, Turner."

⇉⇉⇉✦⇇⇇⇇

LATER, JUST AT noon, Kara descended to the entry hall, wearing one of her newly tailored and equipped skirts, and carrying a wrap.

Niall awaited her. He stood at the open door, filling the frame, and she took a moment to admire his broad form and the chestnut locks moving across his shoulders. That overly long hair was yet another of the myriad ways he was so different from the gentlemen she'd met in Society—and one of her favorites.

"What do you think?" she asked as she came down the last step. "Shall we take the train in? Or the carriage?"

He turned, his expression serious. "That depends. Are we planning to ask for Wooten's permission? Or for his forgiveness?"

Her mouth twitched into a grin. "Forgiveness. Definitely."

Amusement and approval showed in his gaze. "I was hoping you would say that. The carriage, then, for sure. We'll wish to have our own way out of Seven Dials, just in case."

She sobered a little and nodded.

Turner emerged from a passageway, carrying a tray. "The post, miss. Shall you look it over while I call the carriage?"

She took up the small stack and sorted through it. All but one she placed back on the tray. "Leave these on my desk in the ivory sitting room. I'll deal with them later."

She held out one folded envelope and waved it to catch Niall's attention. "From the Grove." He raised a brow as she opened it. "It's from Lady Madge." The older woman had written enthusiastically about the progress she and her friends had made on "The Valkyrie's Song," as they had named it. "She's asked me to come by."

She hadn't told Niall about the song or about that part of the conversation she'd had with Lady Madge. She wasn't sure why. She just didn't feel ready to tell him of the self-portrait she was attempting.

"Perhaps we can fit it in today, depending on Wooten's availability later," he said absently. He'd turned back toward the view out of the front door.

"What is it? Do you see something?"

"No. But I *feel* something." He glanced back. "Did you ever have that feeling? As if something lurks on the horizon, out of sight? You know it's there." He drew a deep breath. "And you know it's coming."

"I don't think so." She paused. "Although I can think of a few times when such foresight might have been useful."

»»»«««

SHE HAD CAUSE to amend that answer, though, not thirty minutes later. The carriage was traveling through the village. Kara was gazing out the window, lost in plotting strategies for the coming interview, when she suddenly gasped.

She moved closer to the window. Yes. It was the woman. Red-gold hair, a furrowed brow, and a sharp blade of a nose. The same woman who had glared at her outside Lake Nemi.

As Kara stared, the other woman caught sight of her inside the carriage. She stopped walking mid-stride. Her eyes narrowed. She turned to watch as the carriage passed, never leaving off until they made the turn onto the main road to London.

Kara sat back. She glanced at Niall, but he appeared lost in his own thoughts and hadn't noticed.

Quite suddenly, she knew just what he'd meant about something hovering, waiting on the horizon.

»»»«««

SEVEN DIALS WAS one of the grim spots in London. The streets about the crowded junction were close and run-down, littered with trash. Women stood whispering in doorways, and men lurked in lanes and alleys or leaned on posts, eyeing Kara's fine carriage with hostility or occasional speculation. Misery and want hung about like mist in the air.

Charlie Banks's shop was on the corner of a tiny square. An opportune situation, as it meant a door with the sign of the traditional three golden balls above stood on Little Earl Street, along with a grimy shop window. Featured in the showcase was a dusty set of carpenter's tools beneath a draped gown, slightly out of date, and a suit of men's clothes in a smaller size. But the fortunate part was the other, more discreet entrance off the square. Here the door stood partway open, inviting a quick entrance to the shadowed interior.

Niall declined the invitation. He paused in the doorway, letting his eyes adjust to the gloom before he entered. Kara kept close behind him.

She made a small noise as they were hit with the musty, dusty smell of the place.

He moved toward the short counter. No one waited behind it. In the case below, he spied a coral necklace and a garnet ring, a collection of pewter spoons and knives, and three watches. He doubted any of the timepieces actually kept time.

Silence lay as heavy in the place as the dust. Kara moved toward one of the two enclosed booths that sat beyond the counter. Pressing her ear to the front of one, she shook her head at his questioning gaze. He went to listen at the other. No sound from within. He eased the door open to find the small space empty.

"What is it for?" she asked, peering under his arm.

"A private space for customers to exchange their pledges for cash and a ticket. Most people don't want to be seen in a place like this. They don't wish for any prying eyes to see what they've brought in or hear how much they take in exchange."

Nodding, she moved away, running her hand over a rack of kitchen pots. "Where does that go, do you suppose?" She'd spotted a door behind the counter, perpendicular to the glass surface.

Niall shrugged.

A mischievous grin lit up her face. Leaning over the counter, she reached across, lifting herself up on her toes until she could just reach the door latch. Her fingers closed on it—and the door opened inward.

She gasped and straightened. The man emerging stopped, surprise on his face. "Good morning." He moved out of the room and closed the door, but stayed behind the counter. He gave Kara a thorough look over, and Niall saw him note the quality of her gown, the cleanliness of her skin, and the shine in her hair. "How can I help you?" the man asked.

"Mr. Banks, I presume?" she said lightly.

His expression grew more guarded, and Niall stepped closer.

"At your service, ma'am." Charlie Banks bowed. "I assume, then, that you've been referred by a previous customer? Someone who knows I trade in a few finer objects, along with the more ... regular, common items?" He gestured toward a high shelf covered in bundles with small tickets attached.

She followed his gesture. "What are they?"

"Sunday best, for the most part. The bread and butter of my establishment."

Niall eyed the vast quantity of wrapped bundles, of all sizes.

"I don't understand." Kara smiled uncertainly.

"Clothes. The Sunday finest of many of the workers around these parts. It's a regular service we provide," Banks explained. "A great many folks around here need extra coin to make it through the week, to feed their young ones and still make their rent. They keep us busy on a Monday, when they come in to pledge their Sunday clothes. They use the coin to make ends meet, then on Saturday, after the men are paid, we are kept lively indeed, sometimes until midnight, as everyone returns to redeem their clothing. They wear it to church on Sunday and to their visitations, their dignity intact. Then they come in again on Monday to start it all over again."

"Every week?" she asked, aghast.

"Week in and week out," Banks agreed sunnily.

"And you make a profit, charging them interest."

"So I do. I make a bit of change, and they get to eat and keep their pride both. It works for everyone."

She still looked dismayed.

Banks heaved a sigh. "Listen. I have customers who pledge a blanket in the morning and exchange it for a coat in the evening. I have wives who pledge their bread to get out their kettle. They make their dinner and bring the kettle back to redeem the bread, before they go home and serve dinner. It's a system that helps everyone get along."

He eyed her again. "But you have obviously come for a different sort of transaction." He gestured toward the door he'd come through. "Would you care to step into my more ... formal room? It's there that I keep the finer items. Silver works, brooches, rings and other jewelry, fine linen, and china." He raised a brow at Niall. "You may both enter, of course."

"Are we private? In here? Right now?" she asked.

"Utterly," he assured her. "Until another customer comes in."

"Seeing as it's neither a Monday nor a Saturday, we'll take our chances," Niall said wryly.

"And we'd like to discuss Janet Ott."

Banks's face changed instantly, all affability wiped away, his expression turning dark and shuttered. "Absolutely not."

"We've heard of the ... difficulties that occurred between the two of you," Kara said levelly.

"Who *are* you?" He shook his head. "Never mind. It doesn't matter. I have nothing to say about her."

"That is a shame," Niall said. "Because when the Metropolitan Police hear that you won't discuss her, they are going to move you right to the top of their list of suspects."

"You are not the police," Banks scoffed.

"We are consultants with the police," Kara informed him loftily. "I met her before her death, you know. Janet had a sharp wit."

"And a sharper tongue," he snapped.

"Indeed. Her death has proved to be an interesting case. So many people who did not care for her. Not to mention all those blackmail victims."

"Yes," he bit out. "Why aren't you bothering them instead of an honest businessman like me?"

"Because we've turned up evidence that indicates Janet's murderer was someone who carried an old grudge," she told him. "And your particular grudge seems to have been the loudest and the messiest."

"I do not have to speak with you," he insisted. "Just go."

"No. You do not," Niall agreed. "We thought to do you a service. We come in, looking like a young couple who might have got themselves in a bit of financial trouble. In need of quick funds, we came to a reputable businessman. As you said, it works for everyone. We get answers. You get to keep your reputation intact. But if you will not cooperate, the losses you suffer will be on your own head." He held out an arm to Kara. "Come along. He'll have no one but himself to blame."

"What are you on about?" Banks demanded.

Niall stopped. "You privately and publicly harassed Janet Ott just over a year ago. You made a spectacle of yourself. Caused a lot of talk and speculation. Now she turns up dead, after your public rejection, and you think you can just refuse to answer questions?" He snorted. "The police will have their answers. But how do you think your customers will feel if a police inspector, bringing all of his constables, shows up here? If they linger until you decide to talk? How many folks will wish to come in with so many uniforms about?"

Banks made a noise in his throat.

"A man in your business must be the soul of discretion. Circumspect. If your customers see you hauled off to Scotland Yard, they will begin to worry about what you might say. Your reputation will suffer." Niall lifted a shoulder. "But there are over three hundred pawn shops in London. I daresay they will find somewhere else to pledge their Sunday best."

"Damn you," Banks snarled. "I did not kill Janet. I learned my lesson last year. I wanted nothing else to do with her." He came out from behind the counter to close the side door. "You don't understand. I have a new woman now. A kind and calm woman. Not a wild creature like Janet. It's a relief, honestly. I'm a better man with her, not the walking raw nerve that I was with that virago."

Niall's attention kicked up a notch. "I would imagine your new lady has no wish to hear further tales about Janet or how you behaved with her?"

Banks grimaced. "No. I don't want it all dragged up again."

"But Janet came back several months ago, didn't she? Did she put your new love at risk?"

"Is that why you killed her?" Kara asked baldly.

The man's eyes bulged. "I've just said I didn't kill her, haven't I?"

"She came back to get up to her old tricks again, didn't she? Poaching your customers for her blackmailing schemes? Damaging your reputation. Putting your business at risk." Niall looked to Kara. "It sounds like he had multiple reasons to do away with her, doesn't it?"

"Oh, it does," she agreed.

"Oh, for—" Banks stopped. He slammed a hand against the door before turning to face them. "Yes. She came back. Yes, it was both a slap in the face and wildly inconvenient." He made a distressed noise. "Exactly what I should have expected of the girl! I wanted her gone, right then and there. Why would I have waited all of these months, only to kill her now? I needed her to go back to whatever latest hell she spawned from right away." His shoulders slumped. "I didn't kill her, but I did do ... something wrong. I admit it. I will tell you, but word of it cannot get around."

"We will only share what you tell us with the inspector,"

Kara told him. "But I cannot make promises for him."

Banks sighed and began to pace. "I gave her a name. A customer," he said, low. "A man who had been coming in regularly. He belonged to a large club. I told her she could use him to wiggle in and find more victims to prey on."

"Douglas Saunders," Kara said flatly.

"Yes." Banks looked both impressed and terrified that she'd known the name already. "Janet listened in on his pledge. He was … indiscreet, thinking we were alone. She heard it all. She followed him out, and I never saw her again."

Niall looked at Kara. She shrugged, and he knew she was doubting her own judgment, but Banks's story held the ring of truth, in his opinion.

"You knew her a long time, did you not?" he asked.

"Lord, yes." Banks shook his head. "Since my brother and I came to London as young men, convinced we would make our fortunes. She knew her way around. She grew up hereabouts, you know. She was up to every trick and turn. And a great many scrapes I let her lead me into. She had a few of us young bucks dangling after her when we were young, and she used us in her various schemes as she saw fit. But that was over, for me, after last year. It had to stop."

"If it wasn't you who killed her, then who might it have been? Do you know of anyone who might have nursed a grudge against her?"

"Great Caesar, it might have been anyone! She was not one to make friends wherever she went."

"Names," Niall said curtly.

Banks began to pace. "I don't know. There were plenty of us who ran around together in those years. But many of them dropped away. My brother and I hung in the longest." He gave them a harsh look. "But don't you go getting ideas about him. He cared for her. I can see it now. He held true feelings for her. Real caring. Until I ruined it."

"We spoke to him," Kara said. "He was broken up to learn of

her death."

Charlie Banks paled. "He would be. He thought he could change her. Calm her." He gave a harsh laugh. "I didn't want her changed. I liked her hanging about, stirring things up. For a long time I was happy just to let her add a dash of daring to my life." He gestured around. "Keeping shop is not so exciting, even a shop like this. But as she grew bolder and more successful at her schemes, I grew more interested. I don't know what came over me, really. I wanted more and more of her, like a drunk craves his drink." He fell into a bleak moment of silence. "I think I was a little mad."

"You said there were plenty of you that ran about together," Niall said. "Could it be one of them, who thought to avenge an old wrong?"

Banks made a face. "I doubt it. Why wait so long?"

"Who are they? Where are they now?"

He considered. "Some are dead. Others might as well be, as they've done themselves in with gin or opium, the pox, or even too much time locked away in the hulks." Banks brightened. "It could have been someone she spent time in gaol with, couldn't it? She was the sort to have rubbed someone the wrong way in a close situation like that."

Niall gave Kara another look, but she looked as surprised as he felt. "Gaol? When was this? What was she held for?"

Banks frowned. "Fifteen years ago? No, more. 'Twas back when I was opening up the shop. That famous case, about the widow." He frowned. "I remember it was the talk all over the city. A widow got herself murdered. But I was busy working every day and half the night, trying to get this place started. I wrapped goods with newspaper, and they all had a piece about it, but I never stopped to read it. It was years later that Janet mentioned it when she was hanging about the place. She said they'd held her for a few weeks because she worked for the widow, but they could find no evidence against her and had to let her go."

Sighing, he lifted his hands. "And before you ask, that's all I know about it. I guess, if you need more, you could talk to Todge. See if you can get anything sensible out of him."

"Todge?" Niall asked.

"He came up with Janet from way back, from her earliest days, running wild on the streets. I think his real name is Thomas? But everyone knows him as Todge. Or Mad Todge."

Kara looked to Niall for an explanation, but he had none.

"It's old slang," Banks explained. "*Beat all to a todge*. It means anything beaten to a mash. It happened one too many times to old Todge and went to his brainbox. He's more than half daft. Says and does strange things. But Janet never forgot him. She always looked out for him, and he for her. If anyone from back in the old days moved against Janet, Todge would know."

"Could we trust what he says?" asked Niall.

"That's another thing altogether. But if it's a story from the old days, you'll have better luck. He remembers his younger days better."

"Where can we find him?" Kara asked.

Chapter Thirteen

"**K**EEP YOUR EYES peeled," Niall cautioned.

Kara nodded. She walked at his side, but had not taken his arm. She was on edge. First, that anonymous warning, then spotting that odd, hostile woman so close to home. Now they were on foot, approaching the open space where the old famous pillar with all its seven dials had once stood, for Banks had informed them that Mad Todge was a street sweeper who had claimed the entrance to Queen Street as his territory.

She held herself at alert, carefully watching their surroundings and concentrating on staying balanced, as she'd been taught. Other advice she'd been given over the years crowded her brain. She'd actually had practical lessons on how to move safely through London's streets, in case she ever found herself abandoned or had escaped from an abduction. The knowledge she'd gained had given her confidence, but right now it jangled her nerves.

They'd already broken several rules.

They stood out. They looked too fine, too prosperous to blend in. Their purpose here was not clear, which made them suspect. Already, they had attracted attention. Sidelong looks and silent communications flew between some of the men about them. Niall's height and breadth held them at bay for now, but she knew they could change their minds and strike in an instant.

Crowds of people moved around them. Children darted in and out, some shouting in delight in the chase, others silent with intent. Dogs roamed too. One yellow cur snapped and growled on the children's heels.

"Is that a pig?" Niall said, pointing down a branching street, where the animal rooted in the gutter. "How is not strung up for bacon?"

"Don't pay too much attention to it," she warned. "It will have been claimed already, by someone all the locals are too afraid to cross."

"Queen Street ahead," he said suddenly. "There. That's likely him."

"Oh. Yes. I see him."

Todge was painfully thin and dressed in rags. His hair had gone wild and matted and stood about his head. A large bandage was wrapped around one leg, dirty and bloodstained. He swept the street clear ahead of a man who looked like he might be a clerk. Todge limped as he swept, but moved steadily. The man kept to the slow pace, not pushing past. He tossed Todge a coin as they reached the other side. Todge grinned and cackled, calling his thanks as he tucked the coin away.

"Niall, I think you should fumble and drop something at the street's edge," Kara said. "I'll go ahead and cross with him. He trusted Janet. Perhaps he might be more willing to talk to a woman alone."

The look Niall gave her spoke volumes of his low opinion of such a plan.

"I won't go farther than across the street. I promise."

Lips pressed in disapproval, he nodded. "Be careful. We've caught a bit of attention."

"I've seen it."

Todge had spotted them and come scurrying back as fast as his limp allowed. "A fine mornin'," he greeted them. "Allow me to clear the way fer the beautiful lady."

Niall nodded. He reached into his pocket and pulled out a folded paper. It fluttered to the ground as Todge set off. Kara started after him. Niall waved her on and made a show of fetching the paper, only to drop it again.

She followed behind the sweep, examining his bandage as she went. The bloodstain was rusty and dry. The edges of the rolled linen were worn and dirty.

As they reached the far side, she pulled out a coin. "Thank you. May I ask, sir, if you have had your leg seen to? I know of a skilled medical man who would help."

"Ah, thank ye, ma'am. So kind ye are." He gave a burbling laugh. "But ol' Todge will heal, right and tight, afore long." He slapped his knee and gave her a decisive nod.

She widened her eyes. "Todge? Is that your name?"

"Aye—well, it's how I'm known hereabouts."

Niall had approached, and handed over a coin now as well. "Thank you for seeing to the lady."

"My pleasure to serve 'er, sir." Todge stepped back, expecting them to move on.

But Kara had paused. "It's so odd, but I'd never heard that name before, until recently. A woman I know had a friend with your name." She looked into the man's lined and dirty face. "Were you a friend of Janet Ott's?"

No change in his expression showed. No hesitation or hint of fear. Just speedy, instantaneous action. One instant, he stood before them, the next he was sprinting away, down Queen Street, deeper into the slums.

With no hint of a limp.

Niall cursed and took off after him. Kara started out as well, lifting her skirts and moving as fast as they allowed.

Todge crossed the street at an angle, with Niall hot on his heels. The sweep dived unexpectedly beneath an empty market stall. He slid, feet first, beneath it, then was back up, running again. Niall jumped the stand and followed him as he ducked down an alley.

Cursing, Kara followed, dodging crates and refuse in the narrow passage. She emerged onto a small square with several doorways set into the surrounding walls. Todge glanced back, saw them both still coming, and ducked into a door set into a run-down rooming house on the left.

Kara groaned, seeing him disappear. Many of the buildings about here were likely connected. He might just have disappeared into a warren of connected passageways, hidden spaces, and myriad exits. "Stay on him," she shouted. Their only hope was to keep him in sight.

Niall raced for the pillared doorway. A woman slumped off on one side, sitting on the cold stone steps and leaning against one of the pillars. Alarm spiked in Kara's chest as she saw the woman reach out an arm and grasp something.

"Jump!" she screeched at Niall.

He faltered a step, but managed to obey, hurtling over the rope the woman had lifted at the last moment, hoping to trip him up.

Niall went on, disappearing into the building. Kara advanced, her hard glare fastened on the slovenly woman, who gulped, scrambled to her feet, and scurried away.

The smell hit her first as she stepped into the building. Vile and thick, it smelled of rot, unwashed bodies, and excrement. She had to pause a moment and allow her eyes to adjust to the gloom, and the sight was nearly as bad as the smell. Everything was filthy and decaying. Mold climbed the walls. A layer of dank and sticky dust coated the floor. The footsteps showing clear told her that Todge and Niall had stopped running and resorted to stealth.

She followed their trail, stepping carefully. There were spots in these close, dangerous neighborhoods that had been designed for escape. Where cracksmen and other criminals could lead a chasing policeman to places that had been set with pitfalls and traps—or watchers, like the woman at the door.

Two sets of prints led the way through the coating on the

floor, past a stairway pocked with missing steps. As she passed, she saw through the holes and the gap on the side of the staircase that small casks had been stacked beneath it. She went along to a long corridor on the left side of the house. It ran so far back that she realized it must indeed be connected to another building.

Distant noises sounded. The closing of a door somewhere above her. A sharp cry, abruptly cut off, that might have come from outside. She proceeded slowly, listening for any closer movement, following the trail until the two steps of footprints abruptly dwindled to one.

She drew up short. Niall's larger, booted prints had gone on alone a few yards, stopped, and turned back. Standing still in a large spot, scuffed mostly clear, she cast about. A long passageway branched to the right, but the dust lay undisturbed. To the left sat an alcove, perhaps ten feet square, its floor also still covered in unbroken layers of grime.

Think.

She peered around again. There was a long, low divan against the wall in the alcove, facing the same way she'd been traveling down the corridor. She looked closer, struggling to see in the gloom.

There it was. A dusty indentation in the center of the cushion. But how? How had either man stepped so far without leaving footprints?

She looked up and found her answer. A metal bar had been suspended from the ceiling. She could picture them jumping up, grasping the bar, and swinging to land on the divan.

But why? A trap? Impossible to tell beneath the grime.

Could she make the swing and the leap? She doubted it. She stood shorter than either of the men. She would likely land several feet short of the target.

Struck by a notion, she turned back and retreated to the staircase. On the floor above, she could hear an argument raging between two women.

Reaching in through the gap torn in the side of the stairwell, she was able to reach one of the casks. It was heavy, which would suit her purpose well. She worked to maneuver it close enough to pull it free and half dragged, half rolled it back to the intersection. She struggled to lift it. What on earth was in them all?

No time to investigate. She hauled it into her arms, swung it wide for better momentum, then let go and tossed it right into the middle of the alcove, before the divan.

It hit with a clatter of something metal—then disappeared, falling through a trapdoor and hitting below with a great, ringing crash.

The echo of the women fighting above stopped.

She breathed out a long sigh, shaken a little. Thank goodness Niall had had the instinct to follow Todge's example. Skirting the edges of the hole, she moved to the spot where they must have landed. Where had they gone from here?

It took a moment to spot it. A trick of perspective. Another, narrower corridor led from the far corner across the alcove. The gloom and the warp and weft of the old, worn wooden paneling rendered it invisible until you reached the middle of the small space.

Stepping carefully, she crossed to it. It lay dark and narrow, but not as long as the one she'd left. If she had to guess, she would say it functioned as a passage to another building. She went in, going fast. When she stepped out of it, she found herself in a space not quite so odorous, not nearly as moldy, but still run-down.

This was not a rooming house. It looked as if it had once housed clerks' offices. Doors stood open along more long corridors and many intersections. The floor was clean.

Well, then. She listened again, but this space was quieter. It seemed as if she'd emerged into the back of the building, so she decided she would head toward the front and check for entrances.

A crash sounded above her, and she quickened her pace. After crossing several empty intersecting passageways, she emerged into a large open space.

It took only a moment for her to realize that here, two buildings had been refashioned into one and a significant portion of wall removed. Someone had created a small warehouse, hidden in the midst of a block of buildings. Bulging sacks lined one wall, while stacks of long crates sat about. On the right, a sturdy, decorated staircase descended from the story above. Across from it, on the opposite wall and obviously from a once-separate building, a smaller, narrower stairway hugged the wall and led to a tiny portal in the ceiling.

She shook her head. It was a warren in here, and the rats were human-sized and likely dangerous. How was she going to find Niall and Todge?

A scatter of light footsteps sounded above. She stilled and ducked behind a stack of crates.

At the top of the elaborate stairs appeared a leg wrapped in a familiar bandage. She ducked, but Todge was not looking below. He was actually moving backward down the stairs, his attention focused on something behind him. He hovered, waiting, and she realized he meant to bait Niall—to let himself be seen so that he could likely lead Niall to another trap.

She stood and strode forward. "Todge! Won't you please stop and listen?"

He started violently and stared down at her in surprise.

Footsteps sounded hard and fast above, and he jerked his head back up. Eyes widening, he turned to vault down the stairs.

She moved to intercept him, but toward the bottom of the stairway he took a great leap and landed well beyond her. Without pause, he ran straight across the room and up the narrower stairs.

She turned to warn Niall, but he was already racing down.

"There's a pit at the bottom!" she shouted.

He heard. She saw the jerk of his head. And when he reached the last step, he took a great jump.

He landed and looked ahead. They both saw Todge poking his head through the small opening above, looking back to see if his adversary had fallen.

Niall started running again.

Kara watched Todge. With a sudden chill, she recognized the anticipation on his face as he watched Niall race toward him.

As Niall headed up the stairs, Todge withdrew.

Her heart dropped.

"Niall, stop! Duck! Now!"

He froze, thanks be to all the heavens. He hunched and stayed, locked in place, just as a wooden door flipped shut to cover the portal above. A wooden door set with shining metal spikes.

The longest one brushed the hair on his head.

Fury surged in Kara's veins. If Niall had moved just a step further, he'd likely be dead, and in a most horrific manner. She marched toward the staircase where he stood.

"Todge!" she shouted. "Thomas! This is beyond enough! We mean to help! We are trying to find who killed your friend." She paused, recalling something Charlie Banks had said. "Janet Ott never forgot you, Thomas. How can we give you her last gift if you keep trying to kill us?"

The spiked door creaked upward a bit. Niall hurriedly backed down several steps.

"A present from Janet?" Todge's tone was uncertain.

"Yes, indeed." She stepped forward. "We need your help. Can you talk with us, please? And we need to tell you about Janet's wish for you."

"You knew my Janet?"

"We did." She drew up at the bottom of the stairs. "Come down now, won't you?" she asked, just as the floor dropped out beneath her.

"KARA!"

Niall's heart plummeted when he saw the floor give way. She flung her arms up and disappeared as he bolted down toward her.

"Kara!"

"Niall!" she cried. "Hurry!"

He crouched down on the last couple of steps and braced himself to peer over the pit that had opened beneath her, afraid of what he might see.

Only to find her scared face peering back at him from only several feet down.

"Hurry," she gasped. "I cannot hold on much longer!"

He reached for her even as he marveled that she'd been able to grab a hold of the edges of the trapdoor. Past her was a long drop. Twelve feet, perhaps? It might have killed her. She could have snapped her neck or broken her back. At the very least, broken a leg. Or two.

Anger surged as he stretched out. He couldn't quite reach her hand. He felt his foot slip off the stair he'd braced against.

Her grip slid a little. "Niall!"

"Yes. Hold on!" He stood and hopped over to the side. Lying flat on the floor and stretching out, he reached for her again. "Give me your hand."

Wild-eyed, she stared at him.

"All I need is your hand, Kara," he said calmly. "I am not going to let you fall."

She nodded. He could see her mentally bracing herself, then she let go with her closest hand and flailed for him.

He caught her arm and clasped it tight. "Now the other one," he urged. She hung there, swaying, and he adjusted his position a little so he could reach further. "Come on now, you can do it."

She let go and reached for him, panic in her eyes.

"I've got you." He dragged in a deep breath and began to haul her up. It took only a few moments, but she was shaking as he helped her to her feet. Her hands clutched him hard. He hesitated a moment, but then pulled her in close, holding her tight while she trembled.

It was a new experience. She was so independent. So endless-ly capable of taking care of herself. He'd never seen her so shaken. He suspected that she'd never allowed herself to be so vulnerable with another human—save perhaps her father. Or Turner. He felt the singular honor of being admitted to such ranks. And he was consumed with a wash of tenderness like he'd never felt before.

"My Janet sent you?"

Kara stiffened. Gently, he unwrapped his arms from about her. Anger rising again, he turned to face the man who had led them on such a dangerous chase.

Todge looked sad, though, and only slightly expectant, as if he didn't dare allow his hopes any latitude.

Niall sighed and nodded at him. He laid a hand on his shoul-der. "Let's find a place to talk, shall we?"

Chapter Fourteen

"**S**HOULD WE FIND a coffee shop and feed him while we talk?" Kara asked quietly. Her ire and anxiety had faded, replaced with the warm comfort she'd found in Niall's arms—and the growing hunger for more. Now she let her concern for this thin, forlorn figure push all of that away.

For now.

"No. We cannot go outside," Niall said.

"I won't run," Todge vowed. "I heard ye. Ye said ye wanted to help Janet and poor Mad Todge."

"Yes, but someone from around here might think you need a rescue. And the less we are seen around here, the better."

Kara noticed the uneasy glance Niall gave the stacked goods around them. "There are offices further back," she said. "We might find some chairs."

Niall nodded, and she set off, heading back the way she'd come. Todge trailed her, and Niall brought up the rear.

She opened the first door she came to and stopped short at the sight of the large casks filling the room. The smell of sulfur wafted out, along with a sharp, metallic tang.

Niall pushed closer, drawing in a breath. Going in, he tested the weight of a cask. It looked to be full. And heavy. "What the—" He looked at Todge. "Gunpowder?"

The man shrugged.

"Who in blazes is storing all of this in here?"

"Angry men," Todge answered, shifting uncomfortably. "Sometimes they shout. Sometimes they gather to whisper around maps. So many maps. They pay the watchers to keep an eye on it all, at least in the early hours. They go about their own business, then they will start to trickle in as the sun dips lower. Best not to be here when they come."

Kara raised a brow. "Who is it, do you think?" She frowned. "Chartists?"

"I doubt it. They presented their last petition three years ago. I thought they'd been quiet since then." Niall gave himself a shake. "It's likely better that we don't know. Come, let's move on."

The next doorway stood open. The bare office held an empty desk and three chairs. Kara dragged one out from behind the desk, closer to the others. "Now we can talk comfortably." She watched Todge perch on the edge of his chair. He didn't look comfortable. "I'm very sorry for the loss of your friend."

Abruptly, he curled over his knees and dug his fingers in his hair. No wonder it stood on end. "My friend," he moaned. "My Janet."

"You've known each other a long time?" Niall asked kindly.

"Always. She's always been there." Todge's voice was muffled. "Since I can remember. Tom and Janet. Janet and Tom. That's who we were. Always together, since we picked pockets and ran in Black Tooth Jack's gang."

"Thomas," Kara said gently, "we have cause to believe that whoever killed Janet held a grudge from long ago. We were told you knew who her enemies were."

His head came up. "Oh, yes. Janet never backed down. Men don't like it when a girl talks back." His eyes glittered. "Black Tooth Jack? He hated it. He tried to break her, didn't he? But we broke him, instead."

Kara sat forward. "Does Black Tooth Jack still run a gang?"

Todge's answering grin made her shiver. "Oh, no. He's gone. Long gone."

"Would you know of any other enemies Janet might have made along the way? Any who might have decided to move now, to take their revenge?"

Todge laughed. "No enemies in London. Not for Janet. None that Todge knew. Todge knows how to deal with them, doesn't he? He knows how to wait. How to watch. How to make it look like an accident."

Niall looked grim at Todge's revelations.

"What of the time when Janet was in gaol, Todge?" Kara watched him closely. "We heard she was held while an inquest into a murder was investigated."

Todge sprang out of his chair. "Yes. The wicked widow got murdered. They thought Janet did it, but she didn't. They had to let her go."

"*Wicked* widow?"

"Oh, and she were a bad one, wasn't she?" Todge was growing more agitated. "*Wicked Widow Wilkins*," he sang, circling the desk. "Oh, she were mean. We didn't like working fer her, Janet and Tom, but she paid in so much pretty coin."

"You both worked for her?" Kara asked. "What did you do?"

The manic glee faded a bit. His face shuttered. "We helped with the farming."

"The farming?" she asked, mystified.

"She took their shame," he said, calming a little. "The widow told them all she would take it, hide it away, safe. Their sins would grow, free and happy, far away from their own world. But she didn't, did she? She buried that shame and turned it into coin."

"Buried it?" Kara was starting to grow alarmed. "What are you talking about, Thomas?"

"Not Thomas," he said sharply. "It were Todge who did it fer her."

"What did he do?"

But Niall had reared back in his chair. "Was the Widow Wilkins a baby farmer, Todge?"

"Yes," Todge whispered. He folded up suddenly and sank down, scurrying to sit with his back against the wall, his hands circled around his knees. "She took the girls who had sinned. She hid them away. No one knew where. But Janet knew. Janet watched the girls fer her. When the babes were born, the widow were meant to bring them back to support them. Those rich nobs paid every month for their keep and their schooling."

"She didn't keep the babes?" Kara whispered, horrified.

"She kept a few. To have on hand to show off, when she needed to."

"And the others?" Niall demanded.

Todge closed his eyes. Kara shuddered to think of the things he had no wish to see again.

"What happened to the other babes?"

He started to rock.

"Did you kill the babes, Todge?" Niall's tone was deadly calm.

The man's eyes popped open. "No! No, not me. The Wicked Widow did it herself. She fed the wee ones laudanum to make them quiet and calm. Then she cut their throats."

Kara gasped in horror. Niall looked ill.

"What did the widow ask you to do?" he asked.

"I was to toss them in the trash, after. Or off a bridge."

"Did you?"

"No." Todge looked up suddenly, directly at Kara. "Did you ever hear the church story? The one about the baby Moses?"

"Yes," she replied, startled.

"I heard it once. It was so cold. Tom and Janet hid in a little church to keep warm. We stole one of those fancy cloths and wrapped up, hiding in one of those little side rooms. We were tired and hungry, but the vicar was telling the story. I liked it. The basket and the bulrushes. The babe floating down the river to a better life." He sighed. "I always remembered it. And when I could, I snuck some of those babes out of the house. I stole a basket from the market, wrapped them up warm, and took them along the river to an abbey. If I waited until the sisters were out working in the garden, I could send the basket floating toward them and they would take them in." He looked at her again. "The quiet ones I had a chance at. The criers, the widow got to them quicker."

Kara's heart twisted. So much tragedy. And an unexpected, raw sort of heroism.

"Did the widow find you out?" asked Niall.

"No, but she wouldn't have given two squats where they were going, as long as she didn't have to support them."

"What of the others, Todge?" Kara couldn't help but ask. "The poor babes she killed? What did you do with them?"

"The basket girl weaves rush mats, too. Stacks them up to sell. I liked that idea. Rushes, like the baby Moses. I wrapped them in there and gave them to the river."

They all sat in silence for a moment. Tears threatened, but Kara fought them mightily. Later. Later she could mourn.

"Janet found out, though," he said after a moment. "She yelled at me. Told me I was soft." His breath caught. "And then she cried."

Niall sighed. "You said Janet didn't kill the Widow Wilkins, Todge. Did you do it?"

"No. No." He shook his head. "It happened at the birthing house. Todge was never allowed there."

"Did they catch the widow's killer?"

"No. No one knows who did it, now that Janet's gone." His lip started to shake again.

"Wait." Niall straightened. "Are you saying Janet Ott knew who murdered this woman?"

He looked at Kara, and she knew they were both thinking the same thing. It sounded like a reason to kill.

"Yes—'twas a ghost, she said."

"A ghost killed the widow?" Kara asked. She looked again at Niall. Was this poor man's mind slipping?

"Janet said so. Stabbed the wicked jade through the heart with a scissors." He started to laugh. "I wish I'd seen it. The old witch deserved worse. And I wish I'd seen the ghost walk right through the wall. Janet was there when it happened." He suddenly burst into tears. "It's just Todge now. No more Janet and Tom."

"We need to speak to Wooten," Niall whispered to her urgently.

"We need to take care of him first," she insisted.

"I don't think we are going to get anything else out of him."

Despite everything, she hated to see the man so miserable, so thin and wasted, sobbing into his hands. "No. I think you are right."

"Why did you tell him you had a present from Janet?"

"Because I remembered that Charlie Banks said she never forgot him—and I thought it might persuade him to talk to us." She paused. "And I think Janet would wish to know he was taken care of."

"But what will you offer him? Money?" He looked over at the sobbing man. "I doubt it will make a difference."

"No. I know a place. My mother sponsored it before her death, and my father carried on the tradition. It's a place for those who are too addled to get along anywhere else. They are watched over. Kept safe. Sometimes, they admit those who are just ... alone. Like him. They just have no one or no place else. He will be well cared for."

"He's dangerous. You heard what he said about taking care of Janet's enemies."

"The staff is experienced. They will watch him and be ready."

She stood and went to kneel in front of the poor man. "Todge, do you recall I said Janet sent us with a present for you?"

He lifted his face, the tears running in tracks over his dirty face, and nodded.

"It's more of a plan than a present. We know of a place we'd like to show you. A place where you might wish to stay."

"Stay? Out of Seven Dials?" He sounded perplexed.

"If you'd like. It's not far outside the city. You could have a room to yourself, either in the house or over the stables."

He blinked. "Stables? Stables are warm."

"Indeed. A bunk of your own. Blankets aplenty. They would feed you from the kitchens, and they have several long walks that would need sweeping."

He brightened. "They need a sweep?"

"They do. We'll try it out, shall we? See if you like the job? They wouldn't pay you in coin," she warned. "Just the room and plenty of food."

"And blankets. And sweeping. I might try it," he said, nodding.

"Excellent. I will make the arrangements. And once they are ready for you, I shall come to Queen Street in my carriage to pick you up."

His mouth dropped. "Mad Todge in a carriage? Won't they all gawk?"

"I imagine they will." She stood. "Now, won't you show us safely out of here?"

≫≫⟪⟪

"WE NEED TO get to Wooten straight away," Niall said as he handed Kara into her carriage. "We need to find out all we can about that widow's murder." He stopped, looking at her drawn face. "But it's been quite a day, I know. Are you quite well? Shall I send you home and go on to Scotland Yard myself?"

She darted him an almost hostile look. "I should like to see you try."

Still standing in the street, he looked up at the afternoon sun. "We should be able to make it there before the inspector departs for home."

"Let's go, then."

He climbed in, and they set off, slumped in opposite corners, wrapped up in their own thoughts. Niall marveled at the sight of her. Her skirt hems and hands were coated with filth, odd smudges lay in other assorted places, and her mind had been filled with tales of horror. But she sat quietly, frowning, lost in thought. Likely planning their next steps.

"The day started out with a threat and ended with you nearly thrown into a pit, with a visit to a dollyshop in the midst," he began.

"Not a dollyshop," she answered absently. "This Banks, at least, is legitimate. I saw the license displayed behind the counter." She shook away her thoughts and looked at him. "And I very much doubt that will be the last of this day's surprises."

He didn't answer. Odin's arse, but he had to see this all the way through, and quickly. He had to find this killer before any other disasters could befall her.

"I can see what you are thinking," she said, suddenly and fiercely. "And I will thank you to stop right now."

"How could you know what I'm thinking?"

"The worry haunting you is writ all over your face. Allow me to ease it. You are a dear friend. The best I've ever had. But I am not your responsibility. You don't need to save me." She paused. "Well, you did need to save me today, and I thank you for it."

He raised a brow. "I seem to recall several timely warnings from you during that chase. We saved each other."

"Exactly. And you see it and appreciate it and are not angry or threatened or disapproving—and that's exactly why this friend-ship has meant so much to me. But I can see the wheels turning in your head. Why not send me home, where I'll be safe? Find this murderer quick, before something dangerous happens again."

He couldn't deny it.

"As I told the inspector, I am an independent woman, and I intend to remain that way. I won't be wrapped in cotton wool. I would far rather race through a booby-trapped hovel with you, even if it does mean nearly falling to my death, than spend my days serving tea, exchanging petty gossip, and waiting for some spoiled lordling to deign to dance with me."

She paused to draw a deep breath. "Janet Ott was a person. Dark and complicated and, yes, a villain at times."

He gave a grunt of assent.

"The men and women of my class, the ones you and Inspector Wooten keep urging me to join more fully, they serve tea and gather in corners at balls and whisper about my odd ways. But Janet Ott? They won't care that she was murdered. They won't care who did it."

"Unless if it was one of them," he murmured.

"Especially then. They would rather one of their own go free than a woman like her find justice. They would scarcely recognize her as the same species as themselves. But she was. I don't condone how she took advantage of people, but neither can I forget that those of my class take advantage of her kind every day." She pointed a finger at him. "By all means, let us solve this case quickly."

He finished her thought. "But let us do it for her."

Niall saw the relief roll through her. "Yes."

He understood how she felt. Once again, they stood in accord about something almost no one else would.

"Someone murdered her," he said. "Perhaps to cover up their own crimes. She deserves justice for that, at the very least. Larger forces than us will judge Janet for her sins. But we cannot let her killer get away with his crime, not if we can stop it."

Her breath caught. She looked pained, almost. "Yes."

He sat back. Kara was clearly caught up in something. Her chest rose and fell quickly. He kept quiet and gave her time to gather herself.

It was several moments before she spoke. Her breathing had calmed and her voice broke the silence softly. "It's going to be very hard on me when you leave," she said quietly.

He stilled. Caught. He tensed, afraid of what was coming.

"But I want you to know that you were right. About me.

About how I was hiding away, burying myself in my work to avoid people, to avoid the judgment and all the ... pressure. To change. To conform. I've heard you, though. You've helped give me the confidence to do as you suggested. We will find Janet Ott's killer. And you will move on. And I will change—in the way that *I* want to."

"Nothing about you needs changing," he said roughly.

"No. You were right. I do need to make connections. I'm going to do it. I'm going to continue to learn and create, but I'm going to find friends. I'll have adventures. I'll use my gifts to make life better, for myself and for others."

His heart swelled. He was so damned proud of her. She was magnificent. He recalled the day he'd first met her. Beautiful but quiet, distant but determined. She'd labored alone to turn bits of metal into wonderful creations, to bring them to life. Now she was bringing herself to life, and he felt privileged to see it. He ached to tell her he would adventure at her side, but he dared not. Not yet.

Perhaps she'd sensed the direction of his thoughts.

"Perhaps someday I'll find a man to love, someone willing to be a partner, a co-conspirator, someone willing to share adventures, through days and nights." She lifted her chin proudly. "Until then, I am going to give them all plenty to gossip about over their tea."

She'd meant it as a blow, and damned if it didn't strike home. It felt like a hook to his gut, pulling out things that were meant to stay coiled and hidden. But how was he supposed to envision her sharing all that they meant to each other—and more—with someone else? It made him want to shout a denial to the universe. To throw caution to the wind and claim her now.

Except ... it actually could throw her in the path of danger. It was what he'd been told his entire life. But was it right?

She was waiting for a reaction.

He was going to corner Stayme the first chance he got. Hash it out with the old man. Make some demands of his own.

"I cannot wait to see what you get up to," he replied in the meantime.

It was all he could give her. He saw in her face that it was not enough. She watched him for a long moment, and he struggled to keep his face composed.

Finally, she sat back and looked away.

And he tightened his jaw and did the same.

Chapter Fifteen

THEY ENTERED SCOTLAND Yard to find a very young officer at the high desk in front, and nearly all the desks beyond deserted.

"Inspector Wooten is not here," the sergeant told Kara when she asked. "He's out on a case and took nearly a regiment of constables with him."

"Any idea when he might return?" asked Niall.

"None," came the answer. "Could be in five minutes, might not be until tomorrow."

She looked up at Niall. "Shall we wait?"

He still appeared utterly unruffled by her passionate declarations in the carriage. The infuriating *man*. She didn't regret a single word she'd said, though. Everything they were learning about Janet Ott, and the others who lived in her orbit, had been working on her. Setting her to thinking about life and how she wished to live it, whom she wished to live it with, about the kind of person she wished to be and the legacy she would leave behind.

"We might as well, at least for a bit," Niall said. He gestured toward a nearby bench intended for the purpose. "After you."

She settled in, folding her hands in her lap. She'd made her move. He'd recognized it, even if he hadn't responded. But she could wait.

And wait they did, for thirty minutes or more, before Niall leaned over. "Perhaps we should turn our attention elsewhere?"

"Where?"

"Imogen Berringer, perhaps. I'd like to know what her situation was when the widow was murdered."

She shook her head. "We need to be armed with all the facts about that case before we consider who might be involved or consider them a suspect."

"I suppose you are right." He pursed his lips. "I might know someone else who would be able to recall the events of the case. From the public side."

"It's better than sitting here, I suppose. But hold a moment. Let me try something." She let out a pronounced sigh, stood, and proceeded to pace the few steps between the desk and the door. Back and forth. Back and forth.

They had been far easier to ignore when they were seated quietly on the bench. The few men seated at in the open collection of desks began to notice her now, though.

"Oh!" She held up her hands as if she had just realized their grimy state. "Excuse me." The young man at the front looked up warily. "Is there a room where I might wash my hands and freshen up a bit?"

"There is, miss." The boy made a face. "But I don't think you would care for the state of—"

"Nonsense!" One of the men seated at a desk rose to his feet. He smiled as he approached. "There is a fine facility on the next floor up, near the commissioners' offices. Just take the stairs at the end of that corridor." He pointed.

"But ... but ... I don't think—" the young man began.

"Don't be daft, Greene. Miss Levett is too fine a lady to be subjected to the facilities down here." The man nodded at her. "You'll find it on the right."

Kara smiled. "Thank you very much, Mr....?"

"Constable John Norland, miss. At your service."

She inclined her head, climbed up, and did indeed take the opportunity to repair her appearance as best she could. She felt better, and as she returned, she made sure to pass by Norland's desk to thank him.

"Not at all. It *is* Miss Levett, is it not?"

"It is."

"And is Mr. Turner still with you?"

She smiled. "He is, indeed."

"Please pass him my compliments? There are still men here who remember the fine work he did to save you, so long ago."

"Thank you, sir. I will tell him you said so. I do like to remind him how wonderful he is when I can. It unsettles him horribly."

Norland laughed.

She looked him over, calculating. "If you have been with the police force as long as that, sir, I would imagine you have quite a few fascinating stories to tell."

He leaned in confidentially. "More than a few, miss. More than a few."

She raised a brow. "How I should love to hear them." She let a moment slide past. "I've only just heard of a notable case. The murder of the Widow Wilkins? That must surely be a quite a tale."

He looked grim. "That it is, but it's one we rarely like to speak of. Unsolved cases. Bad publicity, you know."

"Well, I am very interested in that particular tale, and I am also quite famished. Mr. Kier and I are waiting on Inspector Wooten's return, but he might not be back for hours. Is there a coffee shop or chophouse nearby that you can recommend?"

"Carlisle's coffee shop around the corner turns out a delicious sausage roll and offers other assorted pastries. And their coffee is the best around."

"It sounds perfect. If you have time to join us, I should be happy to buy you a meal." She paused a beat. "And to listen to your story."

The constable eyed her closely. "The word is that you've

helped Wooten out a few times. Lent the feminine touch to easing the way and calming a nervous or delicate interview subject or two?"

"And so I have. I'm happy to lend my aid as our fine police force searches for justice. If you would consider exchanging your knowledge for a promise of my help in the future, I would find it a fair exchange, sir."

"Excellent." Norland held out a hand for her to shake. "Very well, then. Let us all head over to Carlisle's."

Kara hadn't been fabricating her hunger. She finished a sausage roll, a raspberry tart, and several cups of tea while Niall and Norland plowed their way through more significant mounds of food. At last, though, they were all sated and ready to talk.

"Why the Widow Wilkins case?" The constable shook his head. "That was an ugly one. It still wakes me at night occasionally."

"You worked on that investigation?" Niall asked.

"I did. I was still green, just a couple of years on the force. It's still one of the worst I've seen, and that is a statement that means something."

"We heard you held a girl in gaol while the inquest's investigation was ongoing?"

"We started out with *three* girls in custody. And an infant," he added. "But only one stuck," he finished bitterly.

"Excuse me? What was that?" asked Kara.

"Let me start from the beginning, if I'm going to tell it."

She nodded for him to continue.

"It happened in Bermondsey. That Widow Wilkins had a house there." He shuddered. "Evil. There's no other word for what she did."

"We heard what happened to the babes that came into her care," Niall said carefully.

"It was a scandal." Norland sighed. "The press got a hold of the story, and it was all anyone talked about for weeks. She murdered those innocents. And you would not have believed the money those toffs were paying her every month. Room, board, schooling. She charged an exorbitant amount, all for babies she'd outright killed." He paused. "Of course, none of those fine men could come forward with formal complaints, lest their secrets come out."

"But how did you end up with three girls in custody?" Kara asked.

"There had been unrest in that area. Feuding shopkeepers, if I recall? A lot of bluster and crowds and rocks thrown through windows. We had extra patrols scheduled in the area. One night, late, they came upon a group gathered outside a home. Neighbors who heard an unholy amount of screaming coming from inside. More than one person, they said. The door was locked, but our boys broke in. Inside, they found a girl with a brand new babe, a midwife, and two other girls, one of them bent over an old woman breathing her last."

"Stabbed with scissors?" asked Niall.

Norland blanched and then braced both hands on the table. "How is it that you know that?"

Niall met his gaze. "It was in the account we were told."

"And who told you?"

"Finish your story, and then we'll share ours."

The constable looked between them. "We kept that bit to ourselves. The scissors. They were from the midwife's bag." He nodded, his gaze unfocused. "The midwife, the locals could vouch for her. They knew the widow, too. The other girls, no one knew them. We took the three girls and the infant into the public office. Put them in a holding cell, all together, for the night. They were meant to see the magistrate in the morning. Except, the thing is, in the morning, only the one girl was left. The new mother, the babe, and one other girl had all disappeared. No one saw a thing."

"Not even the girl left in the cell?" Niall asked.

"Not even her. She was dead asleep. We could barely wake her, and she was groggy and confused."

"Drugged," Kara said flatly.

"Or else in on the escape," suggested Niall.

"She would hardly agree to be left behind," Kara mused. "Was she in the family way?" she asked Norland.

"Not that we could tell."

"Someone in the public office had to have done it. Or helped. Or looked the other way." Niall sat quietly, his eyes fixed on Norland.

"Another reason we don't like to discuss this particular investigation." The constable sighed again. "Now, tell me how you know about those scissors? We kept that out of the press. And yes, by the way, they had been plunged into the widow's black heart."

"The girl in the cell? That was Janet Ott," Niall said.

Norland's jaw dropped. "Never say it!"

Kara, watching him closely, judged the constable's surprise to be true.

Norland's gaze narrowed. "None of us made the connection. How on earth did you?"

"She's been known to use false names," Niall replied. "But we've been looking into her past. We heard it from two separate sources who knew her back then."

They all stared at each other in silence.

And all three jumped a little when the door to the shop flew open with a bang. Wooten strode in, looking like thunder.

Norland shot to his feet. "Inspector."

Kara nodded. "Good evening, Inspector Wooten."

Niall only looked mildly amused. "Your lead did not prove useful, I take it."

Wooten sat down. "No." He glanced at Norland. "Whatever you've heard from these two tonight, forget it."

"Come now, Inspector," Niall said. "Constable Norland has proved extremely helpful. And you need to hear all that we've pieced together."

Wooten sighed. He waved at a waitress. "Coffee, please." He

took out his notebook. "Very well. Go ahead."

They caught him up, and the same heavy silence fell over the table as their tales finished.

"Did you know of the widow's case?" Kara asked Wooten.

"I knew of it, although not the details." He took a long drink from his cup. "I was part of a special unit investigating in Hampstead for most of that year. We were after a particularly cunning highwayman."

"And Two-Choice Thompson was brought in due to your excellent work, sir," Norland said. "I've heard the stories."

"Two-Choice Thompson?" Kara asked.

"Never mind," Wooten said with a sharp look at the constable. "So, you are thinking we should be looking for a woman? A woman who birthed an illegitimate child, then killed the widow before she could take the infant?"

"A young woman of wealth or breeding or both," Kara added. "Who else could have secured an escape from the cell in such a manner?"

Wooten looked at Niall. "And you are still leaning toward someone from the Druids?"

"Now that we know that neither of the Banks brothers killed her, it makes the most sense. Unless you have another woman on Janet Ott's blackmail list?"

"One. But I've already spoken to her. She was blackmailed over a painting. Certainly not over anything like this."

Niall sighed. "The Druidic Bards admitted women from the outset. I cannot forget that all of the members had knowledge of and access to those plants."

"And don't forget that woman, the maid that looked to be avoiding Janet Ott during the party in the gardens," Kara added. "She had an odd gait. And I thought I heard a hitch to the step of the woman I surprised at the plants later that night."

Wooten gave Niall a steady look.

"I was not thinking of Lady Madge," Niall protested. "She was there that night and definitely not dressed like a maid. For all that's she's older and could be said to have a slow gait, she's far too direct to have waited this long. She would have tracked that girl down right after it happened. Not to mention, if she had waited all these years, she would have had this investigation quashed right at the start."

"Who were you considering, then?" Wooten asked.

"I was thinking we need to look again at Imogen Berringer. She knows more about the maids employed at the Grove than anyone else. And there is also the matter of the newspapers." Niall told them of the delivered threat, the newspaper, and the project in the summerhouse.

Wooten frowned. "I don't like this."

"It was just a note," Kara said.

"It was a threat, and I don't like it at all. But I did look at Mrs. Berringer's background, early on, before we spoke to her and Towland. If I recall, she would have been a young, married woman at that time. She would have had no need to hide a birth."

"Unless her husband was away at the critical time?" Niall pointed out. "Or the babe was going to look decidedly different from him? Who knows what goes on in a marriage?"

"You said Lady Flora was with her?" Kara thought back. "Do you remember when I asked about the Celtic knot on her gown? She admitted she designed it, and that it symbolized mother-hood."

"Lady Flora Copely?" The inspector sounded aghast. "The daughter of the Earl of Chawford? The woman who has served as Queen Victoria's woman of the bedchamber for multiple terms? She's spent half her life at court! Not to mention she's so kind and unassuming. I doubt she would harm a fly."

"She did mention her knot was a reference to Mother Earth," Niall reminded Kara. "Which makes sense, when you consider her devotion to gardening." He made a face. "Like the inspector, I have a hard time pegging her as a murderer."

Kara pursed her lips. "Well, then, Lady Madge might recall

any gossip from that period. She's been a member since the beginning. Also, she's already asked me to come see her about another matter. I shall see what light she can shed on this."

"I'll start looking into the Berringers' marriage," Wooten said.

"Let me help with that?" Norland asked. "I'd like to help you all see this through. I have personal reasons to find some of these answers."

Wooten watched him a moment. "You were on duty at the public office that night, then, weren't you? When the girls disappeared?"

Norland flushed deeply. "I was, and I never heard a thing. And before you ask … no, I did not fall asleep on duty. I have no idea how they did it. I tried to find out. Looked into everyone there that night. Someone had to turn a blind eye, at the very least, but it wasn't me. And whoever it was, they hid it well and kept silent."

"Likely paid a king's ransom to do it," Wooten said cynically.

"Well, it didn't help my career any, carrying that millstone around my neck. I've been looked at with suspicion, passed over for opportunities and advancements. That night, it has haunted me for years. I want to help. I want to know."

Wooten conceded. "Very well."

Kara leaned forward, struck by a thought. "Inspector, about that other woman on Janet Ott's blackmail list?"

"Yes? She confessed her part in it, on condition I didn't tell her family of her shame. Apparently, Janet saw her pawn a family painting. When the woman went back to claim it, Janet had bought it. She came to her home and offered to sell it back to her. When the woman agreed, Janet turned over a copy, not the original. The woman knew she was being fleeced and accused Janet of it."

"What happened?" asked Niall.

"The jade freely confessed. She'd already sold the original, so there was naught to be done. Janet was paid twice for the same painting, and the owner took the copy rather than be discovered by her family."

"Was the woman young? Pretty? Red-gold hair and a long, sharp nose?" Kara asked.

"No. I remember her differently, but let me check to be sure. I would have written it down." Wooten flipped backward in his notebook and consulted an earlier page. "She was short, middle-aged, and gray."

"Oh. Very well, then. Thank you."

Niall frowned. "Why do you ask?"

"It was just a thought."

He continued to frown at her, but she ignored it. She didn't know why she hadn't told him about the strange woman. Perhaps because she wished to have a secret or two of her own. Or perhaps it was because of the obvious disdain the woman had shown her.

Wooten stood. "Well. It's late. We all have our tasks. Let's see what we can accomplish tomorrow, and then we'll meet again to discuss our findings. Here again? Tomorrow evening? What say you all?"

Murmuring agreement, they all took leave of one another and went their separate ways.

Chapter Sixteen

NIALL CONSIDERED STAYING in the city in his rooms at the White Hart, but Kara fell asleep as soon as the carriage started to move. He couldn't just send her on, alone and out for the count, so he gritted his teeth and endured the ride out to Bluefield.

Exhaustion settled over him and coalesced into an ache in his chest, but there was no possibility of sleep for him. Not after this hellish day. Not after so many unexpected surprises and so many things left unsettled and undone. His mind kept whirling from one to the other.

When they pulled up before the house, Niall craned to look out, but there was no sign of Turner or any of the other servants. The hour must be late indeed. Gently, he reached out to wake Kara.

She came awake slowly, turning her head and opening her eyes. She caught sight of him and gave a sleepy, contented smile.

It made his heart twist painfully.

The bond of their friendship ran deep. How much better might it be if he were he free to take it further? What might it be like to open his eyes every morning to that smile? To know the day ahead—all the days ahead—would be full of her wit and laughter and talent and beauty?

He longed to find out. And his urge to follow that thread was growing as strong as the worries that prevented it.

He climbed down and turned to assist her. The bracing night air prodded her awake, although she gave a great yawn that left him smiling.

She squeezed his hand. The carriage moved on, heading for the stables. They stood alone in the dark, with the sky full of the sparkling beauty of a multitude of stars and his heart full of conflicting emotions.

"Thank you, Niall."

It was thanks offered for more than his help out of the carriage. He heard the breadth of her meaning in her tone.

He smiled in answer, returned the squeeze, and let her go.

With a sigh, she began to move toward the house. He watched her for a moment, before turning toward his forge and the loft above.

The sound of her footsteps in the gravel stopped.

"Niall?"

He turned around. She faced him, her hair coming down a little on one side and wafting in the night breeze. He drank in the beauty of her. She was a mad combination of exuberance, stubborn determination, extraordinary vision, and the lovely sweetness of her soul. It almost hurt to look at her.

And suddenly, she was moving. Lifting her skirts and racing toward him. As she drew closer, she let go and reached out—and leapt into his arms.

He caught her. Staggered back a step. And her lips were on his and he was lost.

Her fingers were in his hair. Her legs wrapped around his waist. He braced one hand across her back to hold her close and the other beneath the curve of her bottom, to keep her, high and hot and pressed against him, with her mouth locked to his.

She'd gone soft and pliant. Need sprang to heated life in his chest, and he felt the answering sensation in her. Together, their longings rose and combined, whirling between them, spiraling higher and fueling the fervent, dangerous beauty of their kiss.

She was inexperienced. He showed her subtly, delicately, how it was done. An enthusiastic pupil, she let him coax her mouth open. Their embrace deepened, transforming this encounter into something more demanding and desperate. Something that fought and railed against the cold knowledge of its fleeting nature.

She moaned, a low sound of aching want, and he clutched her closer still, wishing he could pull her right inside, so that this might never end.

But end it did. She pulled away and looked down at him, her face filled with sorrow. Slowly, he let her drop, felt the forbidden slide of her down the front of him. But he could not let go, not yet. He bent his head so that their lips hovered close.

"I wanted to know," she whispered. "When you are long gone and I am lying awake, making myself miserable with what might have been, I want to know exactly what I will be missing." She ducked her head, pressing against his chest and gripping him tightly for a moment, before looking back up, her expression gone stern. "Perhaps I wanted you to know, too."

She whirled, then, and was gone, running for the house.

He stood, reaching for balance in a world that had abruptly shifted. He had no memory of moving, but suddenly he found himself in his forge. The dark pressed in on him, a tangible impression of his loneliness and sorrow, of his fears and worries.

In a sudden burst of motion, he tore off his coat. He lit a lantern, and even by its dim light, he could start up the forge. After shifting coals to burn hot and high, he left them to get going and ran up to change his clothes. He slid into his old kilt with a sigh of relief. Within the hour he was pulling metal from the fire to the anvil.

With each swing, each blow, he pounded away at his frustrations. This. This was how he defeated, destroyed, or controlled his emotions. He pummeled them into submission with fire, with the power of his arm and the strength and discipline he'd learned to wield in his mind.

Except there was no subduing the desire she'd awakened in him. No wiping away the glory of that kiss or the incredible *rightness* of their rapport. And that stubborn resistance opened the door to all of his other worries.

He didn't give up, though. He pounded away at them all.

At the person who had dared to threaten Kara. At the image of her panicked face as she swung over that pit. At the conundrum she'd put him in, informing him she was going to move on after he left London, and her, behind.

He wiped his brow and thrust the long rod he was flattening back into the furnace. Wasn't it just like her, though? No tears, no wiles, no wounded glances or sighs. Just acceptance of his plans and a flat-out declaration of her own. And a heart-stopping, glorious demonstration of what might be.

Odin's arse, but he loved that about her.

He loved her.

He started hammering again. Against the worst of his fears. The cold shiver that had run through him when she asked that question of Wooten. About other women who might have been Janet Ott's blackmail victims.

About a pretty woman, with red-gold hair and a long, straight nose. A very specific description.

Pound. Pound.

Entirely too close to the mark.

Pound. Pound.

It couldn't be.

Pound. Pound.

Could it?

Cursing, he thrust the rod into the fire again. It could not be a coincidence. Not so soon after Marston began creeping about and asking questions. But what had happened? And why hadn't Kara told him? Had something been *said*?

The apprehension that gripped him translated into a flurry of blows that finished out the flattening of the rod. He forced himself to let it all go as he focused on the work. On heating it again and working on one jig, then the next. Heat and turn. Heat and turn. He concentrated with mind and muscle until the nondescript metal had been transformed into the winding shape of a vine covered in roses, delicate and sturdy at once. It would fit into the wide arbor he was creating on commission.

But not now. When he finished, he thrust the piece into the water and let it steam, his mind clear at last.

The first graying of the approaching dawn was showing on the horizon. After banking the forge, he went up to his loft, where he washed thoroughly and dressed carefully. He checked to be sure the fires were safely contained before he walked out into the dawn. At the drive, standing before the bulk of the dark house, he hesitated.

But no. He needed to speak to Stayme alone. There were things that they could only discuss in private. He needed answers. And Stayme was the only one who could give them.

He walked on, into the village, where he caught a ride on a farm wagon to the train station in Hammersmith.

He slept on the train. When he disembarked in London, the city was just awakening. Wagons rumbled toward the markets, and maids with baskets over their arms hurried after them, hoping to get the best, freshest choices of the day. Other servants swept steps. Shopkeepers unlocked doors, and clerks hurried out into the streets. Barrow vendors ducked down alleys and back streets, eager to sell straight to the cooks in their kitchens.

Ignoring the indecent and utterly impolite hour, Niall marched right up to Stayme's door and made loud use of his slightly naughty knocker. It was time. He didn't want to exist in this foggy half-a-life any longer. There had to be a way for him to break out of the strictures that had held sway over him.

The door opened surprisingly quickly. Stayme's butler inclined his head in greeting. "Mr. Kier."

"Watts." Niall stepped inside. "Not even this ungodly hour can ruffle your feathers. I congratulate you." He handed over his hat and coat. "Apologies, but I must see the old man. Now."

"His lordship is dressing, sir, and should be downstairs quite soon."

"So early? I'm shocked. I'll wait in his study, then, shall I?"

He strode past the servant but had barely placed his hand on the latch when Watts spoke, low and urgent. "No, sir. Not there. Why do you not step into the dining room and I'll have cook send up some breakfast?"

Niall turned and frowned at the man in surprise. Stayme *never* invited anyone to dine in his home. He routinely stated he had enough dinner conversation elsewhere and preferred his own company in his own home.

"I'm sorry, sir." Watts stepped close so he could keep his tone low. "His lordship already has a visitor awaiting him in the study."

"At this hour?"

"Indeed, sir." The butler gave him a wry look. "Shocking, isn't it?"

"Very well, then." Niall turned to follow the servant to the dining room, but paused when he heard the door open behind him.

"Niall? I thought I heard your voice."

He looked over his shoulder and stopped dead in his tracks.

"How did you know I was here?"

"Kara?" he said roughly. "What in blazes are you doing here?"

"THERE'S A QUESTION I should love to put to each of you."

Niall turned his head. Lord Stayme stood on the stairs, as neat as a pin and his narrowed gaze sharp as a tack.

"I'm impressed, sir," Niall drawled. "I thought perhaps this once I would catch you off guard and in your dressing gown."

The viscount glared at him, then snorted and turned a softer look on Kara. "Miss Levett, I shall, of course, be happy to speak with you about whatever topic has brought you, but first I hope you won't mind if I see Niall a moment? I have rather an urgent task for him."

"Of course," Kara replied. "I do apologize for descending upon you at such an early hour."

Stayme waved her apology away. "Think nothing of it. Men of my age rarely sleep much, in any case." He raised a brow at Niall. "Upstairs, if you will? We will speak in my private parlor."

Mystified, Niall followed him up. He'd never been permitted in this part of the house. Nor in any part, save for the study and the formal parlor next to it.

At the first landing, he followed Stayme down a passage lined with portraits, each with a stern gaze and more than a few with the heavy brow the viscount used to such advantage.

Stayme approached a wide set of double doors, all carved wood and grandeur. He swept inside. Niall followed behind, then stopped to gape.

The room was large and brightly lit. The walls were covered in bookshelves and large, framed maps. He recognized Paris, Lisbon, Vienna, and Moscow, all done in exquisite detail, down to the street level. A globe took up one corner, an astrolabe on a plinth another. A large telescope on a tripod sat near a massive desk, although the one big window showed only out into the garden and the mews beyond.

Chairs were grouped before the hearth and the desk. On the desk, another map of Paris had been unrolled and weighted down. It was even more detailed and had been marked with several colored dots.

Stayme marched around the desk and lifted a weight. The map rolled itself up as the viscount shot Niall a look full of venom. "What are you playing at?"

Niall drew up straight. He'd heard Stayme's nasty tone before, but never directed at him. "You'll have to be more specific."

"Did I not expressly forbid you from interfering?"

He frowned. "With Marston, you mean?"

"Yes, with Marston, you fool! What have you done?"

"Nothing!" Niall hesitated. "Well, I had him followed in Paris, but the report I received assured me he hadn't caught on to the tail. Nor was he chasing miniatures. Instead, he's been visiting. Parisian elite, for the most part."

"He's been visiting *my* friends and acquaintances, and asking questions about *me*," the viscount raged. "The upstart little weasel! First, the search for the miniatures, then a host of inquiries about me, my friends, and my travels?" He blew out a breath. "He knows something."

"What could he know?" Niall took a moment to comb back through his memories, but he was as certain now as he had been then. "He could not have learned anything from her."

"Surely he must have. Or perhaps he's received some sort of clue from elsewhere and is just fitting it in with her observations and speculations. Clearly he suspects something. And now he's gone and got himself knocked half-dead."

"Excuse me? He … what?"

"He set out for home and was attacked in Le Havre. Clearly it was an assassination attempt. Worse, it wasn't me who arranged it." Stayme cast a cold look over him. "Was it you?"

"No! Of course not."

"You've more reason than anyone to see the dastard dead."

"If I wanted revenge, I'd make sure he lives. Surely he's suffering by now. A man can only tolerate so much manipulation and drama at home. Are you sure you didn't have anything to do with it? It occurs to me you have the perfect scapegoat."

Stayme raised a brow.

"Me," Niall clarified.

"Oh. No. Had I wanted him dead, he'd be dead. As it is, he was merely injured. He's being kept in bed a few days, then he'll resume his journey home." The viscount's expression grew serious. "You are sure the miniatures are safe?"

"Utterly."

"And the documents?"

"They are all safe, as I've already said. They are stored where none can retrieve them. None but me, that is."

Stayme dropped into his chair. "Thank the heavens for small mercies. Now." He gave Niall a direct look. "You have to go."

Niall stilled. "I cannot."

"You must."

"I cannot. Kara has been threatened."

The viscount covered his eyes. "Is it this murder business?"

"It is. She's had a direct threat. I cannot leave her in danger."

"Niall, if someone is truly pursuing information about the miniatures, about me, then you know what a hornet's nest might get stirred up. If word of this becomes known ... *everyone* will be looking for you. You need to be far out of reach before it comes to that." His expression softened. "Leave Miss Levett to me. I will protect her. You go."

"Is there no chance of putting a stop to this instead?"

"There is, but the odds ... It's too risky. Something is afoot, and I don't have my thumb on it."

"I know how you hate that."

"I need you safe, lad. All told, it's easier for you to go. Safer."

Niall slammed a fist on the desk. "And if it's not easier? Not this time? Not for me?"

Stayme frowned, his gaze running over him—and Niall saw comprehension dawn.

"Oh, no. No, Niall."

"Why not?" He refrained from slamming the desk again, but only just. "I deserve more than half a life. An existence in the shadows."

"You know why it must be so. You've always known."

"I'm tired of paying and paying for sins that were not my own!"

"Yes, I've heard similar sentiments before," the viscount reminded him. "And you see how well that's turned out."

Niall quieted. "I deserve that, I know I do. But this—there is no comparison. I was young then, a randy fool with grand ideas of playing the hero. This could not be more different."

"Yes, and all for the worse! This one is blue-blooded. Always in the spotlight." Stayme's eyes widened. "And good heavens, the money she has! You'll send them all into a tizzy at the thought of what you might do with it."

"It's no more than I've done to myself. I was going to go, you see. I had it planned, before it all progressed too far. And then it was too late. She needed me. And I'm afraid I've seen, at last, how much I need her, too."

Stayme heaved a sigh. "Spare me young fools in love."

Niall gripped the back of a chair. "I'm serious, sir. This is so much easier. Better. Truer. It's *real*. I know you understand what I'm saying. So talk to the Privy Council or to the twice-damned queen herself, if you must. But help us."

Stayme rubbed his brow. "Take her with you, then."

"How can I? Without telling her all?"

"You cannot tell her! Not yet. Not until you know she can be trusted."

"I already know she can be *trusted*. But what if she decides she has no wish to deal with ... everything? If she's run off with me, it will be too late. She'll be ruined."

"And she'll know it all and be furious, besides. Oh, damn it all to hell," Stayme muttered.

Niall went around and sat in the chair he'd been holding like a lifeline. "There's more."

"How could that be?"

He told the viscount about Kara's very specific question for Wooten.

"What in seven hells am I supposed to make of that?" demanded Stayme.

"I wish I knew."

"Are you her target? Is it you? Or is it Miss Levett?"

Niall shook his head and shrugged. "You know all I know."

"Nothing at all, then. All the saints in heaven. What a mess."

"Yes," Niall agreed grimly. "What are you going to do?"

"First, I'm going to talk to the girl. See what's brought her here and what she knows." Stayme sat back. "What are you going to do?"

"I'm going to solve that cursed murder," Niall vowed. "And then I'll see what's to be done."

Chapter Seventeen

"PLEASE, DO FORGIVE me, my dear. I'm sorry I've made you wait."

"Not at all, sir." Kara stood and curtsied as Lord Stayme entered. "I shouldn't have come at all." She shook her head. "I see that now. It's just, perhaps you know how it is when you are so tired, but your mind is too full to let you sleep? The solution to your problem looks so clear there, in the dark. But it doesn't always hold up in the light of day."

"Please, sit." He waved her into a chair and took the one behind the desk. "I do know just what you mean, dear girl. But I should love to become the solution to your problem. Why don't you tell me about it?"

"It seems incredibly small and silly when I say it out loud, but it doesn't *feel* small."

The viscount's gaze sharpened. "Trust your instincts, child. Tell me what's bothering you."

"Well, it's only that Niall has spoken, sometimes, of a friend who has vast acquaintance and knowledge of Society. I realized, after your visit, that you must be who he meant."

"You wish to know something about someone in Society?"

"Perhaps. I've come to ask about a woman. She certainly dresses as if she has access to Society dressmakers. Or at least to a great deal of wealth."

"But you do not know her name?"

"No. I've not met her. But I've seen her twice. Once outside Lake Nemi." She paused to see if he recognized the name of the club. He must have, as he nodded for her to go on. "The other time, I saw her in the village near my home. And my maid said someone of the same description called at Bluefield Park, but she would not leave a card when she was turned away."

"Were you alone when you spotted her?"

"Once. The second time, I was in a carriage with Niall."

"He didn't notice her?"

"No."

"Do you have any idea why she is seeking you out?"

She shook her head.

He leaned back. "So, a description is all you have?"

"Yes. She's a young woman. A little taller than me. She has the sort of strawberry-blonde hair that shines like rose gold in the sun. Blue eyes and a long, sharp nose. She's very lovely."

"That's not very much to go on. Is there anything else you can tell me?"

She hesitated.

"Ah. There *is* more. In for a penny, in for a pound, girl. What is it?"

"It's only … the woman has appeared quite … disdainful of me, both times I've seen her. Almost hostile."

He looked more interested. "Does she, indeed?"

Kara flushed. "It must sound ridiculous, like nothing—"

"No," he interrupted. "I will look into this for you, my dear. I will let you know if I discover anything substantial."

"Thank you. Your help is much appreciated." She cast him a curious look. "Do you mind if I ask you a question?"

He smiled. "Of course. I've been shooting them at you, and you've been quite accommodating about answering."

"Why did you ask me about Becky Sharpe the first time we met?"

"Ah." He smiled. "You have been thinking about that, have you?"

"I have."

"You are perceptive, I see."

"It was some sort of test?"

"Perhaps a small one. Do you care to change your answer?"

"Not at all." She leaned forward. "Does that mean I passed?"

"Perhaps you might see it that way." He shrugged. "It is something I use to gauge a person's temperament, their way of thinking, of viewing the world around them. I don't believe there is a right or wrong answer."

"You think I am naïve, not believing Becky's character would kill her husband?"

"I think you are a kind, caring woman. One who has empathy for others. One who would never contemplate such an act and would find such an idea shocking, even when proposed for a vain, self-serving, and impatient creature like Becky."

"I think perhaps you read too much into such a simple question."

"Never worry. I have other ways of gauging people."

"You've got one thing wrong, at least," she told him.

He looked interested. "And what is that?"

"I don't think I would be shocked." She frowned. "I've seen so much, so many different sorts of people. So many of them are quite creative in coming up with ways to hurt others. Or themselves." She sighed. "I'm not sure anything shocks me now."

"Don't tempt fate by saying so, Miss Levett. It is never wise." He stood. "Come now. I've already sent Niall into breakfast. Let's see if we can catch up to him before you both go about your day."

He offered his arm, and she took it, admittedly with the smallest bit with trepidation. In the dining room, they found Niall making his way through a bowl of oatmeal and reading a newspaper.

Guiltily, he folded the paper and tossed it back to the head of the table. "Apologies if I creased your ironed pages," he said.

Lord Stayme waved the apology away, although Kara thought his mouth looked a little pinched. He seated Kara next to his spot at the head of the table and across from Niall.

She looked at the viscount, at the richly flocked wallpaper, at the plate a servant set in front of her. Anywhere but at Niall. The memory of what they'd done together swamped her, raising a heated flush to her cheeks. Stayme saw it, looked between them, and sighed.

"Eat up, the pair of you," he ordered them. "I should think we all have a busy day ahead."

Kara bent to her plate, spreading jam across her toast, while a servant approached Stayme with a silver tray. "The first post, my lord."

The viscount took the stack of mail and began to riffle through it as he ate. When he encountered a small, folded note, he opened and read it straightaway.

Kara looked up when he made a strangled sound. Now *he* was flushed red—with anger. "What in blazes?" he demanded, waving the note. "Why am I receiving notice that the pair of you were seen leaving Boyd's Yard?"

Kara exchanged questioning looks with Niall. "Were we?"

"Off Queen Street in Seven Dials?" Stayme said sharply. "Ringing any bells?"

"Oh, yes. Yesterday," she replied. "We were literally chasing a lead, but I don't believe either of us knew the name of the place."

He blinked furiously at her, then turned his anger on Niall. "You fool! Idiot! Do you know anything about what is going on in there?"

"We do now," Niall replied. "I should have mentioned it. Looks like someone intends to stir up some trouble." He took a sip of his coffee. "They are stockpiling supplies in there. Do you know who it is?"

"I've spent the better part of a fortnight trying to figure that out. Whoever it is, they are organized and practically invisible.

And now you have let yourself be seen there? Do you realize what you've done? What *others* will think?"

"Oh." He set down his cup. "But it's true. We were led there by someone we wished to talk to about this murder we're looking into. I've nothing to do with whatever is going on in there."

"Oh, I'm sure they will all just take my word for it," the viscount said sardonically. "Can you not see how it looks?" He glanced over at Kara, who was still watching, bewildered. "And see how it complicates ... things?"

"Damn it, I do." Niall looked grim now, too. "But perhaps if I explain—"

"Bah! Don't be ridiculous. It's me who will do the explaining. As always!" Stayme tossed down the note and pushed back his chair. "Just ... go. Now. *Think!* I have to think about all of this." He grabbed up a pastry and the post and stalked from the room.

Kara stared at Niall, wide-eyed.

He sighed. "Well, then." Clearing his throat, he stood. "I'm going to pin down Towland at the courts. Ask him about Imogen and about any other scandals he can recall at the time."

She stood as well. "I'm going to go to the Druid's Grove. Lady Madge will be in the music room sometime today. I'll wait for her. And I'll see if she knows anything that could help."

"You brought your carriage?"

She nodded.

"And footmen?"

"Of course."

"Very well. Don't make any stops," he warned. "And keep your eyes open. We still don't know who wrote that threat."

"I'll be careful." She had a thousand more things she wished to say to him, but his face was carefully blank. Closed off.

Well. She should not have kissed him. That much was clear. She'd spooked him again. Perhaps she'd hastened his leave-taking. Their goodbye.

"I'll meet you at the Grove later." He spun around, stopped, and looked back. She thought he might say something, but he pressed his lips together and strode off.

She thrust her chin in the air. She didn't regret it. Couldn't. She needed that measure to carry on with her. A kiss born of feelings, real and true. The standard by which she would judge every other further embrace.

Throwing down her napkin, she followed him out.

A GREAT CLAMOR of booing, hissing, and disparaging remarks sounded beyond Arthur Towland's office.

"And that is the reason I am glad to be sitting magistrate today, and not presiding," Towland said.

"What is it?" asked Niall as he took a seat.

"Old Barrel Belly Belmont got taken up on another drunk and disorderly charge. He's made a thrashing mess of one too many pubs and shops in Marylebone. The locals want him gone. Sent off to the penal colonies or down to the hulks, they don't care which. All that noise is just him being brought out before the court. Just wait until the testimony begins. It'll be all sorts of bother trying to keep order in there, and it will likely bleed over into the rest of the day's cases, too."

"I don't think I realized how rowdy your court could get." Niall had to speak loudly over another round of abuse heaped on poor Mr. Belmont.

"Why do you think I'm always so anxious to keep the Grove a place of peaceful learning and retreat?"

Niall sobered at his words.

Towland noticed. And drew the correct conclusions. "It's come back around, has it then? You are thinking it's one of us?"

"It does look to be a greater possibility now." Niall met his friend's gaze. "As you are part and parcel of Her Majesty's system of justice, I won't hesitate to tell you all that we've found, but I will ask you to keep the details to yourself."

"Of course."

"Even from Imogen Berringer."

Towland's shoulders slumped. "You cannot think it was her?"

"We think it might have been a woman." Niall told the magistrate about the Widow Wilkins and Janet Ott's connection to her.

"Good heavens. I recall the case, but only from the papers, as I hadn't been appointed yet." Towland sat back, staring at the ceiling and trying to piece it all together. "So, you believe one of those girls who disappeared from police custody might be a member of our Druids?" He made a face. "It's certainly a clear motive—covering up a killing you got away with all those years ago. But honestly, Kier, it doesn't make sense that it would be Imogen. She's always mourned the fact that she and her husband never had children. In fact, it was hard on them both. It was one of the first things she told me about her marriage."

"I see."

"We actually did discuss it, you know. The fact that she might be suspected. She was worried at one point, after I had been cleared. All the whispers about her. She heard them. She was afraid the police might lend them credence."

"What did she say about it?"

"Well, you know how interested she is in the Triple Goddesses. Maiden, mother, and crone. She considered the killing from each aspect and wanted me to know her thoughts about it. She said she doubted a maiden would have a reason or the boldness to do it. A mother might, especially if a child were threatened."

"Which, interestingly enough, might turn out to be the inciting incident of this entire mess," Niall said.

"Yes. And I could see it affected her, the thought that she'd never experienced such a powerful connection. Would never experience it. She sadly said that she was closer to the crone than any other aspect and that any woman should fear usurping the judgment and duty of Atropos."

"Interesting. And I am relieved at anything that casts doubt on Imogen." Niall thought a moment. "It certainly could be another member. But there's one more thing." He told the tale of the threat in the post and the paper flower project in the summerhouse.

"Oh, yes. I heard all about that." Towland frowned. "Imogen had all the maids cutting up newspapers for days, though. It could have been any one of them who crafted that warning. Should we, perhaps, take a closer look at the staff?"

"We were considering that the escape from the cell might point more toward a member of the Druids. Someone working as a maid now would have been unlikely to arrange such a thing back then."

"You might be right. That's a significant loss of status. But perhaps the maid was the other girl they found? Another young girl hiding her pregnancy from the world?"

Niall straightened. "Or perhaps an ill-gotten child led to the woman's fall from her place in the *beau monde*?"

"Either could be true. A woman forced to find her own way in the world and she lands a stable, secure job at the Grove. Years later, she recognizes the newest member. Realizes that she was, long ago, the Widow Wilkins's assistant. They might have recognized each other in the crowd during the induction party. Even the servants must have been all abuzz about Janet Ottridge's poem that night and her bold hints at blackmail. Our mystery lady would have had cause to worry."

"It's worth looking into, at the very least." Niall hesitated. "Lady Flora was helping Imogen with that project. You don't think there's a chance that she …"

"Good heavens." Towland looked truly shocked. "I cannot imagine it. Lady Flora is a lovely woman, in a friendly, 'talk for hours about varieties of roses' sort of way, but in all of the years I've known her, I've never seen her even flirt with a gentleman. Not a bat of an eyelash or a second look at a man. I don't think there's ever been a whisper of a suitor for her. Her life revolves around the court and her gardens, both here and at her family's estates."

"No gentlemen, you said. But could there be a possibility of a lower class of man?"

Towland frowned. "She does enjoy a thoroughly obvious friendship with the head gardener at the Grove. It might give me pause, if I did not know her to be just as close with the man's wife."

Niall nodded. "I had to ask. Thank you for your time, Arthur. Miss Levett means to be at the Grove today. She wants to talk to Lady Madge about female members and possible scandals, back at the right time period. I think I will take up your suggestion and head out there to start to look into the staff."

"Tell Imogen I've asked for you to be given full access to her files. I'll come out, too, after the courts wrap up this afternoon."

"Thank you." Niall grinned as another wave of abuse sounded next door. "I'll see you later, then."

Chapter Eighteen

M USIC FILLED THE library, swirled around Kara, and flowed
like magic in her veins. The Bardic Tradition was nothing
short of magnificent. Lyre, lute, harp, and bodhran—they had
taken her description of the song in her head and made it into a
haunting melody, primitive and searching.

She could see it so clearly. Her Valkyrie moving through the
fields of the dead. Quiet, intent, and reverential, seeking the
warriors who would be chosen to rise. But then the music
changed, quickened. It grew more upbeat, with repeated rises in
tempo. She imagined each one was a new man gathered up,
called by the Valkyrie's will.

And then it changed again, a slow rise to a thrilling crescendo,
and she pictured the new host as it was borne off to Valhalla, the
warriors welcomed as heroes with feasting and rivers of mead.

The song ended with a merry, trailing trill, and Kara sat, tears
welling, her hands clasped under her chin, unable to even
applaud, so moved was she.

"Well, lads, I'd say she liked it." Lady Madge's tone was full of
dry humor.

"She loved it!" Kara sprang from her seat and clapped her
hand over her mouth. "I don't know how to thank you," she said
after a moment. "At least, not without crying."

"Go ahead and cry," the gentleman who had played the lute urged. "Music is meant to move us. And this one? This piece is special. Your heart would have to be made of stone not to feel it."

"Thank you for pulling us in to work on it." The musician who had played the bodhran gave her a nod.

"Oh, good heavens, all the thanks must go to all of you!" Kara said. "It was … You were … You've done so much more than I expected. I can *see* her. Feel her. You brought her to life. And now I cannot wait to finish and show you all my Valkyrie."

Lady Madge was smiling softly. "I think we've seen a glimpse of her already. But you have given me an idea. We have several literary-minded Druids about. Imogen is one of them. Why don't we invite her to write a few words about your Valkyrie? Then we can give a combined performance. An unveiling of your sculpture, a reading of poetry, all while we play in the background."

"Oh!" Kara's heart filled. "That sounds so wonderful. Will the others be interested enough to attend, do you think?"

"Of course. This is exactly the sort of thing this group loves. And in any case, they will come if we call. They may joke about the Merry Minstrels, but none of them wants to get on our bad side. Those who do tend to find we've come up with a catchy little tune, the sort that plays again in your mind, with less-than-flattering lyrics pointing their way."

Kara laughed. She sat enthralled as the group played the song again, stopping in places to ask her opinion or to discuss composition among themselves. They all stayed a while after they finished, talking of music, history, and performances past.

It thrilled Kara down to her soul to be included in such a collaboration. She hated to see it end, but gradually instruments were packed away and the other musicians drifted from the music library, until only she and Lady Madge were left.

Heaving a sigh, Kara forced herself to drift down from lofty artistic heights and face the other reason she had come.

Almost as if she'd seen the transition, Lady Madge eyed her. "Something else going on in that pretty little head of yours, girl?"

Kara blushed a little. "Yes. I did have something else I wished to discuss with you. If you won't mind."

The older woman eyed her closely. "Very well. But it's unseasonably warm out there today. Put on a wrap and let's go sit in the garden while we discuss whatever it is that's making you flush."

Kara adjusted to Lady Madge's slower pace and carried her lyre for her. They headed to the same spot under the spreading oak they had sat beneath once before, during the initiation party. "They keep this chair out here for my use," the older woman explained. "It fits my old bones just right, and it's shaped well enough that I can sit and play here, too."

"It's a lovely spot." The sun shone warm. Enough leaves were gone from the oak that Kara could lift her face to feel it. The air was still and lovely, full of the sound of the stream not far before them, and the scratching of a squirrel in the leaves on the ground. Beyond the stream lay the flagstone circle where she'd been initiated. Past it, the ground sloped slightly up to the start of the terraced boxes. A swath of ground had been dug up before the first terrace. It lay bare, awaiting some fall planting. "Lovely," she sighed.

"Yes, yes. Now, why don't you tell me what is agitating in that brainbox of yours?"

"I almost hate to ask. It feels like gossip."

Lady Madge snorted. "Then it likely is."

"Honestly, it definitely is. Old gossip, specifically."

"Old gossip? You've set my own brainbox to rattling, young lady. If you are still chasing after Janet Ottridge's killer, then you must think it happened because of an old grudge?"

"Perhaps. Or perhaps because of an old crime."

"Ah." The older woman's gaze sharpened. "What is it you wish to know?"

"We had wondered if you know of any scandal or secrets that might have occurred among the Druidic Bards. It would have been not so long after the split from the main branch and the establishment of the Grove." Kara explained the relevant time period without mentioning the Widow Wilkins's killing.

"That far back?" Lady Madge seemed surprised. "Hmm. Let me think." She laughed suddenly. "I believe *I* was likely the biggest scandal of that year. My second husband had died, and I did not wait the expected time of mourning before taking up with an Italian artist. Ah, such long, dark hair and eyes like burning coals." She sighed. "Not a very skilled artist, it turned out. For a portraitist, he had a great deal of difficulty depicting hands. But the skills of his own hands more than made up for that small deficiency."

Kara's eyes widened at the older woman's smile of remembrance.

"I might have got away with it, had I not gone about looking like the cat that got into the cream, but it had been so very long since I'd been played so well, it showed clear on my face." Kara choked back a laugh, and Lady Madge grinned. "Well, and there's a blush like I haven't seen in a while. So refreshing, to be around young people again."

"Can you recall any other bits of gossip that made the rounds back then? Other than your own, please."

"But focused among our members?"

"Yes."

Although her gaze had fixed upon a gardener carrying a large shrub out to the prepared soil, Lady Madge had clearly turned inward, toward her memories.

"Well, I seem to recall that Mr. Lloyd Humphries spent that summer in debtor's prison." She brightened. "Oh, and Sam Clausen made a fool of himself, claiming to have discovered a new comet. He submitted the paperwork, but didn't wait for the confirmation before he announced it everywhere, even in the papers. He named it after himself. But it turned out his math was wrong. Or was it that his telescope was smudged? Both, likely, knowing Sam. He took quite a ribbing over it all. Still hear a tease or two about it, occasionally."

"Oh my." Kara couldn't help but chuckle. Then she couldn't help but stiffen as Niall strode out of the summerhouse. He was far enough away that he moved quickly past their spot, without glancing their way or seeming to notice them. He crossed the stream, stepping lightly on the rocks, and paused in the flagstone circle to remove his coat. Throwing it over his arm, he stretched mightily. His hair looked disheveled, as if he'd been thrusting his hands through it. She warmed, thinking of how just last night she'd run her own fingers through those soft, thick locks.

"Now, that's the sort of blush I like to see on a young maid's cheek," Lady Madge said. "Why don't you leave off chasing nasty killers and set out after that strapping young man, instead?" She eyed him with an appreciative gleam in her eye. "Those shoulders. Comes from all that forge work, I suppose." She glanced askance at Kara. "Were I a bit younger, I'd give you a run for your money, girl."

"You'd have to run fast. Unfortunately, the strapping young man is skittish. He's making plans to leave London soon."

"Ah. Showed your hand and he's running like a fox with the hounds at his heels? That's too bad." The older woman shook her head. "It's hard advice to take, but you should let him go, dearie."

"I am trying," Kara said quietly, her hand clutched over her heart. "It seems to involve several steps, this process. And they are all horrible. But I know I have to let him go."

"I'm glad you understand. Take the word of a woman who has been in and witnessed countless relationships, both successful and supremely *not*. Letting him go is the only chance you have. If he comes back, he will be yours." Lady Madge raised her brows as Niall set off again, over the lawn, heading for the spot where a passage between two terraces led to the back end of the gardens. "If he doesn't come back, he's a fool." She patted Kara's hand. "But I don't think he's a fool."

"Thank you," Kara whispered.

"Not at all. Now," Lady Madge said briskly. "None of those scandals I've dredged up seem to be what you are looking for, are they?"

"Well, we had thought there might be something more ... salacious?"

"More salacious than my affair with a sloe-eyed Italian painter?" Lady Madge sounded surprised.

"Love affairs certainly would be of interest. As would be the ... unexpected consequences of such a relationship."

"Illicit loves and secret babes? Come now, girl. This isn't cheap theater. Why don't you stop beating around the bush and tell me what it is you are looking for? Or should I say, *whom* you are looking for?

Kara drew a breath. "Mrs. Berringer?"

Lady Madge reared back. "Didn't I tell you not to listen to spiteful gossip? Imogen did not kill that girl."

"I don't believe so either, but there is a reason I must ask. What do you recall of her?"

"From so far back? Not much. She was not a member here yet." She frowned. "She was out in Society at the time. I remember her as a happy, young, newly married girl. Bright-eyed. Sunny. Nothing salacious there."

Kara's mouth twisted as she thought about it. Could they have been wrong about the woman or women from the Widow Wilkins case being a Druidic Bard? "What about the staff?" she said. "Any scandals there?"

"I don't believe I would know. Imogen might. But staff that has been employed here since so far back? I doubt there are any, save for the cook. The only scandal that revolved around him was when someone at Brooks tried to hire him away. We had to double his salary."

Kara let out a huff of frustration, but was distracted by a call from nearby. After a moment, it came again.

"Martin? Do you have those trees ready? And the heathers?"

Searching, Kara realized she'd missed a figure kneeling and working in the upturned soil by the terraces. "Oh, is that Lady Flora working there? Her gown blended in so well, I hadn't noticed her."

Lady Madge peered across the stream. "I would imagine so. She's always mucking about in the gardens here, just as I muck about in the music library." She waved a hand. "We owe all of this to her, you know. It's been her pet project, and she's a dab hand at it."

Kara sat back. "Yes, I suppose it is a grand day for fall planting."

"Coming, my lady!" An answering call sounded as a gardener emerged from the passage Niall had taken. The gardener was carrying a small tree, and behind him emerged Niall carrying another.

"Is that why Mr. Kier went out toward the tool sheds? Have you set him to questioning the gardener while you wriggle old gossip out of me?" Lady Madge asked lightly.

"I don't know what Niall is up to." A thought crossed Kara's mind. "Has the gardener, perhaps, been here since the start of the club?"

The older woman frowned. "No. Actually, he got the job when Lady Flora was initiated. These were all just weedy meadows and hills back then. She took on the gardens as her special project and recommended Martin for the job, as she'd worked with him at one of her family's estates."

Kara blinked.

"Oh no! All of these salacious rumors have muddled your head. Don't let your mind wander there. The man took the job and brought his wife with him. They live in a cottage at the back of the property. Lady Flora is very friendly with them both." Lady Madge snorted. "To suspect Lady Flora? You would be grasping at straws there. There's never been a whisper of scandal attached to her name. She's highly placed at court and valued as a trusted friend by the queen."

"But she's never married? It's unusual, isn't it? Her family must have wished for her to marry, if only for dynastic or financial purposes."

"That is the way of it, as I'm sure you know. But Lady Flora is one of those ... different people. Touched, my mother would have called her. Not quite of this world."

Kara frowned. "I've found her quite lovely. I hadn't noticed anything odd."

"Not *odd*, not in that way. It's just that the woman knows everything there is to know about practically every green, living thing, but she has no real interest in the practical, pragmatic realities of life. She moves between the rarified bubble of the court to the bubble of her own making, her gardens. And back again without touching the sordid bits the rest of us have to deal with."

"And she's never had any suitors at all?"

"Not that I know of, nor would she know what to do with them, I should think. Now, if she could find a gentleman interested in ornamental shrubs ..." Lady Madge stopped, tapping her fingers along the crossbar of her lyre. "No. Wait a moment. There was talk of a match, long ago. I recall it now. Before she came to the Druids. He was a German count from one of those small German duchies. He was part of the Duke of Saxe-Coburg and Gotha's entourage, and accompanied the duke here several times when he came to visit his brother, Prince Albert. There was talk of an engagement."

"What happened?" asked Kara.

"I don't know. Nothing much, I suppose. Lady Flora went on a tour of the Continent, I recall. There was talk that she might come back engaged, or even stay abroad as a married woman. But none of it happened. She came home, still single, and went on with her life. She joined us Druids not long after her return. And she's been here, working on all of this, ever since."

Kara's mind was racing. Lady Flora had a *tendre* for a gentleman at court. She'd disappeared to "travel abroad," but came back, still alone. She soon after became a member of the Druids, and she brought the gardener and his wife with her ...

"Lady Madge, when the gardener and his wife moved into

their cottage on the grounds, did they have any children?"

The older woman brightened. "They did, indeed. A brand new little lad. Just a babe. I cannot recall his name, but he grew up here. We'd see him running about when he was small. Towland never minded, not as long as he was kept away from the ceremonies. But as the boy grew older, he began to help his father with his work. He's a young man now. Apprenticed with a landscape architect. I remember Flora speaking of it. Likely, she arranged it." She paused. Her gaze went out to where Lady Flora knelt over the soil. "You are not thinking what I think you are?"

Another shout rang out at that moment. "Mary? Are you still up there?"

It was Lady Flora, but this time she was on her knees and directed her call upward.

Kara saw a head pop up over the foliage in the terrace above the spot where the others had gathered. Was it Lady Flora's maid up there?

Niall had placed his root-bagged tree where the gardener had indicated and been squatting next to Lady Flora, peering at the soil she was turning over. He looked up in surprise when the maid answered her mistress's shout.

The maid's reply was too low for Kara to hear. Lady Flora beckoned, then turned back to speak to Niall.

"It's absurd," Lady Madge declared, looking horrified. "I cannot believe what you are thinking. Not for a moment."

"Mary!" They both turned to watch as Lady Flora called again, impatient and louder. "Bring that bucket down at once!" She spoke again to Niall, too low to hear.

The maid's head popped up again. She said something equally low. Lady Flora's reply sounded insistent.

Mary dared to hesitate a bit longer, then she turned and moved toward the stairs that met the lawn down by the beginning of the long, overturned strip of soil. Her movements were half hidden by the foliage, but she reached the stairs and made her careful way down, carrying what looked to be a heavy bucket.

Kara held her breath as Mary stepped out across the lawn, moving with a deliberate, limping gait.

Niall watched too. He stood. And then he turned to look directly at Kara.

"Stay here," she said urgently to Lady Madge. "Don't move. Don't draw any attention to yourself."

She took off at an angle, eyeing the uneven terraces and their random entrances and stairways, mentally plotting her route.

Chapter Nineteen

NIALL'S SEARCH THIS morning amongst the maids' files had turned up nothing at all. None of them had been with the Druids for more than five years. Hell, none of them were even old enough to have been a participant in the saga of the Widow Wilkins's murder.

Imogen informed him that the two longest-serving members of the staff were the chef and the gardener. He started with the chef, who sat him down in his office, fed him golden pastries filled with berries and French cheese, and denied any knowledge of scandal, either among the Druids or the staff.

"There is no gossip allowed in my kitchen," he declared. "If their tongues are wagging, then their fingers are not working."

Niall decided to give it a try with the gardener. He or his laborers must surely have borne witness to more than a few scandalous embraces in the bushes. But he fell flat there, as well. The man insisted he and his staff kept their noses down and out of anyone's business. He turned the soil, cared for the gardens, and followed Lady Flora's orders.

"It's like I tell my son, sir. Care for those who care for you."

Niall had to respect his loyalty. He gave the man a hand, carrying a pear tree out to where they were being placed in a new bed. He found Lady Flora there, her hands in the soil.

"Good morning to you! I'm amending the soil. I've found it markedly increases the success of new plantings." She told him at length of her own formula, developed through trial and error. "It smells to high heaven, but it works wonders."

She called for her maid to bring down the bucket she'd taken to the terrace above them. "The roses up there do better with a good dose to help them survive the winter."

Her maid was slow to respond, and then reluctant, and then resistant. Lady Flora looked shocked, then became insistent. "I don't know what's got into Mary lately."

Curious, Niall watched the servant come down the stairs, careful with the noxious bucket. And then she reached the lawn and her chin went up as she came haltingly toward them.

Sudden, abrupt signal fires flared to life in his head. Facts and theories and utterances all intertwined to form one thread that snapped tight, suddenly whole.

And he knew.

He slid his gaze down to Lady Flora, who had sunk back down to her knees and returned to loosening the soil. "Your maid, Mary. Has she been with you long?"

"Oh, yes," Flora replied absently. "Ever so long. Since I was a girl, ready to make my debut and be presented at court." She sat back on her heels. "Mary's so much of the warp and weft of my life, I scarcely know what I'd do without her. But she has been acting so odd lately."

"Odd?"

"Just … off. She will scarcely let me out of her sight. She starts at every shadow." Lady Flora shook her head. "She stopped following me out here to the gardens years ago. Oh, she'll come to the occasional ceremony, when I am more likely to need her, but now she comes every time I set foot in the Grove." She looked over to see the woman had made it about halfway across from the stairs. "And I have no idea what's wrong with her this afternoon. Perhaps her leg pains her. Or she's had too much sun?"

But Niall thought he knew what was amiss, and Kara had

been closer to the truth than any of them. He looked to meet her gaze where she sat with Lady Madge. Where he had pretended not to see them earlier, so that she could ask the questions that might help them find the killer.

But the killer had paused not far from him. If he was correct.

Mary followed his gaze and saw Kara, and judging by her expression, she put a few puzzle pieces together herself. Abruptly, she tossed the contents of the bucket at him and turned to flee.

She was too far away for the mess to reach him, but the smell hit him like a wall as he took off after her.

"Mary!" Lady Flora gasped after them. "Whatever has got into you?"

The maid moved faster than he expected, but she had no hope of outrunning him. Still, she made it to the stairs, and as he drew near, she whirled about, brandishing a sharp, shining pruning knife with a hellish curve at the end.

"Stay back!" she ordered him from several steps up.

"Mary. Stop now. There's no need to run. Let's just discuss everything that's happened."

"No, thank you. I know what's what. I know you are working for the police. Both of you. Why couldn't you just leave it alone? That wicked hag deserved to die. Nobody mourned her."

"That's not true. Janet Ott did have friends who mourn her."

"I don't care. You don't understand! You don't know what she did!"

"I think I do know. She worked for the Widow Wilkins. She watched you." He looked back to where Lady Flora stood, pale, wringing her hands. Martin, the gardener, had gripped her shoulders to keep her still. "The pair of you. She reported on you both to the widow, didn't she?"

"How?" Mary's mouth worked. "How could you know?"

"We traced it back. All the way back to Bermondsey."

A great shudder ran down Mary's form. "That place. How I hated it. Close and ugly. And the smell." She made a face and pointed with her chin. "Worse than that mess. The stink from the tanneries, the sharp wafts from the leather markets—it all mixed with rank food smells from the factory where they were tinning meat."

"Your mistress was sent there by her family, wasn't she? Because she was with child?" Niall spoke quietly, hoping to spare Lady Flora from reliving the nightmare.

"Yes." Mary glanced at her mistress and kept her voice quiet as well. "Though it wasn't any fault of her own, so don't go thinking that of her!"

"What happened?" he asked gently.

"It was that vile German cockscomb," she spat. "A friend of the prince's brother. All she did was flirt with him a little. Just for practice. But he took it for permission to go too far. She told him no. Told him to leave her alone. But he came back, again and again. Finally, he caught her alone and he attacked her. He forced her. He *hurt* her." The last part came out with a sob.

"I'm so sorry."

"I took care of her. Bathed her. Let her cry and cry. I put liniment on all her bruises and I tucked her up and kept everyone away, told them she was ill. It was hard enough to get through, but then she turned up with child. We tried to hide it, but she was found out."

"Her family sent her the Widow Wilkins, then, didn't they? They sent you both."

"She needed me. They sent us out to that house on the other side of the river. I had to fetch the food, do the marketing and all the errands. She couldn't be seen outside. Not so much as a glimpse. She was supposed to be off on the Continent."

"You protected her then, just as you meant to protect her from Janet Ott, didn't you?"

"She needs protection. She doesn't understand how ugly life can be."

Niall took a step closer. Mary backed up a step. "Lady Flora must have understood some of the difficulties of life, though. Assaulted, raped, hidden away. And then, somehow, the pair of you must have realized what the Widow Wilkins meant to do with the child. How did you find out?"

Mary's face twisted into a snarl. "The widow let it slip herself. She came right after the birth. Oh, but she was three seas over. Staggering. Smelling of gin. She praised my lady for being so strong, for giving birth to a fine, thriving boy, but she forgot to wait until she was out of earshot before she told Janet to give the babe a good dose of laudanum. *The brats bleed out so much quieter, that way.* That's what she said."

"Odin's arse," he whispered. "You both heard her?"

"We did. We stared at each other, scarcely believing such a horror."

"Who killed the widow, Mary? You? Or your lady?"

"My lady rose out of the bed. She snatched that babe right out of Janet Ott's arms and thrust him into mine. Then she took up the midwife's scissors, broke them apart into two, and went after Widow Wilkins." She choked back a sob. "That evil woman didn't go down easy. They fought—and my lady just risen from childbed! But she had the strength of the furies. It was something awful—the babe screaming and everything breaking and flying about. My lady stuck her with the shears, but they didn't go in very far. It enraged the widow something awful, though. She looked down at 'em sticking out of her, and she growled like a dog. She rushed Lady Flora, but I grabbed her out of the way. I stuck my foot out and tripped the widow. She went down, and the scissors went all the way in."

Mary fell silent. Niall looked over to see Lady Flora sobbing into her hands. "The police came, didn't they?" he asked Mary. "You were all taken to gaol, except for the midwife. How did you get out that night?"

"Lady Flora's brother did it. I don't know how he knew. Mayhap the widow sent word about the babe. Mayhap the family had a watch on the house. But he came. I found out later, he paid one of the watchmen to drug us all. They must have carried us out, dead asleep. We woke up the next day in her father's hunting box in Somerset." She looked suddenly to her crying mistress, and her gaze sharpened. The knife in her hand rose. "It wasn't her fault. None of it was her fault. You cannot let them hurt her."

"There is not a jury in England that would convict a mother for saving her newborn infant from a murderous baby farmer," he assured her.

Her shoulders slumped. "Thank God. Thank God."

Niall stepped closer again. "What about Janet Ott?" he asked gently. "Did Lady Flora know about her?"

Mary's head snapped up. Her fist tightened on the knife, and she thrust it forward. "No! She didn't know anything about it! She didn't meet her that night, and that's all you need to know."

"I can help you, Mary. Tell me what happened and I can speak up for you."

"Will you?"

"I promise it."

"Swear it," she insisted.

"I swear it." He saw her indecision and prompted her, "You were here that night. You saw Janet?"

Her eyes closed. Her head tilted back. She nodded. "My lady saw the woman from a distance and kept trying to place her. But I knew. I knew her right off. I will never forget the way she moved into that house, when my lady's time drew near. We didn't know if she was another girl in the family way or someone sent by the widow. Not until she tried to act all friendly. A million questions, she had. She was pumping us for information to send on to the widow. About my lady's family. About the court. She reported it all, every move my lady made, every bite she ate. I found her once, adding up all the cost of the food we ate. I had to plead with my lady to stop answering all her questions." Her tone turned fierce. "When I thought about it later, I figured she had to know what the widow was doing to all of those babes. I wished then I had killed her with the other half of the scissors."

"And then you recognized her here, in the garden, that night."

"I almost turned up my toes from the shock of it. Seeing that hard, spiteful face again. And that poem! She was announcing her intentions right out loud! I knew we had to go, and fast. But she saw me. And she knew me. I got away from her, though, before she could speak."

"But you came back that night, for the poisonous bits of the plants."

"Yes. I knew I had to get rid of her before she ruined Lady Flora. My lady saved her boy. I would do my part and save her."

"Did you?" Niall asked. "Did you poison her drink that day at the Crystal Palace?"

She hesitated. But then she looked over at Lady Flora once more before she drew a deep breath and nodded. "Yes. At first, I was frantic, trying to figure out how I could get here without my lady, so I could slip it into her drink. But then I heard there was to be a party at the closing ceremonies, and that woman meant to be there. I thought it was perfect. A crowd like that? No one looks, and if they do, they aren't sure of what they saw. Perfect. And so easy. All I did was tell her the drink wasn't meant for her, but for my lady and her nerves. She snatched it and drank it right down, laughing. She practically did it to herself."

As if the words snapped her back to her perilous situation, she took a step further up the stairs. "You stay back, sir. Do you hear? I won't hang for her death. Not when it was so deserved."

"No, Mary. You've done the right thing, explaining yourself. I will try all I can to help you. I promised. I meant it."

"You won't," she whispered. "No one has ever helped Mary Freane, except for my lady. She'll go free, that what's you said. That's what's important." She turned a pleading look on him. "Let me go, sir! I'll disappear. You can tell the whole story. I'll just … go. I won't ever hurt anyone ever again. There's no need of it."

"I cannot, Mary," he said softly. "I'm sorry."

"You must!"

"I cannot."

She backed up another step. Just one step from the top now, she raised her head and looked around the nearly empty garden. His gaze followed hers. Kara had disappeared. Lady Madge sat frozen in her chair. Lady Flora had turned and was crying into the gardener's shirt.

"Looks like your lady has gone for help. I have to hurry." Mary took another step higher. "I'm sorry, sir. I've seen a hanging. I won't go through it. Not for ridding the world of such venom. And forgive me, but even lame as I am, you are the only one who can keep me from getting away."

"Mary, don't be—"

Hoisting the knife high, she launched herself down and toward him.

He widened his stance and braced himself, his gaze focused on the knife in her hand.

From the side, higher even than Mary, came a blur of motion. Suddenly Kara was there, crashing into Mary in midair. She hit her hard enough to shift her trajectory, but they still clipped his side.

They all went down in a tangle of limbs.

Niall landed on his back with both women sprawled on top of him. The breath whooshed out of him even as the pair of them erupted into a flurry of blows and shrieks.

He wheezed and grabbed Kara, rolling her to the side to get her out of Mary Freane's reach.

Cursing, Mary was scrambling to get away. She got to her knees and fought to get herself to her feet as Niall struggled to pull air into his lungs.

Then she was up, and Niall rolled over and reached out, grabbing her ankle and sending her back down. Still gasping, he subdued her the only way he could—by crawling over to lie across her.

Still fighting for air, he lifted his head to grin at Kara.

The grin quickly faded.

Kara was stretched out on her back. The pruning knife was

buried in her shoulder. Blood was spreading rapidly across the bodice of her gown. She reached a hand toward him, but it fell, limp, as her eyes closed—and his heart dropped right out of him.

Chapter Twenty

S HE WAS SWIMMING, swimming, swimming.
No. Her limbs were not moving. Floating, then, on a sea of warm, lapping water. She'd never felt so free. Unattached. So utterly peaceful. Stretched out, arms and legs akimbo, she rocked in the embrace of the water. So calm.

A touch startled her. She swore she could smell her mother's scent. Feel the caress of a soft hand across her cheek. Hear a faint echo of the lullaby her mother had sung softly over her, so long ago. She drifted into it and off to sleep.

When she awoke, she found she had washed up onto a beach. Her face was pressed into the small, worn rocks of the shore, so she turned over onto her back and luxuriated in the warmth of the sun. It felt right, after the water, to absorb the light head to toe. With a sigh, she basked and closed her eyes again, content.

After a while, though, she realized it was too much. She was too hot. A ray of sun had pierced her shoulder. It was on fire. She began to thrash. Why couldn't she rise? What was wrong with her?

A blessedly cool shadow fell over her. Her father. She stopped fighting and smiled up at him. His gaze was full of love, and she just wanted to drink it in. He pressed a cup against her lips. "Drink, child," he whispered.

She had a sudden, horrified recollection of a drink with berries and leaves in it and turned her head away. But he kissed her brow and urged her again, and she obeyed him, because she always had.

It tasted terrible.

"All of it, now," he whispered. "It will help."

"I love you, Papa," she whispered.

"And I you, my sweet." His smile was full of pride and love, and his touch on her brow was wonderfully cool. It spread all the way down her body. The pain eased away.

"Sleep now. You must gather your strength. You have trials ahead of you."

She nodded and slept once again.

WAKE UP.

Kara came awake with a gasp. Her eyes snapped open. "Niall?" Frantic, she looked around. Where was she? "Niall?" Had that been his voice? Panic sent her heart into a gallop.

"Kara? You're awake. Finally."

She relaxed a little as Gyda stood up from a chair at her bedside. The relief in her voice was clear. Still, Kara cast about until she realized she did know the place. The woodland chamber at the White Hart. She had stayed here once before, earlier in the year.

"Niall?" she asked again. "Where is he? Is he all right?"

"Yes, yes. He's fine. He's downstairs, pacing and wearing a track in the taproom floor, worrying and waiting for you to wake up."

"Oh, good." She frowned. "Why am I here?"

"It was closer than Bluefield. You needed a doctor, and quickly. Niall insisted we come here, also partly because he knew there were plenty of us to keep watch over you."

The door opened and a slight figure entered, carrying a tray.

"Jenny," Kara said with pleasure.

The head chambermaid broke into a large grin. "Ah, miss! You're awake!"

Kara started to sit up, but fell back with a gasp as pain exploded, stabbing her in the shoulder and down through her chest and left arm. She clutched it with her right hand and only then realized her left arm was bound to her chest tightly enough to immobilize it.

She looked at Gyda, not understanding, but then the memory hit her. "Oh! The knife! She got me with it?" Her eyes widened at Gyda's solemn face. "How bad is it?"

"It's serious," Gyda said softly. "You bled quite a lot. The doctor says that you are not to move your shoulder or disturb the wound at all for some time. If you wish any hope of healing, that is."

Jenny set the tray down and came closer. "You were feverish, miss, and thrashing something awful. The doctor dosed you with laudanum to keep you still and quiet, and we bound your arm and shoulder to keep it as still as we might."

"It will likely come to drive you to distraction, but you'll have to keep it bound for a bit, I think," Gyda said apologetically.

"Now that you are awake, you must drink a full cup of my sister's special tea," Jenny said. "It will help with the fever and the pain. And she's sent over her best tinctures and potions to help you heal."

"Tell Ellie I send my thanks," Kara told her. "And could you please help me to sit up? I'll hold still, but I would feel better upright, I think."

They did better, carefully getting her into a fresh night shift and standing her up while they changed her sweat-damp linens.

"There now." Jenny handed her a mug when she was tucked back in with pillows at her back. "Drink all of this, and I'll go down and tell them all that you are awake. Don't go to sleep," she warned. "They'll all be up to check on you. Mr. Kier will be here in a second flat, once he hears."

Kara nodded, but despite her best efforts, she was asleep before Jenny left the room. She had no idea how long she slept, but when she woke, Niall sat in the chair, bent at the waist, half draped onto the bed and asleep. As soon as she shifted to ease her shoulder, he sat up.

She grabbed his hand as he started to move away. "You're all right?"

"I'm fine. You are the one who leapt from nowhere and let a killer stick you with a pruning knife." He clutched her hand back. "You were on the terrace above?"

"Yes. I crept up to a higher level and then down on the other side of the one above you. I went as quietly as I could. I heard her ask you to let her go."

"You scared the life out of me. I'm so glad you are on the mend."

"They said I would heal, if I am careful?" She watched him anxiously, knowing he would tell her the truth.

He nodded. "You must do as the doctor says, but there is a good chance you won't face lasting complications if you do."

Relief rushed through her. "Thank you." Eyeing him closely, she asked, "But it's true? Mary did it, then? When I saw her start to walk across the lawn with that halting gait ..."

"I know. You were right all along."

"She confessed?"

"She did. She killed Janet Ott to protect Lady Flora. To keep Janet from blackmailing her. Mary didn't trust Janet not to tell the story, in any case, and she wouldn't risk her mistress's life being ruined."

"They were the two girls, then? The two who disappeared from the cell?"

"They were. Lady Flora's family arranged the escape." He sighed. "It was Flora who killed the widow. Widow Wilkins arrived right after the birth, apparently drunk enough to let slip what she meant to do with the boy."

"Flora couldn't allow her to leave with the babe once she knew. Any woman would have done the same."

"Others have agreed."

"Why? What's happened?" she asked.

"The coroner convened his jury, and they committed Mary for trial. She's being held at Newgate in the meanwhile. I intervened and got her moved out of the dungeons and into the state area, at least."

"And Lady Flora?"

"Her family has tried to send her to a far-flung estate, but she refuses to leave Mary. She's visited her twice already."

"What about her crime? Will anything happen to her?"

"Nothing. They convened a special meeting about it all. Quite an illustrious gathering. Towland went to tell the story. At the table were one of the police commissioners, a privy counsellor, a judge from Old Bailey, and a representative from the Foreign Office. Someone from Lady Flora's family attended, as well. Together, they all decided that she will not be charged with the crime."

"I'm glad for her, but still, I worry. The whole sorry tale will come out at Mary's trial."

"Yes. There's naught to be done about it, though."

Kara sighed and shifted again. "It will cause an uproar. A great scandal. Her life will never be the same. We can only hope the boy will escape all the attention."

"The boy?"

She explained about the gardener's boy.

"So, she got to see him grow and be a part of his life after all." Niall sounded impressed.

"She provided all she could. Shelter, love, and conditions to thrive," Kara answered, recalling Lady Flora's words that fateful night in the gardens. "As any mother would."

They sat quietly for a few moments, with her hand still nestled between his. The warmth of it spread over her. Her eyelids dropped.

She shot awake when the chair creaked and he withdrew his hand.

"Don't go," she whispered.

"You need your rest."

"Niall." She reached for him again. "Don't leave. Not without saying goodbye."

He knew what she meant. He ducked his head. "There are things I must tell you. I have made mistakes. There is one in particular I must fix, before ..."

"Before." Hope and despair swirled around each other, forming a funnel cloud in her heart. She nodded. "But please, come and say farewell first?"

"I promise. I will be back. But you rest now."

He slipped away, and she lay there alone, shedding a few tears for all of them before finally drifting off to sleep once more.

※》》《《※

THE NEXT MORNING, Kara awoke to find Turner cleaning the room as if each speck of dust was a personal affront. He rushed over when he saw her awake and pressed her hand tightly—a rare show of emotion from her oldest friend.

"I'm fine," she assured him. "But I am so glad you are here."

"I've brought your nightwear and robe, the post, and a selection of your favorite pastries from Cook." He leaned down. "And she's sent a fig and apple tart along for Mr. Kier."

"Bless you both. But will you send Jenny in first? I think I need to get ready for the day ahead."

Jenny, bless her, came in like a whirlwind, bringing the doctor with her. Kara endured a dressing change, and the doctor approved the idea of the binding, although he adjusted the angle of her arm, which greatly improved her comfort. Afterward, Jenny was free to focus all of her energy on Kara, as the room was already spotless.

"You'll feel a hundred times better if we get you bathed, even if it is just at the side of the bed." She carefully washed Kara's hair, brushed it until it shone, and gave her loose coiffure a few finishing touches with the heated tongs.

"You'll want to look your best. You have a distinguished visitor coming today. A police inspector, no less!"

"Good," Kara said. "Then I should like to meet him in the armchair, rather than the bed."

She was ready when Wooten arrived. He brought her a great bouquet and offered several compliments on her fine reasoning and interview skills.

"Thank you. I hope you also complimented Niall for his good works," she teased.

"And so I will, don't worry. I hope to speak to him when he returns."

She stilled. "Returns?"

He nodded.

"Where has he gone?" She fought to keep the shrill note out of her tone.

Wooten sobered. "No one has told you?"

"Told me what?" She clutched the sides of the chair.

"It's Mary Freane. She was found dead in her cell last evening."

Shock coursed through her. "What? How? I thought she'd been removed from the crowded cells?"

"So she had been." Wooten turned his gaze onto his hands. "Her death looked remarkably similar to Janet Ott's."

She covered her mouth.

"Mr. Kier said she told him several times that she feared a sentence of hanging."

"Lady Flora has been visiting her," Kara said flatly. "Do you think Mary asked her to spare her a hanging? Or did Lady Flora wish to be spared the scandal that would have come with a trial?"

"I think both reasons would have been important to Mary Freane. And I think they reached the decision together, as they did so many things." He sighed. "But Lady Flora's family has banished her to the wilds, and they refused to allow Mary to be interned in the village near their main estate. Mr. Towland arranged for her to be laid to rest in Shoreditch, but they thought it best done quickly. He and Niall are attending the burial today."

Setting aside his cup of tea, Wooten looked at her directly. "Now, I've one last thing to tell you."

"This sounds like the start of a lecture."

"You might call it that. Perhaps it will sound contradictory, especially as I've just gone and told you what fine work you did on this case. That is absolutely true. But, my dear, that is enough."

"Enough?" Honestly, it did feel like he was intruding past usual boundaries.

His expression held earnest. "I find you a remarkable young woman. I am proud to know you. But you have had a whirlwind of a year, ever since the start of the Exhibition in May. Nonstop work, excitement, *two* murders involving either yourself or someone close to you. You've been going at a full run, reacting with emotion, pivoting on too many turns, leaps, and decisions. Now, things will have to change." He gestured toward her shoulder. "You will be forced to slow down. I urge you to take advantage of it."

"How?"

"Stop and think. Reflect. Use this time to decide what is important. How do you wish to spend the gift of your one life? Who shall you spend it with? Just … relax. Think. Dream. And when you are healed, move forward with intention."

Abruptly, her eyes filled. "That is actually kind and good advice, sir. It does sound like something my father might have said to me."

"I was honored to meet your father once. I am even more honored to know his daughter."

"Thank you. For everything. I will think on all that you have said."

"That is all I could ask." He stood and bent to place a kiss on her hand. "Good day to you, Miss Levett. I sincerely wish you well."

Kara spent a few moments alone with her tears and her handkerchief. Was she going to cry after every visitor? Once she'd recovered, she rang for Turner.

It wasn't her butler who entered, but Lord Stayme.

She gaped at him as he ran a sharp gaze over her. Once again, she was glad she'd allowed Jenny to take the time to make her presentable and drape her into her finely embroidered robe.

"Oh, my dear. I do admire a woman who doesn't allow a little thing like a bullet to keep her from her toilette."

"It was a knife, sir, but I thank you for the compliment."

"You deserve many more, or so I am told. I congratulate you on the resolution of your murder case. It is all neatly tied up now, is it not?"

"It's a tragedy, not something to celebrate."

"Two tragedies, or so I hear."

Her surprise must have shown.

"Oh, don't worry. It's not common knowledge."

"Nothing about your knowledge is common, is it, sir?"

"Not at all." He sat back. "But that is why you came to me with your problem, isn't it?" He sighed. "Unfortunately, I do not have answers for you. Only sad tidings."

She raised a brow.

He dropped the flippant attitude and grew serious. "Niall is in danger. From more than one direction. His safekeeping is in my hands, and I feel he must go away. Disappear. For his own good. You must not stop him, my dear."

"He told me he had made mistakes, and one in particular. I'm assuming that mistake has strawberry-blonde hair and a sharp nose."

"You are perceptive. Yes, that particular mistake has come back to haunt him. Unfortunately, even I underestimated her sly nature and her extreme willingness to do whatever it takes to get what she wants."

"Shocking," she said wryly.

"It is, actually. If only you knew." He sat up straighter. "In any case, there's been another killing, and by no account can either you or Niall get involved. I've made arrangements for him to get out of London. He must go. I know you care for him, but it is imperative you let him."

"Yes," she said quietly. "Everyone does seem to keep telling me that."

"Good. You are an intelligent girl. I know I can trust you to do the right thing. Let me handle this. Let me get him through it alive. And then the pair of you can … revisit your feelings."

"Thank you for informing me of the situation, my lord. Of course I wish you to succeed." She hesitated. "Perhaps you will keep me informed?"

He stood and bowed low. "I will try, Miss Levett. I hope you heal quickly, but for now, I must go."

Kara rang again as soon as he left. She was shaking with fatigue as she got settled back into bed, but she didn't sleep. She sat, staring out the window, lost in thought, while the daylight faded and darkness moved in.

She sat there still, knees drawn up, long after midnight struck and her door swung silently open.

"You're still awake," Niall said quietly.

"I didn't want to miss you."

He stared, his countenance more open, vulnerable, and full of conflicting emotion than she'd ever seen it.

She reached out. "Will you help me up? I think I need to be out of the bed for this conversation."

He got her settled on the settee, then pulled a chair over. He started to sit, but then cursed and pushed the chair away. He perched next to her, his hip pressing into the curve of her waist, their bodies touching and their faces close.

"You are going away." She reached out to turn a lock of his hair around her finger.

In turn, he touched her brow, the shell of her ear, the line of her jaw. "I was so frightened when I saw you lying there. So much blood. I was frantic, but I had to keep my wits, see to you, then Mary and Flora."

"You did, and now I am fine." She winced as he shifted his weight. "Or I soon will be."

His touch moved over her hair, down the nape of her neck. "You are a wealth of contradictions," he whispered. "So strong and yet so fragile."

"I am strong," she insisted. "And I can bear whatever it is that you have to tell me. I know you carry burdens. I can share their weight. Lighten your load."

"There are not so many burdens," he said slowly. "But there are a great many *rules*. Rules that have been ingrained in me since birth." He sighed. "The sins in my past are not my own, but I must live with the consequences of them. Which means limits have been placed upon me. I have lived easily within them, for the most part. I stretched a few occasionally. Only once have I broken them, though. A colossal misstep, it turned out, but I was stubborn and foolish."

"A colossal misstep—she of the red-gold hair and intimidating stare of disdain."

"Don't you dare be intimidated by her," he insisted. "You are worth more than a thousand of her."

"By all that is holy, what is her *name*?" Kara asked, exasperated.

"Malina. Her cursed name is Malina."

"You loved her."

"God help me, I did." He lowered his head. "She was a beauty, but the thing that caught me was her smile. She kept directing it at *me*," he marveled. "The first one hit me in the chest, harder than my family's mule could kick. She fooled me completely with her soft smiles, admiring words, and sighs. But it didn't last. She grew bored and restless. I wasn't enough for her. She needed more. We didn't part well."

Kara thought about it. "And now she sees you as a success? A man who can give her more?"

He snorted. "Now she sees me as a tool to use to get herself more."

"I don't understand."

"I cannot explain it all. Not yet. But I want you to know, after she left, I didn't hate her. I was just … weary. Wary of women, honestly. She wasn't the only one to pick me up like a rag doll when it suited, and toss me away when it didn't. I thought that was what women were."

"It is what some women are," she said, thinking of her cousin's erstwhile fiancée.

"Some. Not all. But I didn't know that. I needed a change. So, I went traveling. I buried myself in art and history and the craft of forging. I became enamored of Norse design and mythology, and I thought—those were the sort of women I'd like to meet. Strong, opinionated, and forthright. I thought I'd been born in the wrong century." He grinned. "And then I met Gyda."

She laughed. "A strong woman, indeed."

"Yes. Ah, the adventures we got up to." His expression melted into a smile. "And then I met you."

She flushed as he took her hand.

"Here you were. So intelligent. Talented. Intrepid. Kind. You are genuinely special, Kara, and I am continuously impressed that you don't act like it. You don't puff yourself up or tear others down. You just go your own way, being honest and caring—and I couldn't help but want to spend more time with you."

"But now you must go."

"I must. A man has been killed. It's possible I will be blamed. But in any case, it has focused unwanted attention on me."

Frowning, she took a fistful of his coat in her free hand. "I know. You've said it. Stayme has said it. You have to leave. And if feels as if everyone around me has wisely counseled me that I must let you go. I convinced myself it was best." She pulled him closer and spoke fiercely. "But I will be damned if I will."

He started to speak, but she cut him off. "No. I hear you. I understand. It's dangerous. Leave London if you must, but you won't be leaving me. I won't have it. I haven't picked you up like a doll. I've picked you. Chosen you. You are the only man who hasn't winced at my insane upbringing. Who hasn't flinched at my devotion to my work or my wildly varied interests. Rules and limits be damned, Niall! Expectations can go hang. We will forge our own way. Make our own rules. Together. Because *I will not give you up.*"

He surged forward, even as he gently cradled her head. His lips slid over hers, and they were not gentle, but primal, hot, and demanding. She came alive in his arms, awakening to a new level of heat, desire, hunger.

But he pulled away. Their breath mingled. Breathing him in, she knew they were one, united in this spot, in this point in time.

"Thank you," he rasped. "I had no idea how much I needed to hear that."

"Remember it," she ordered him. "I am limited as to what I can do for now, but I will heal. And we will see this through."

"Together."

"Yes."

"I must go." He glanced toward the clock on the mantel. "Let me get you back to bed."

When she was sitting up in bed once more, he kissed her lingeringly. "I'll send word."

And he was gone.

No tears this time, either. She sat awake, planning and plotting, before she drifted off to a far easier sleep.

THE NEXT TIME she opened her eyes, dawn's light was filtering in. It caught and held in the red-gold hair of the woman glaring down at her.

She blinked, then deliberately yawned. "Malina."

The other woman reared back in shock. "He's told you of me?"

Fiendishly glad she was still propped upright and not lying vulnerably flat, Kara glared back at the woman. "I'm not some animal in a menagerie. You are not free to come in and stare at me while I sleep. What is it you want?"

Malina's eyes narrowed. She wore another rich scarlet gown. The color of rubies ... or blood. "I want to know if he told you I am his *wife*."

Shock, hurt, and betrayal bloomed in her chest, worse than the pain in her shoulder. No. No. She wouldn't believe it.

But wait. Scotland. He grew up in Scotland.

She scowled at her unwanted visitor. "The handfast bond dissolves after a year and a day if both parties don't agree to make the marriage permanent. And you were long gone before that day, weren't you?"

Malina huffed out a breath. "I had you for a moment." She snarled. "You think you are so clever, don't you?"

"Clever enough to know he is no longer bound to you."

She laughed. "He is bound to me by other ties. By ties of want and need. Of long nights and shared days." She paused. Lightning quick, her face darkened. "He's bound to me because I say he is. I will have him dancing at the end of my strings again." She leaned down to meet Kara face to face. "And you will stay out of it, do you hear? You think you are very fine with your money and your vast estate, but I can make sure things go very wrong for you, if you do not back away."

Straightening, she gave a sniff and swept out of the room.

Kara sat for a while, watching the door. When the inn began to stir, she rang her bell.

Turner came in moments.

She told him what had occurred. Most of it, in any case. "I will need your help."

"Always."

She gave him a fierce grin. "Good. Call Jenny. And call the doctor back today. I want to hear again everything I am to do. And everything I am not. You can take notes so we get it right. Then start preparing to get me back to Bluefield. Enough of this lounging about. I've ready to move ahead. With intention. We have work to do."

ABOUT THE AUTHOR

USA Today Bestselling author Deb Marlowe grew up with her nose in a book. Luckily, she'd read enough romances to recognize the hero she met at a college Halloween party – even though he wore a tuxedo t-shirt instead of breeches and boots. They married, settled in North Carolina and raised two handsome, funny and genuinely intelligent boys.

The author of over twenty-five historical romances, Deb is a Golden Heart Winner, a Rita Finalist and her books have won or been a finalist in the Golden Quill, the Holt Medallion, the Maggie, the Write Touch Reader Awards and the Daphne du Maurier Award.

A proud geek, history buff and story addict, she loves to talk with readers! Find her discussing books, period dramas and her infamous Men in Boots on Facebook, Twitter and Instagram. Watch her making historical recipes in her modern kitchen at Deb Marlowe's Regency Kitchen, a set of completely amateur videos on her website. While there, find out Behind the Book details and interesting Historical Tidbits and enter her monthly contest at deb@debmarlowe.com.

CPSIA information can be obtained
at www.ICGtesting.com
Printed in the USA
BVHW051715280423
663245BV00009B/108